Concord High School Library
2331 East Mishawaka Road
Elkhart, Indiana 46514

S0-ARV-569

THE SURVIVALIST

Other books by Giles Tippette

SATURDAY'S CHILDREN
THE BRAVE MEN
THE TROJAN COW
THE BANK ROBBER

THE
SURVIVALIST
GILES
TIPPETTE

Concord High School Library
2331 East Mishawaka Road
Elkhart, Indiana 46514

75 - 96

MACMILLAN PUBLISHING CO., INC.

New York

Copyright © 1975
by Giles Tippette

All rights reserved. No part of this
book may be reproduced or
transmitted in any form or by any
means, electronic or mechanical,
including photocopying, recording
or by any information storage and
retrieval system, without
permission in writing from the
Publisher.

Macmillan Publishing Co., Inc.
866 Third Avenue
New York, N. Y. 10022
Collier-Macmillan Canada Ltd.

**Library of Congress
Cataloging in Publication Data**
Tippette, Giles.
The survivalist.
I. Title.
PZ4.T594Su [PS3570.I6]   813'.5'4
74-22042
ISBN 0-02-619020-6

First Printing 1975
Printed in the United States of
America

To Ann

Hence, **Survi·valist** (*nonce-wd.*), one who holds a theory of survival.
THE OXFORD ENGLISH DICTIONARY

PART 1

I traded the station wagon in on a pickup. It was a squat power-ful-looking International with four-wheel drive and a small power winch on the front. It had overload springs, heavy-duty shocks, and stiffened suspension. It was an ideal vehicle for off the road. As a last measure, I had the regular tires replaced with mud grips.

Chris was startled when I brought it home. But as long as I didn't fool with her Mercedes, she wasn't going to get too disturbed.

"What in the world!" she exclaimed.

"It's for the trip," I told her enthusiastically.

"Are you crazy?" We were standing out in the front yard, looking at the pickup parked in the driveway. It was the only vehicle of its type in the neighborhood. "I'm not driving around the country in that thing!"

"Why not?"

"I'm just not. For one thing it would be uncomfortable."

"Oh, no!" I said. "Come look in this cab. Seats just like a car. Air conditioning. Power steering, brakes, radio. Very luxurious, my woman. Let's go for a drive and you'll see."

"No thanks," she said frowning. She looked over at me. "Franklin, what are you up to?"

"Nothing," I said.

She looked doubtful. "I don't know . . ." She glanced at the pickup and then back at me. "What are you planning? Besides this trip I mean."

"Nothing that I know of," I said. And I really didn't know. I don't think it was the old case of the right hand not letting the left know what it was doing. There was no specific plan in my mind. I just knew I wanted certain things, and I felt better for having them. I was just making moves that seemed right. What the hell; it couldn't hurt. And I'd have them, *just in case*.

Chris shook her head and started for the house. "I certainly hope they gave you a lot of money in difference between that thing and the station wagon."

That was Chris. She didn't know much about vehicles. In fact, the truck had cost the wagon and four thousand dollars. But it would take a man just about anywhere he wanted to go. A city-bred station wagon and little pieces of green paper couldn't do that.

I don't know exactly when the idea came. It had been in my head for a long time, years maybe, but only as a hazy, pleasant speculation; the kind of thing you put yourself to sleep with at night. I'm not talking about leaving the city and moving to a chicken farm somewhere out in the country. I'm talking about a man grabbing up his family and fleeing, running from society as he might hide from a dangerous enemy.

The decision (if it could be called that) was made somewhat easier, I guess, by the fact that there were only Chris and I. Though we'd been married nine years, we had no children and there weren't any close relations to worry about. My parents were both dead, and Chris's lived in South America. Not that I'd let them interfere anyway. Chris's daddy was a retired Air Force Brigadier General, SAC no less, and he'd consider what I wanted to do as traitorous, mutinous, and probably perverted. But, no matter. I had no concern over country or loyalty or "a better way" or any of that hogwash. I was simply afraid and angry and frustrated and set on a clean course of action in which we'd be the only arbiters of our fate. I wanted out. Clean. Split. Surgery if you please, doctor. I wanted to leave whatever it might be called; system, society, civilization, government, custom—take your pick. I wanted Franklin Horn to be all his own man without any help or hindrance from anyone else.

I remember playing poker over at Leslie Coker's house one night. We played for a long time, and we talked about a lot of the things middle-aged, average men talk about. Some things were very bad in the country and the world, and we talked about these things, worried about them, and wondered where it was all going to lead. We did so with the intensity of our generation, the generation that had learned that what you read about in the newspapers today is going to affect you directly tomorrow, and we kept saying, "Yeah, but what can you do about it?"

Just little instances like that. Nothing big; nothing important. I remember working on my taxes one night and getting madder and madder. "Goddamnit," I finally exploded to Chris, "I'm getting tired of this charade being played with my life."

Chris said quietly, "You have to pay taxes, Franklin."

"Why?" I demanded. "I thought the goddamn income tax was a temporary measure. Like all the other goddamn temporary things governments do. I don't even have a say in what they do with my money. That's a point that seems to be overlooked."

She said dryly, "You can vote, Franklin. That's your say."

"Don't needle me, Chris. I'm mad."

"I can see that. But you always get mad."

"The young people are angry and that seems to be all right. Well, I tell you, I'm about as angry as a frustrated forty-four-year-old French–Indian–Jewish–English diamond importer can get. It's not just taxes. It's everything. Every goddamn restriction, every goddamn new law, every goddamn interference. Listen, I'm about to get tired of some son-of-a-bitch two thousand miles from here screwing about with my life."

"Take it easy. There's nothing you can do about it."

"Don't be too sure."

"What?"

"I don't know. But don't be too sure."

One evening, while reading the paper, I said to Chris, "Look at this. Just look on this front page. There's stories about eight separate riots. Where in hell is it going to all end?"

"Whenever everyone gets what they want, I guess," she said.

I looked over at her. "That ain't possible. Too many people want what some other people have, and if they go get that, then those people are going to riot. One of these days, all these little riots are going to link up into one big one and then it *will* affect us. If you start enough brush fires, you can set the whole country on fire. And, besides, everytime one bunch starts trouble and gets away with it, it just encourages some other group. I'm tired of it."

"You want a drink?"

"Yeah," I said, "a big one."

I watched her going across the room. She was thirty-five and a very good-looking woman. I'd been lucky in a lot of things, and Chris was about the best of it.

I took the whiskey she brought me and drank off half of it, thinking I was drinking and smoking too much and just in generally bad condition. Probably the worst of my life. Oh, I'd never been any Tarzan. I'd been a pretty good athlete in my younger days, but I never had been in more than ordinary shape after that. Ordinary was a pretty good word for what I'd become, I thought to myself. I'd helled around a little and been a touch on the adventurous side at one time, but now I'd pretty well settled down. We had a nice home in a nice suburb in an ordinary city in the south. I had a nice business that made us about thirty thousand dollars a year. We had a nice circle of friends whom we didn't consider any duller than they considered us.

"This energy crisis, this gas and power shortage. I'd love for it to just go on and get worse. I'd love to see us go back to the horse-and-buggy days, back to a man depending on his own muscle and sweat and skill. It'd be wonderful."

"You wouldn't like it. You just think you would. God, I'd hate to think of working like women had to in the eighteen-hundreds."

"Listen, it'd be great. I'd like to see all the fucking engineers and technicians and scientists put slam out of business. All the machines and computers, all that shit. Zap! No more. Listen, a man felt like a man then. It was he and what he could do with his brains and his hands. Now, those fucking machines got you hemmed in on all sides. That's what's the matter now, Chris. People are frustrated. They've gotten away from the simple, basic way of life and they're just not made to live like that."

I was getting excited.

"I mean it, I'll bet that's what's causing all the trouble now.

Taken all in all, a man is still an animal and he's not meant to live the soft life we do. Hell, that's why we're all going crazy. No wonder we have riots and wars. At least it's something to do, something for a man to react about. I hope they run out of every goddamn gallon of gasoline and oil. It'd suit me just fine!"

Chris dampened my spirits by saying, "They'll just invent something else to take its place. Nuclear power."

"Yeah," I agreed, "no doubt." I sighed, "Goddamnit, there's no way out. Let's move to Mexico and hide in the mountains. And we wouldn't even have to live in a cave. I'd build us a cabin. What do you say?"

"I say I wouldn't like it. Listen, why don't you have another drink and forget about it. You'll feel better tomorrow."

"I'll have another drink," I said, "but I'm not going to feel better. Anyway, I'm going to cut down on my drinking. I'm going to start getting in shape. What do you think about that?"

"I think it's wonderful," she said.

"You also think I'm talking big. Well, I might fool you. I think a man ought to be in shape. God knows what's going to happen tomorrow." I started out of the room and stopped and looked back at her. "Don't be too sure I'm not kidding on the square about hiding in the mountains somewhere."

"You wouldn't like being a hermit, Franklin."

"Hermits don't have wives," I reminded her.

"That's what I said. You wouldn't like it."

It was the first time I'd mentioned the great idea to her. Maybe it was the first time I'd mentioned it to myself, in that form, anyway.

Diamonds, with prices jumping wildly and the market uncertain, had gone into very short supply as everyone sat back waiting to see what would happen. But I had accidentally uncovered a source that would net me a quick profit if I could make the deal before the sellers woke up. The transaction took me to South America, and I thought of my plan or idea or whatever it was as we flew over the Colombian interior. Below the plane were miles and miles of jungle and wilderness. From our altitude the ground looked green and soft and welcoming, and I thought just how easy it would be to hide out in such a place and never be heard from again.

It was chance that the deal took me to Bogotá, where Chris's parents choose to live. Or, I should say, where the general chooses to live. His wife, a timid little birdlike woman, just did what she was told. I'd had absolutely no intentions of even letting them know I was in town, but when my plane connections got fouled up, I called and went out to visit them for the afternoon.

The general and his wife received me in the sunken living room of their big, cool house. The general was wearing sport clothes, but he still contrived to make them look like a uniform. At sixty-eight he'd gone to paunch and his hair was just a fringe over his ears. But he still had the military bearing, and when he walked into the room, your immediate impression was that he'd just returned from inspecting the squadron.

What to call the general was a problem. I reserved "the general" for sarcasm. Mister Mayberry was a little formal, but I certainly wasn't going to call him Harry, which was his first name. Mostly I just avoided the issue.

"Well?" he barked at me. "And how do we find you here?"

I told him I'd come in on business.

"You want a drink?"

"Sure," I said.

He turned to his wife. "Fix a pitcher of martinis. Mind you, don't stir it too hard."

His wife ordered off, he turned back to me. "How is my daughter?"

"Chris is fine," I answered. "She sends her regards."

"Fine," he said. He turned to look at his wife, monitoring her business with the martinis. It was impossible for me to be around him two minutes without getting mad. I could feel several sarcastic remarks edging their way into my mouth.

"Your business in good order?" he asked me peremptorily.

"It's okay," I said. "I'm about to sell it."

"You're what?"

"I'm going to sell," I answered. It was the first time the thought had crossed my mind. "We're going to move. Chris and I."

"What!" The general, even though he's a small man, has large, shaggy eyebrows. They seemed to positively bristle as he stared at me. Suggestion of change made the general angry. He wanted us placed and classified.

"Yes," I said easily, "we're thinking of emigrating to Australia." That, too, was a virgin thought. It had the anticipated effect on the general. He swelled up in his chair, his face going almost purple.

"People don't migrate *from* the United States!" he told me angrily.

"Why not?" I challenged him.

"They just don't!" he shouted. "Goddamn, what a question."

At that moment his wife put the drinks down on the coffee table. "Oh, Harry," she said, "I think these are all right."

I took mine and thanked her. I don't like martinis, but the general decides what everyone drinks.

The general tasted his and slammed the glass down on the table. "Goddamnit, June," he shouted, "you've bruised the gin! This is London gin. It costs twelve dollars a quart in this goddamn country! What is the matter with you!"

"Oh, Harry, I'm sorry." She brushed her graying hair back. "I thought I was being so careful."

"Mine is fine," I said helpfully. "I like it."

The general glared at me. "Have you gone crazy?"

I didn't know which he was talking about—my opinion of the martinis or what I'd said about Australia. "No," I said, "I think the martinis are good."

He brushed that aside with an angry gesture. "What is this talk about Australia! About moving!"

"Why," I said, "I'm merely invoking the right of all oppressed people to get the hell out of a bad situation. I feel oppressed so we're going where things are better."

"You're not taking my daughter to Australia!" he ordered me.

"I'm not?"

"Not my daughter!"

"She may be your daughter," I told him, "but she's my wife. And that outranks, general. You're just a buck private in this game."

I could see it kind of hurt the old man. I began toning things down, a little ashamed of myself for having provoked him. But like a fool, I tried to be rational with him, to seriously explain my position. "Look," I told him, "I'm not saying that patriotism is not important. It is at right and proper times. When the enemy is at the gate, I think you've got to do a little flag waving for everyone's sake. When you've got an army coming at you, there's no time to sit down and reason things out on an individual basis. But now's a time when I think the individual has got the right, the duty, to look to himself and to what he can work out for his own little gang. I'm not knocking the country. It's a great country, if I know what that means. I'm not serious about Australia, but not because I wouldn't leave the United States. I just don't think that moving is the answer. Trouble's all over. I think a man had better start looking out for himself any way he can and to hell with all the side issues. Remember, general, the birthright came before citizenship."

The general was a phony and a demigod and a man looking out for old number one; nevertheless, I think I'd still put my money on him if I had to get a fleet of bombers in and out of a target.

The deal on the South American diamonds turned out better than I'd expected, and I made a clear twenty thousand dollars. It was a windfall, a profit above and different from my normal business earnings. I suppose if it hadn't happened I'd never have bought the gas generator. For some reason, ever since my thinking had turned the way it had, I'd wanted one. I guess it was symbolic of some sort of independence.

The day it was delivered I moved the International out of the garage and set the generator in its place. After I'd uncrated it, I called Chris out to look. I was very excited.

"It certainly is big," she said, not at all sure what she was seeing or what it was for.

"Not so big," I said. "You can haul it easily in the back of the pickup. That's part of the beauty, you've got a mobile power source. As long as you have gasoline anyway."

"But what's it for?"

"For? My gosh, you could darn near hook this thing in and have enough electricity to power our house. Think of being independent of the electric company. Man, that *is* fighting city hall."

My practical wife asked, "But what would you want to do that for? Isn't—I mean, wouldn't this be more expensive?"

"Oh, sure," I said, "of course this would cost more to run. But that's not the point. The point is independence. Hell, if a man had one of these and his own water well and a septic system he could snap his fingers at the world."

"How about the telephone?"

"Oh, that. That's just a bother."

"And garbage pickup?"

I frowned at her. "My God, Chris, show a little enthusiasm for the idea."

Going back in the house, she asked, "You say it runs on gasoline?"

I told her it did.

"I thought you said you hoped they ran out of gasoline."

"Just as long as there's enough for us."

"What about everyone else?"

I put my arm around her shoulders. "Sweetheart, you better understand right now that I'm not interested in anyone else. Just us."

Next day I bought four fifty-five-gallon drums of gasoline. These too I had stacked in the garage. Chris didn't take this, however, as one of my boyish whims. She didn't like it. "Franklin, that's dangerous, all that gasoline. You shouldn't have bought that."

"It's not dangerous," I insisted. "All these drums are hermetically sealed. No chance of an explosion or fire."

"What if the house catches on fire?"

"Then we better run like hell. Com'on, Chris!" Then, suddenly, "Listen, let's take a vacation."

"All right."

"No, I mean it," I said. "Let's really do. We've got that extra money." She knew about the twenty thousand. "And things are going to be slow for a time with the business."

Actually, my business was pretty much a one-man operation, done mostly out of my head and a briefcase. I had a little office and a secretary whose principal function was answering the telephone. There was no reason I couldn't get away.

"I said it's okay with me. You know me, I'm ready to go. I think it would be fun. Where'll we go?"

"Well—" I began. "I've been thinking. Let's take a driving trip."

"A driving trip? That doesn't sound so hot."

"Sure it is," I urged. "Let's go look at the country. Go all over the Southwest. It's been a long time since we've really gotten out and looked around. Let's go see what's happening. Go to all the little places. Get off the main highways."

She gave me a searching look. "Franklin—" she said, cocking her head to the side just a little.

"What?"

She studied me a moment longer. "Nothing."

"Got to be some real places left somewhere."

"How long will we be gone?"

"Oh, two weeks," I said, offhandedly.

"That's a long time to just drive around."

"We'll stop some," I promised her. "You'll love it."

"And when do we leave?"

"Pretty quick," I answered. "Let me get a few things cleared up."

Nick Pfeiffer was an unusual man. He was a doctor who'd rejected the medical profession, calling it, "Devious, greedy, useless, self-serving, ignorant, and above all, mystical." He had taken up the ministry and become a pastor in an orthodox, formalized religion. He'd said, "If I'm going to assume a godlike demeanor, it's not going to be with a stethoscope around my neck, but in the proper clothes." I called him variously, "Your Reverence," "The Old Nick," and "Your Holy Pulpit."

We had some lovely conversations. Once, I'd said something that had caused him to growl, "Watch it, buddy, I'm a man of God." I'd answered, "So what, so am I. Aren't we all?" And he'd said, "Yeah, but I got the business card to prove it."

He was a thin, aesthetic-looking man with a spade beard that he cultivated to a dagger point. The main thing I liked about him was his jaundiced honesty. He made no attempt to hide that he was playing a role. "You bet your fucking ass, sweet buddy, and if Hollywood ever discovers me I'll get the Oscar with halo."

I told him about the trip and he raised his eyebrows. "You're taking the lovely Chris Horn touring around the sticks in a pickup?"

"My God, Nick, she's not that fragile."

"Neither is that her mode."

I felt it necessary to be stubborn on that point. "Chris is pretty tough. All women are. They can stand a lot more than you might think."

He was eating a crab cocktail, so he waited before saying, "Any reason why they should have to?"

"You never know," I said. "Isn't it you that's always predicting dire disasters?"

He tossed his head in annoyance. Nick has a very high opinion of his intellect, and he prefers that it be treated with due respect. Besides, you've got to be careful with Nick. He's the kind of son-of-a-bitch that just likes to argue for the sake of proving his mental superiority. He'll take either side. "Oh," he put in sarcastically, "I don't believe I've ever said anything just so."

"Everything's great then?"

"Neither did I say that. But maybe you ought to get to your prayers."

"Seriously, Nick, what do you think is going to happen in the country, even in the world. I suppose everybody would be affected by a serious change here."

"Well I don't think we're going back to the caves."

"But it could be bad, couldn't it? I mean, if the economic structure broke down."

"Why? Why the big interest?"

"Oh, I don't know. Just the things that are happening. The dollar's under attack. We're having all sorts of economic and industrial-type crises. That and a fair amount of social unrest could make things a little hairy. I don't really pretend to understand what keeps a country going. I still don't comprehend the gold standard. Seems as if so much is built on a very uncertain foundation of mutual trust and confidence. What happens if that structure gets a little shaky?"

"You're right about one thing," he lectured. "It is like a row of dominoes. Let's hope the first in line doesn't get knocked over." He turned and waved at the waiter. "You want another drink?"

"Not me."

He asked, "Where you going on this trip?"

"Oh, the back country. The hinterlands."

He was looking at me.

"I want to look the land over." I hesitated. "Maybe buy a little piece somewhere."

His eyes went shrewd. "A little retreat, Franklin? Little hidey-hole?"

"You never can tell," I said laughing. "Want me to find you one?"

"No. I'm making some small plans."

I looked up quickly to see if he was serious. "Really?"

"Who knows," he answered carelessly.

I had a sudden thought. "Say, what's happened to the bread basket of the world? We used to be able to feed the world, and now half the families in the country can't afford to buy food. Where have all the surpluses gone to?"

Nick cocked a wry eye at me. "Price supports, my man."

"So?"

"Well, price supports are expensive. We can't afford them and food."

"Is there less food available, then?"

He shrugged. "Who knows? What is all this? When did I become your economic adviser? I'm just a simple country pastor trying to get by in the big city."

I bought Chris and me a sleeping bag and some other camping gear. She looked at my purchases with a disinterested glance. "I don't see what I'll need with that in a motel."

"Well, you never know," I said. I'd also bought a 30.06 rifle with a telescopic scope. I had it out, admiring its deadly simplicity. "A beautiful machine," I told Chris.

"I don't like guns," she said.

"Guns are very useful when you need one," I said. "It's a stupid attitude to condemn an inert piece of machinery because it's been misused by some people."

"I still don't like them," she insisted. There is a stubborn streak in Chris that is not always open to reason. But she would have to have a great many more faults before I could love her any less. A great many.

I had other guns. I had a fine Browning superimposed 12-gauge shotgun that I'd bought when I was interested in skeet shooting. For handguns I had a .357 Colt revolver and a 9-mm Browning automatic. I made a note to myself to buy up a quantity of ammunition. There'd been persistent rumors that the government was going to restrict its sale, and I wanted to be sure to lay in a good supply before such a thing happened. Already it was difficult to buy a gun, especially a handgun.

The night before we were to leave, there was a coincidental item on the television news, a report on the rising purchases of dehydrated and long-term storage foodstuffs. One company, which had been used to selling a half-million-dollars' worth a year to campers and outdoorsmen, was suddenly doing ten-million-dollars' worth of business. The food was being bought by ordinary people for no specific purpose. The reporter interviewed a number of them, but they were vague in their responses saying things like, "Well, you never can tell," and "Just want to have it on hand. It won't spoil." None of them would say they expected any one specific thing to happen, it was just the case of being ready. But significantly, they were vague about where their storage places were. They'd say they were putting it in a summer house or in a ". . . little place we've got in the mountains," but nothing more specific than that. The reporter, talking into the camera, finished by noting, "These people will tell you anything you want to know about their emergency food supplies—except where they are. Or what might cause them to be used. . . ."

I turned to Chris. "What do you think about that?"

She had a little frown on her face. She was tucked up on the sofa, wrapped up in a bathrobe. The ends of her blond hair were still damp from her shower. "I don't know," she said slowly. "I suppose there are people who panic at the slightest thing. I don't see how we could run out of food."

"Oh, we won't," I agreed, "under normal conditions. But what if something happens to just tip the scales a little. Panic. Then you've got shortages."

"I'd feel silly buying that stuff," she said. "Dehydrated bananas and soybean meal. Good heavens. Think how ridiculous they're going to feel five years from now, staring at all those cans they never opened."

I do not know a great deal about women. I married later than most men and I never, before Chris, had the closeness to a woman that marriage creates. Most of my affairs had been hit-and-miss propositions involving a lot of emotion and intense sex and very little sharing or knowing of each other. Chris, as a woman, sometimes baffled me in her logic. She's stubborn, and she's also a touch selfish. I can't much blame her for this. In her father's household it was necessary to look after her own interests or else end up like her mother. Also, I was not her first husband. She'd been married once before to a young lieutenant in one of her father's commands. It didn't last long, and I expect she may have married just to get away from home. It didn't matter. But, for me, it did explain some of Chris's ways and make me more patient with her. Maybe she's resisting change, even to the point of denying reality. There were things happening that spelled trouble as plain as day to me. But I could tell that Chris didn't see them or didn't want to.

We toured Central Texas the first few days, passing through towns like Boerne and Comfort and Junction and Mineral Wells, staying away from the big population centers. I insisted on stopping in quite a few of them, looking over the surrounding countryside, visiting with real estate agents. I was particularly interested in the hill country because of the broken terrain that was arable, yet rough enough to provide a kind of remote concealment. But I could see that the country was growing up too fast. It was a beautiful area with a fine, unspoiled climate and people who could afford it were pouring in to live. In ten years it would be overpopulated.

The first night out, we stopped in a motel and I put on a pair of running shorts and shoes that I'd just bought. Chris looked at me in some amazement. "What are you going to do?"

"Jog," I answered. "Out in the parking lot."

She laughed, looking over her shoulder. She was dressing for dinner, standing in front of the dressing table mirror in just her panties and bra, making up her face. "Are you serious?"

"Certainly." I went up behind her and put my arms around her, spanning her soft belly with my hands. She smelled very clean and good after her bath.

"Franklin!" she exclaimed, twisting in my arms. "You're still dusty from the road. You'll mess me up."

"I'll mess you up," I growled in her ear, kidding, yet feeling that copper taste come into my mouth.

"You'll be too tired from jogging," she said.

"Wait and see." I let her go and stepped back, admiring her shape and the rounded symmetry of her bottom in the tight nylon panties. "Care to fuck?"

"Franklin!" she said, the word coming out mouthy because she had her lips pulled back the way women do when they're applying lipstick. "Why are you doing it?"

"What? Jogging? Because I need to get in shape."

"You don't look bad."

"I've got no stamina. I couldn't do hard work for an hour without falling on my face."

I'm a little over six foot. In my better days I'd weighed 190. Now I was up to 225 and feeling it. Worse, the extra weight was straight fat distributed over bad places like my belly and the sides of my back and my thighs. It was true, though, that I didn't look too bad. I had a big chest and heavily muscled arms, and this development kept me from appearing like an out-of-proportion fat man.

Chris turned and got a dress out of the suitcase. While she pulled it over her head she said, "Why should you have to do hard work? Are you going to start digging ditches?"

"You never can tell," I said.

I don't know why I was unwilling to completely discuss my fears with Chris. I suppose I didn't want to scare her.

But, next day driving along, I said, "You know, honey, things seem in a very uncertain state to me. I'm not like Nick Pfeiffer, predicting the collapse of the world 'as we know it' unquote, but I am concerned about what could become a very bad economic and social period."

"Well, what can you do about it? God, I've just gotten to where I shut my eyes and don't worry."

"That's just it—I think we can do something. There have been other bad periods in the country's history—depression, civil war —and the people that came out the best were those out of the line of fire and with some method of making out for themselves until things got back in order."

"That certainly sounds good. But how do you do that?"

"Well," I said carefully, "I was thinking we might buy a little piece of land somewhere. Somewhere remote. The kind of place we could run to if things got too hot for comfort."

She was pensive; I watched the road and drove, letting her think. Finally, she asked, "Is that the purpose of this trip?"

"Not altogether," I said evasively. "I really wanted to find out how things looked around the country, our half of the country anyway. The only information we really get is out of the television, and I felt it was time we ran a check ourselves. And I did think we'd have fun."

"You really fooled me," she said dryly. "And of course this *is* my idea of fun."

"Now, Chris," I said, "don't be like that. I don't believe you're as finicky and soft as you'd like me to believe."

Then, unexpectedly, she said, "I think it's a good idea. About buying a piece of land. If there were some kind of trouble, we'd have it. And then, we could always use it as a vacation house or something. And there's no better investment than land, is there?"

"Not now," I said. "Not the way things are. Except maybe for guns it's about the safest."

She tossed her head in annoyance when I said that about guns.

"Listen," I added, "I agree with you about the vacation house business. You know, we could make this a lot of fun."

"But can we afford it?"

"I don't see why not." I took my hand off the steering wheel and shook it to get the numbness out. The pickup didn't really ride like a Cadillac, and the stiff suspension sent deadening waves up through the steering wheel that put your hand to sleep. The road was gradually climbing as we neared the New Mexico border. It was summer, but the land—where it wasn't desert and cactus—was clean and green.

"I've been figuring up," I said. "I think we could cash out, if we had to, for about a hundred and fifty thousand dollars. That's just talking about the stuff that's easily convertible like some stocks and that little property we have toward town and that private supply of diamonds I've been hoarding."

"Do we want to do that?" she asked, looking a little alarmed. "We better not be too hasty, had we?"

"I think it'd be a good idea anyway," I said doggedly.

We had just crossed into New Mexico and the first gas station we passed had a sign out limiting each customer to five gallons.

"Look at that," I said. It had been ten gallons in Texas.

"Your dream is coming true."

"I want it to hold off for a while." I lit a cigarette. "No, Chris," I said. "I think it would be a good idea to be a little more liquid anyway. The stock market is nervous. Everytime the least thing happens it fluctuates like a jet Yo-Yo. And that property—there's no telling when it might be right in the middle of a riot. No, we ought to get ourselves into a more flexible position."

"Well," she said uncertainly, "I guess you know best about that."

"In fact, I hate to even keep it in cash. I don't even trust that too much. I wish you could still hold gold. Or something like that. Land, I believe, would be the safest."

"And gas generators and pickups?"

I looked over at her and winked. "Now you're getting the idea."

She shook her head. "I can't believe we're really talking like this. Do you know what my daddy would say about this? My God, this is treason. We're supposed to have faith."

"I have faith," I said, "in human nature. You let things go from bad to worse, and you'll have people jerking food out of each other's hands."

"Well, what do you see happening?"

"Probably nothing," I said. "But I don't think it would take much of a trick to make the game turn serious. Not with all the shortages we already have. You get people scrambling after basic needs and they can turn pretty ugly. Remember, dear, I've spent time with some pretty primitive people, and I know what lurks in all our breasts. Trouble starts; I just want to make sure we're not one of the innocent bystanders that gets caught in the cross fire."

After much persuasion, Chris had finally agreed to camp out. We made it into Lincoln National Forest a couple of hours before dusk. I had brought an ice chest full of steaks, fresh produce, and other edibles. I was determined to make it as pleasant for her as I could. But she was already worrying about such things as showers. "Where," she asked me, "do you go to the bathroom?"

We were bumping up a little mountain road that qualified more as a trail.

"You'll figure it out," I said.

She looked out the window at the rough country. "I'm not going out in the bushes," she said flatly.

"Why not?"

"Are you kidding? God knows what's out there."

"Nothing to hurt you, my lady love," I said. "You're under the protection of the national government on these lands. You're a citizen, aren't you?"

The day had been warm but, when we finally stepped out of the cab, high on the side of a mountain, the air was crisp and cool and delicious.

"This *is* nice!" Chris said, standing by the pickup looking around.

"Isn't it?" I agreed. I'd located a little flat clearing. All around us was the bigness of the sky and the mountains, seeming to stretch away forever. We were up high enough that the distant clouds seemed on a level with us. Behind us our mountain rose another two or three thousand feet, its sides carpeted with shrub and underbrush and some kind of pine.

"Listen," I told Chris, "we better kind of hurry and get camped. Don't want dark to slip up on us. You gather some wood while I unload and get us set up."

She looked doubtful. "Where do I find firewood?"

I indicated the line of trees. "Just in there. Don't try to carry anything too big."

"I'm not going in there."

"Why not?"

"Well, snakes for one thing."

"No snakes," I said. Too high up. No snakes in the mountains," I told her, having not the slightest idea if it were true or not.

"Are you sure?"

"Certainly. Now go on."

"Well. . . ." She still looked doubtful, but she walked over to the edge of the clearing and began picking up a few branches.

I started unloading the pickup. We hadn't brought a tent, but I had a couple of large tarps. I spread one of these near where I planned to build the fire, then inflated the two air mattresses and placed them side by side on the tarp. Then I buttoned our two sleeping bags together, making one big one, and put it on the mattresses. It made a very cozy-looking bed, and I knew it would look even better as it got colder. The ranger at the entrance had told me it got down to forty degrees at night up high. When I had the bed fixed I got out the ice chest and set it near the fire. Then I poured a five-gallon bucket full of water. That was for Chris, for any washing and bathing she might want to do. The cooking water was in a separate keg. I'd even brought camp stools and a little folding table. I had done everything I could think of to make Chris comfortable because I wanted her to enjoy herself and feel amenable to certain parts of this kind of life. She came up bearing an armload of wood and I took it and praised her for her efforts, even though it was the wrong kind. It was mostly pitch type that would put out an oily black smoke, making it unusable as a cooking fire. But it would do all right to start with, and I'd find some hardwood later.

I laid my fire carefully, first clearing off a patch of ground and setting a circle of rocks to protect against the wind and to use as rests for the grill.

"Why is it," Chris asked me, "that the man always cooks in the woods and the woman in the kitchen?"

"I never thought of it," I said, lighting my tinder. The pitch wood caught quickly, and I laid on larger and larger twigs until the fire was soon consuming fair-sized branches. "That's a good question." It was becoming twilight faster than it should have by my watch; but that was because of the encircling mountains. I knew the light would be around long enough for us to get set up.

I left Chris tending the fire, took the other tarp and a Coleman lantern, and walked twenty or thirty feet off in the brush until I found a tiny little clearing. I strung the tarp from a limb, making a sort of screen, lit the lantern, and hung it from a nearby limb. This was to be Chris's bathroom. I spent a moment looking the ground over, making sure there were no snake holes or ant hills or anything else dangerous. On the way I picked up several seasoned pieces of oak that would make nice coals to cook the steaks over.

Chris was sitting by the fire, staring out across the mountains.

She turned her head and looked at me. She was wearing slacks and a becoming blouse, and she had her yellow hair done back some way in a blue bandanna. She looked wonderful. "Gosh, it's pretty," she said.

"You betcha. I feel very right here."

The pine wood was burning rapidly so I laid on my billets of oak, knowing that the pine would be all consumed by the time we were ready to cook. Then I mixed Chris and me a drink in paper cups; scotch and water for her, bourbon for me. I made them strong. Lastly, I sat down beside her. "There," I said, "we're set."

I turned her head and pointed to the glow of light from the lantern just back in the woods. "Your privy, madame. Free of snakes, mountain lions, and screened from leering sex maniacs."

She leaned back against me, sipping her drink. She sighed. "This is nice. I thought it would be all bugs and dust and gritty food."

"Well," I said, "we haven't eaten yet."

Now it was becoming dark, and I got up and lit the other lantern so there'd be plenty of light for cooking. With the night came the sounds of the forest; the suspicious rustle of nearby brush, the far-off hooting of an owl, the rasp of crickets.

"What's for supper?" Chris asked.

"Well, let me see." I opened the top of the ice chest. I had enough food laid on to camp a month, practically. "Steak, of course. And how about a baked potato. No salad. Too much trouble. But I'll give you an apple or orange. In fact," I said, "I better get the potatoes on right now. The coals are about right, and they'll take at least forty-five minutes." I got up, took two potatoes, washed them, then rolled them in aluminum foil with butter and salt and pepper. I put a double roll of foil on the outside to make sure they didn't burn. If we'd been near a creek I'd have gotten some clay and coated the outside of the foil with that. That's the way to cook potatoes.

With my hatchet I shoved aside a heap of coals, dug a little hollow in the ground, laid in the potatoes and then recovered them. While I was up I got the grill and laid that over the fire.

"You're certainly efficient," Chris said.

"Ain't I hell," I agreed. "Not over eighty or ninety million people could do this as well. I may set up a guide service." I looked over at her. She was sitting on the ground instead of one of the camp chairs. "You comfortable enough?"

"Oh, yes."

"Why don't you sit on the bed?"

"I like it here by the fire."

"All right."

We finished our drinks in silence, staring out at the sky. The first belts of stars were just getting up in the east and I explained to Chris how the stars progress during the night. "You can follow a star," I said, "for your longitude. But you can't get your latitude that way. Stars are more useful to a man on land than at sea."

"I didn't know you knew all these things."

"Oh, yes." I got up and mixed us another drink. I was deliberately showing off for Chris, being careful to do everything smoothly and right. Not that it was hard; much the opposite. I'd had a lot of experience in the past in much rougher circumstances than we were in. But I wanted her to feel confident with me in surroundings we'd never been in together. There was trouble coming, somewhere, and I wanted her to feel that I could handle it, whatever it was.

"The thing to do with the wilderness," I said, "is to not fight it. Give with it, blend, adapt. Man lived like this once, he can again. And a lot easier now with all the stuff we have. Most people don't understand the brush. They've been on concrete so long that they panic when the trees close in over their heads. They fight and struggle and get mad and do everything wrong simply because they won't mix with their surroundings. Listen, there's less stuff out here to hurt you than there is on some city street. And if you'll just take the time and be patient a man can find nearly everything he needs right at hand."

Fifteen minutes before the potatoes were done I put the steaks on. They cooked rapidly over the hot coals. When it was all done I took the potatoes up, burning my fingers a little when I unwrapped the foil, and then served it on the table. We ate across from each other with the lantern sitting to one side as our candle. The food was very good, made even better by the cold clarity of the night air. Chris suddenly laughed, high and pleasant. "God, this is fun."

I fixed us another drink, feeling pleased with myself.

"This is really strange," she said, "sitting here, eating steak and potatoes off a table. And we're way the hell up in the mountains." She was getting a little tight from the drinks. It excited me for Chris has fewer inhibitions in bed when she's had a few drinks. I don't mean she is cold by nature, God the opposite, but the liquor does make her go at things with a greater abandon.

We had one last drink to finish dinner. Then Chris went off to her bathroom to get ready for bed, and I put away stuff and banked down the fire. I kneeled on the sleeping bag, looking out over the valley, feeling good from the whiskey and the night and just things in general. Chris came back, not wisecracking about the lack of towels, but with that soft expression in her face and eyes that I liked to see so well. I pulled back the top of the sleeping bag and held it around her shoulders as she kneeled down to take her clothes off. I was going to let the lantern burn all night, and by its soft glow I could admire her body as she stripped. When her breasts slipped free of her bra, I could feel the lust rising in my throat. I took one in my hand, feeling its incredible smoothness and warmth, and bent my head to kiss the nipple and pull it into my mouth.

Then she was naked. She slipped down under the covers and I tore my own clothes off and got in beside her. I kissed her mouth and neck and ears. I was excited. "I love you," I said.

"I love you."

I slipped down inside the bag, kissing her breasts and stomach, working my way down. It was difficult in the sleeping bag, even though it was a double large one. I could feel her body quivering. All around us was the night and the woods and the sensation of absolute freedom. Because of the confinement of the sleeping bag we could not do the things we normally did. But I held her and she me, and it was wonderful. Finally, I entered her and we seemed to melt together. She was sighing in high, gasping breaths. I could feel us together, and I suddenly knew we were going to do something we hadn't done in a long time—climax together from just straight intercourse. I was so excited I was trembling, and I could feel Chris the same below me.

And then there came a high, curdling scream that rushed at us like the wind. I jerked upward, fighting Chris's legs, fighting the

Concord High School Library
2331 East Mishawaka Road
Elkhart, Indiana 46514

sleeping bag. The violent sound seemed right on us. Beneath me,
I could feel Chris thrashing around. She was screaming. I was
fumbling at the side of the bed for where I'd laid my pistol. I
couldn't find it. And then, just as the terror seemed absolutely
on top of us, the scream went off into a gurgling chuckle and I
knew what it was. It was a screech owl. A little bird no bigger
than your fist. Our light had attracted him and he'd come wing-
ing in, screeching out his horrible sound.

I slumped back, trying to quiet Chris. "It's all right, baby! It's
all right!" It took me a moment to get her attention. When I did
I told her about the owl, trying to explain that there was no danger. I should have recognized the sound immediately, but it had
been so long since I'd heard a screech owl that I'd forgotten what
they were. And then I would never have connected them with
such a place. All the frights they'd given me had been in the
South, down near some river.

Chris was unnerved. Even after she understood, she still
couldn't calm down. Now, after such a suggestive sound, there
might be danger anywhere and her every nerve was on guard. I
couldn't blame her. A screech owl sounds something like the
scream of a panther, and I'd myself thought for an instant that
that was what was coming at us.

Of course the moment was lost. We gave it up for the night. I
fixed us both a straight shot, but Chris never did relax. All night
I felt her tense and alert, pressed right up against me. Well, it
was a hell of an ending to what had been turning out to be a
perfect night. I lay there thinking of the lecture I'd given Chris
on how you had to blend and mix with the wild country. Well,
it seemed that it wasn't always that easy. I suppose if I'd been a
little more experienced I could have handled the screech owl
scare, but it would still have messed up the wonderful love we
were making. I bitterly regretted that, as well as having the very
pleasant flow of things interrupted.

We got away first thing next morning. Chris was restless and
eager to go, and I couldn't really blame her. I'd wanted us to
take an extended hike, but right after breakfast, I loaded the
truck and we bumped our way down the mountain. Chris said
she felt grimy. "I couldn't really get clean taking a whore's bath
out of a bucket."

I sympathized with her, but at the same time I wanted her to understand that she might be called on to make certain changes of attitude. "Listen, babe," I said after we'd regained the main highway, "I want you to understand that we haven't been talking just to exercise our mouths. It could be that we might actually have to take to the mountains. And I want you to be a little acquainted with the life. I—"

She broke in. "Listen, I don't care how much I practice, I'll never get to where I like feeling dirty."

"You know there's more to it than that. Com'on Chris. Of course we wouldn't have to live as rough as that, but there are certain things to learn, basic skills and approaches."

"I understand that," she said.

"I mean, you see the point?"

"I see, but I still think it's not going to be necessary. Or at least I hope not."

I didn't answer, other than to say we'd stop early that night and she could take a long, hot bath.

I was just as glad to be moving on. We still had a lot of country to see, and I wasn't impressed with anything in that part of New Mexico. As if she were reading my mind, Chris asked if I'd seen any land I liked.

"Not really. This is remote and rough enough, but the soil looks very thin. It's actually too rough. You could hide a cabin all right, but you'd have a hell of a time doing any farming. And the one condition is just as important as the other. I think we'll just drive straight on through and have a look at Arizona."

"What about Colorado, or Oregon? They're pretty. Or remote, as you'd say."

"They're also cold as hell in the winter. No, see, we've got to find a place that's remote enough to hide in, but also arable— that means farmable—and with a reasonably mild climate. I don't mean mild like Miami Beach, just where it doesn't snow and freeze six months out of the year. We need a fairly long growing season, and then we also aren't going to have central heating." I lit a cigarette. "I think we'll run through the middle of Arizona, then swing back and hit Oklahoma and Arkansas. I rule Louisiana out because of the too warm climate. We need a little cold weather for processing slaughter meat. We wouldn't have refrigeration, you know."

"Why not?"

"No electricity."

"What? That doesn't make any sense. You're not planning on buying land that doesn't even have electricity running to it, are you?"

I looked at her in astonishment. "Well, of course. Listen, if we have to hide, we want to hide. You can't hide with a power line running right up to your front door. Might as well put up signs."

"Oh . . ." she said, looking vague as if she didn't completely grasp the idea. "But what about your precious generator?"

"That's just for emergencies. You couldn't run that all the time. You'd use your gasoline up in nothing flat."

"You could get some more, couldn't you?"

I looked at her and didn't answer. There wasn't anything to answer. Sometimes we seemed to be talking about the same things and other times not.

Arizona wasn't suitable either. We confined our looking to the northern half of the state. I knew the southern part well, and what wasn't desert was overpopulated. Upper state had the type of terrain I was looking for, but the growing season wasn't long enough. There was also the feeling, hard to define, that everyone was a little too interested in the other guy's business. I didn't know how I formed that impression from the little looking and talking we did, but I said to Chris, "I'm developing another criterion, we want to find a section where people are not so goddamn *neighborly*. I want 'em to have no more interest in us than if we were another rock on a hill side."

I thought Chris was taking the trip very well. She couldn't really be having a lot of fun—not her kind of fun—on a trip that I'd originally proposed as a vacation. She'd eaten meals in borderline cafés, slept in something less than the best hotels on occasion, and ridden several thousand miles in what she called, ". . . one step down from a Mexican bus." She asked me, "Does this thing have square wheels?"

But I thought we were getting a lot accomplished. We hadn't found what we were looking for, but we'd at least eliminated a lot of country and that can be just as important. However, I was worried. It might be possible, I thought, that what I was searching for no longer existed. What had begun as a hazy idea was taking on more and more form, and I was visualizing a large tract of property, remote and hidden, arable, in a sparsely settled area, and at a price we could afford. Maybe there wasn't anything like that anymore.

We were accomplishing something else; we were seeing and feeling and learning about a lot of the country. I didn't know how much value it was going to be to us, but we were finding out that there were two basic groups, at least in the sections we visited; those who were bored and tired of all the trouble and who just wanted to be left alone, and those who felt so strongly on the issues, any issues, that they were vocal and violent and militant. Of course, this was not much different from what we'd already known in the big cities, but people in the back country seemed more involved with the larger national issues than with what was happening immediately in front of them.

We crossed into Arkansas at Fort Smith, and I told Chris about how the old town had once been a big jumping off place for people heading West. We had just crossed the bridge over the Red River on the west side of town. "That bridge," I said, "represented the last link with organized civilization. From then on, until they got to California, it was wildcat country. Unsettled, no law and order, nothing. It was the Cimarron, you've heard of that. A lot of people went this way who were trying to get away from something. Not too many settlers. Most of those took the northern route that was easier for wagons and stock. People going this way were generally on horseback and traveling in a hurry. Jesse James and his gang crossed that very bridge, just a jump ahead of a posse that had been chasing them all the way from Missouri. But they weren't all outlaws. A lot of them were people just like us, people who didn't like the way things were shaping up."

"But aren't we going in the wrong direction?"

"Not now. We would have been then. But I kind of like the way things look here."

Fort Smith was a raw little town lying just at the foothills of some rough-looking mountains that rose far off to the east. "I'm going to drive up north" I told Chris. "Toward the White River country around the Missouri border. I've got a topographical map that shows the country to be very much like what we're looking for."

"All right," she said, "but let's stop soon, for God's sake. I want a bath and a long rest. Turn up the air-conditioner, I'm burning up."

We worked our way across the state from Harrison, with fifteen thousand people the biggest town north of Little Rock. I knew immediately that I had found the country I was looking for. Most of it was either in or near the foothills of the Ozarks. It was a country broken by deep draws and canyons and knobby, sloping mountains and hills. And yet, as rough as the land was, it was still heavily timbered with beech and oak and hickory and some varieties I didn't recognize; and the top soil, where you found it, was deep and rich. From talking to county agents I learned that the annual rainfall was ample and that a large number of the standard vegetables and eating crops did well. Of course, that varied from section to section, as did the mean temperature. It got cold, but there was a seven- or eight-month growing season and that was all you'd need.

But most important, the whole area, for hundreds of miles, was very sparsely settled. There was no industry to speak of, nor was there likely to be. We spent four days going across the top of the state and then turned back to recross it. After that little time I was firmly convinced that no one in the whole area had much interest in anyone else's business. Everyone we met had a strong strain of suspicion, mistrust, and disinterest in strangers. It was difficult, for instance, to get a waitress in any of the little cafés to do more than take our order, much less give out information. Real estate agents were willing enough to discuss prospective properties, but they were a long mile from gregarious. Some of them even bordered on the hostile. That had me at a loss until I later figured it out. Generally, their opening remark was, "Well, I might have a few pieces of land for sale, but it's gonna be way overpriced." They didn't like it that outside money and buyers had come in and driven the prices up. They didn't like what they felt were artificial price situations created by absentee buyers who were investing and did not intend to live on the land or work it. Most of them were old men who'd dealt in land for many years, and their approach had always been how much corn or truck you could grow or how many cows such-and-such land would graze. They didn't understand about land having a value by just sitting there and being and providing some one with a place to be.

None of the land we were seeing really fit my bill. It was rough and remote and farmable, but I had the feeling it would not stay remote very long. Most of it was on or near a road or near a town or a close neighbor. The story I was giving the real estate agents was that I was buying for long-term speculation, and I wanted the most out-of-the-way land I could find because it would have the cheapest price. I had to give them a plausible story because what we were looking for was not what most buyers want, and you have to give a man something *he* can understand or else he'll be suspicious of your motives. And suspicion created interest and interest was not what I wanted.

But it was not working too well. Those old real estate agents, accustomed to using their own criterion to establish a piece of property, kept showing me deals that were right by the judgments I'd given them, but wrong by my hidden motives. They'd say, proudly, as if they'd done a good job, "Well, look at this one, 659 feet of paved road frontage!" or "Already got electric lights and water. Might even get the phone company to run a special line in." or "Town's moving that way. Here's a real good buy."

I'd explain that it wasn't what I wanted, that I was speculating for the long-term and I wanted *rough, remote* land so it'd be cheap. And they'd say, "Why hang it man, this property is twenty dollars an acre under the market. Buy this and you won't have to wait for a profit." They'd look bewildered and I'd be frustrated. Now and again one would show me something close but it would fail in the final analysis. Once, one of them brought me a beautiful 300-acre tract with 70 acres fronting on the White River. He showed it to me like a man disclosing some well-kept secret. He was amazed that I could turn it down. It was a good buy, very good, and the businessman in me could see this even as the survivalist was turning it away. It was too good, and I could see all the hunters and fishermen that would be coming down that river and intruding.

Chris was getting tired of the whole thing. Mountain View was a semiresort town with a pretty nice motel and we'd head-quartered there. Every day I'd go venturing out, convinced I could find what I wanted if I only stayed after it long enough. But after the first couple of days, Chris quit going. One night she said to me, "My God, Franklin, let's go home! I'm tired of this. We've been gone nearly three weeks, and I don't know what you're thinking of trying to buy land up here anyway."

I asked her to be just a little patient.

"Why? I don't think there's anything in this area we want. Listen, I was afraid you were actually going to buy that piece that was two hundred dollars an acre and over three hundred acres. What was it, sixty-five-thousand dollars? That'd be thir-teen thousand dollars down and God knows what a year. What are you buying so much for?"

I didn't answer the question, but replied to her statement. "It'd be more than thirteen thousand down, Chris."

"Why? Twenty percent is standard."

"Because," I told her quietly, "we're going to pay cash. For the whole thing. Whatever we buy."

She looked aghast. "Franklin, have you lost your mind! You'd put sixty or seventy thousand dollars of our money in a place like this? Why, we'd never get it out if we had to. I won't have that!"

"I may have to do it," I told her.

"Why cash?"

"Because," I said, "if it's to be truly a hideaway it can't be very much of one if you've got to go to the bank to make payments. I want to buy it and have people forget it exists. They can't do that if you still owe them money."

She got out a cigarette and lit it. It was as good an indicator as any how nervous she was since she rarely smokes. "I don't like this," she said. "I'm not sure I want to do it."

We were sitting in the motel room, she on one twin bed, I on the other. "Chris, you're very near telling me that half our money is yours—half of everything. Don't do that. That would make me mad."

She looked up at me. "Well, I don't give a damn how mad you

get. I'm not going to let you do something foolish, even if it makes you furious."

"I will only do what I feel I have to," I told her gently. "I've done a fair job of taking care of you. Don't stop trusting me now."

She looked at me, grimaced, and then put the cigarette out in disgust. "Oh, Franklin," she said. "You make me so darn mad." She got up and started for the bathroom. "I'm going to get dressed and let's go eat. I've been sitting around this damn place so long I'm about to get cabin fever."

Yellville was a little town about thirty miles from our motel. I kept going back there to hound one particular real estate agent because I felt he *ought* to know where what I sought could be found. His name was Chipman. He was old, seventy at least, and he looked it. He'd been around that part of the country all his life, and he knew every piece of property within a hundred miles. On a day when I knew we'd have to start for home soon, I sat in his little store front office and put it to him one more time. "Last chance, Mister Chipman, to skin the city slicker. We're going to leave tomorrow unless you can come up with something near what I'm talking about."

"Now that's a funny thing," he said. He creaked around in his old swivel chair and looked at the ancient plat map he had pinned to the wall. "I was studyin' 'bout ya'll all yesterday evening after supper. Reckon that was why I dreamed 'bout you last night."

"Dreamed about us?"

"Indeed I did."

"What'd you dream?"

"Well, I don't recollect what I dreamed. But it happened to make me think about an old piece of land I do my best to keep shut out of mind."

"Where is it?" I asked.

He flung out an arm in a northwesterly direction. "Oh, about forty miles up yonder in the wild country. But you don't want it."

He shook his head, and leaned over and spit in a cuspidor by the side of his ancient desk. The times I'd seen him, Mister Chipman had always worn the same dress: khaki pants and shirt with a leather, black bow tie. Though his face was seamed and wrinkled, his hair had surprisingly held its color. I never for a moment suspected that he might be dying it. No man who'd wear a leather bow tie and high top brogans could have enough vanity left to run brown shoe polish through his hair. He was a diminutive, dried-up old man and the way he moved, slow and cautious, mainly gave away his age.

But, in the deprecating way he was talking about the land, I felt a little prickle of premonition. "How big is it?"

"Oh, seven hundred acres, more or less. But you don't want it."

"Why not?"

"Why, pshaw, son, it's in country so wild it'd make a bear homesick for town. And it's way, way, too high. Why, if you lived to be twice as old as I am, you'd never see it come to what is being asked. Belongs to an old crank in Tulsa, Oklahoma. He writes down here every year or so and raises the price five dollars an acre. I used to try to tell him it wouldn't sell at any price, but lately I ain't bothered to waste my breath. Just put it out of my mind."

"How much is it?" I asked steadily.

He looked up at the ceiling, as if to remember. "Best I can recollect he's now asking a hundred dollars an acre. Foolishness."

"That is high," I admitted.

"But that ain't the real reason you don't want it," he said. "Or why it ain't ever going to sell."

I was beginning to lose interest. The way Chris was feeling she'd never be willing to spend that kind of money. "What's the reason?" I asked.

"It's landlocked."

I cocked my head.

"What's that mean?"

"No access. No right-of-way. It's bounded on three sides by a great big estate that's been in litigation for twenty-five or thirty years. That thing's been in and out of court as much as the teeth in my mouth. 'Bout four hundred heirs involved. Who you going to get an easement from? You going to go and get a paper from all four hundred? Why, you couldn't get that bunch to agree on what day of the week it is."

I felt the premonition stirring stronger. "I don't quite understand," I said.

Mister Chipman sighed and stood up. "Well, lemmee show you." He eased slowly out of his chair and went over to an old wooden filing cabinet in the corner. "If I can find the danged thing." He pulled open a drawer and began hunting through folders. "You're sure a lot of trouble."

I smiled.

He went on hunting through folders. "Haven't had this thing out in ten years. Might have rotted or the rats might have ate it. I guess this is it." He drew out a yellowed folder and came back over to the desk, taking out an old plat map. It had been folded for so long that the crease marks had turned brown. I helped him spread it out on the desk. For a moment he bent low over the map, having trouble seeing. "Here it is," he said. "I think." He tapped a place on the map. "Here, your eyes are younger than mine. Does that say tract twelve?"

I leaned over and looked at a large square. It was tract 12 of the Joel Wheaton Survey (done in 1881, I noted).

"Well, look here and you'll see the mess." He pointed to a sort of U-shaped tract that bordered twelve on three sides. "That's that big chunk I was telling you was gone to law. Got you cut off from any road on three sides."

"What about down here," I asked, pointing to the other side. "To the southwest."

"That's no help either. This is the property line on this side, a little old dry creek. Then across that you've got the tail end of another big place. Go on across that and you get on a government reservation. Even if you could get an easement from this feller, if you could find him, you still couldn't get one from the government. You can't build no road over government land."

"Hmmm," I said, my excitement rising. I pointed at the U-shaped parcel again. It was big; big and wide. The closest road looked miles away. "Can you at least get in this way? I mean, just cross it?"

"I reckon you could. Damn sure wouldn't be nobody out there to stop you. But you couldn't build a road. Nothin' permanent.

Sure as you went to all that trouble and expense some one of these fool heirs would find out and then you'd be in court."

"But you could go overland," I insisted. "Even if it was trespassing."

"I guess so," he said. "But I'm telling you, you ain't never gonna get no permanent easement. Not until all them suits get settled. And that ain't never gonna happen. And how you gonna sell any of it without you got a road?"

"Let's go see it," I said. I was very excited.

He looked up at me, startled. "Why, you've taken leave of your senses." He shuffled around his desk, spit his chew in the cuspidor, and got a fresh cud out of his pouch of Day's Work chewing tobacco. "Your pretty wife oughtn't to let you run the streets by yourself."

"Listen, Mister Chipman," I said rapidly, "this is near what I'm looking for. Call me an optimist. I bet I could buy that and hold it and make a ton of money someday. I could get an easement. I bet I could. Over the government land. I've got powerful friends in Washington. In the Capitol." I said it without batting an eye. "And I bet this guy would take a lot less. Let's go see it."

"I ain't gonna drive out there," he said emphatically. "It's nearly dinner time."

"I'll buy your lunch," I insisted. "We'll eat on the way."

He came back to his desk and sat down. "Why, what's the matter with you? I just explained it wasn't a good buy."

"I know. But I want to look at it."

He made an irritated gesture and said querulously. "I doubt I could find the corners. I haven't been on that place in a month of Sundays."

"But you could find it. I don't need to see all the boundaries. I just want to get on it and look around. See what kind of land it is. I've got a big, comfortable pickup with four-wheel drive. All you'll have to do is sit in the air-conditioned cab and give directions."

In the end he gave in. "All right," he said grumpily, "but you're just wasting my time and yours. I tell you, you don't want this property." He went out to my pickup, not even bothering to shut his front door.

We went twenty miles out a paved state road, winding back and through the mountains. Once we left Yellville, we didn't see another sign of civilization except for telephone poles and an occasional mountain shanty. After we turned off the paved road, we went for five or six miles down an unpaved one, then turned off onto a worse one that was rutted and rough. Mister Chipman had complained the whole way about the foolishness of the trip and about what a damned fool I was. "If you just want to throw your money away, why, we could have found a rat hole someplace in town for you to chunked it down and not had to made this damn fool trip. I don't see how a man can think of buying a piece of property he can't even—Here! Whoah! You got to turn here."

I slid to a stop on the gravelly road and backed up, looking for some kind of road. I finally made out the dim outlines of a two-track trail leading back through a heavily forested canyon. "Here?"

"Yes," Mister Chipman said grumpily. "I don't even know if we can get through. I bet this road don't get used once every five years. Probably so grown up a snake couldn't make it."

I put it in four-wheel drive and shifted to low-low, and turned off on the little tracks. It was rough going as we jounced and bumped over rock ledges and deep holes. I followed the trail more by the outline of where the trees had been cleared away than by anything else. We were very shortly into some mountainous terrain. Sometimes it seemed we were going straight up, and other times, I'd be worried about the brakes on a down grade.

"We're on that big tract that's got you boxed in," Mister Chipman said. "The Remacher place."

"How will you know when we get on tract twelve?"

Mister Chipman had put on a sweat-faded old felt hat. The whole ride he'd sat tensely forward, staring out the window. "I ain't sure I will," he said. "There's an old lightning-struck oak with a white rock beside it that is right on the property line. Last time we came out here that's where we turned in. It's about in the middle of the eastern line. But who knows if it'll look the same."

The land had flattened off to hilly knobs and low draws and the going got easier. Once we came to a wide band of exposed rock with a little spring running across it. I stopped over it and opened the truck door and looked down, enjoying the sight of the crystal clear water. "Many springs?"

"Oh, there's plenty of springs. Whole damn country's full of 'em. Must be twenty or thirty on that tract you're talking about."

We went on. Mister Chipman had been right; it got very tight in some places. Once we drug high center going over a rocky ledge, and in a couple of places, the trees pressed in so close that I could hear the paint being scratched off as we forced our way through.

Mister Chipman was leaning far forward, staring intently out of the windshield. "It begins to look a touch familiar," he said. "But I can't be sure. It's been so long— Wait a minute. I believe that's that old oak right down yonder on our left."

It was. A huge white boulder was beside it, drug down from the mountain top by some prehistoric glacier. "Turn left here," Mister Chipman said, leaning back in his seat for the first time. "From here on you're on your own. You're on the place."

I drove a couple of hundred yards deep into the property and stopped and got out. I stood beside the pickup looking around for a few seconds. "Yes," I said in the still mountain air, "this is it."

That night I told Chris, so excited that it came out in spurts of bits and pieces. ". . . I mean some draws and canyons you could hide an oil tanker in. Plenty of sites for the cabin where it couldn't be easily seen. But it's not all rough. There's plenty of flat places. Little knoll here, little valley there. You could farm all over the damn thing! And water! Jesus, you'd never have to drill a well. Plenty and plenty of natural springs. Even a little pond. You could stock that and have fish every day. It's cold enough I believe mountain trout would work. I know they have rainbow in the White River and that's not but thirty miles away. God, Chris, you've got to see it."

Of course, she hadn't seen it so her enthusiasm was contained. I think she was relieved that I'd at least quit looking and we could go home. But I wanted to stay one more night.

"Listen," I said, "we'll go up and see it tomorrow. But instead of going straight home, let's camp out there that night. What do you say?"

"I don't know, Franklin, about that. God, we ought to go home. I'm tired of motels and cafés. Say, how much did you say that place was?"

"Well . . ." I hedged. I stopped moving around the room and sat down. "Well, it's a hundred dollars an acre."

"Oh, no," she said quickly. "No way. That'd be seventy thousand dollars."

"Wait," I said, putting up my hand. "Just wait. I'm not going to pay any hundred dollars an acre. Won't have to. Mister Chipman is going to wire the owner an offer of fifty dollars an acre. And he feels sure we'll get it for no more than sixty."

"That's still forty-two thousand," she said. "And you're talking about cash."

"It's worth it," I insisted. "Wait'll you see it. It's mountain land in mint condition. Chris, it's perfect. Listen, we're not going to lose any money. In fact, we'll probably end up making an immense profit." I still had not told her about the plot being landlocked. "And we'll have such fun fixing up a retreat. Building a cabin, starting a farm. You don't know how much fun it's going to be. Listen, we'll knock a home run with this land."

"I don't know," she said doubtfully.

"Oh, stop that!" I scolded her. "Quit sounding like you're my mother and I'm coming to you for permission for something. Now listen, we'll go up late tomorrow morning and spend the day looking around and then camp out that night. Just like in New Mexico—only no screech owls. How's that?"

"Darn you, Horn," she said. "Do I look like Daniel Boone?"

"Better," I told her. "A whole lot better."

We were up at the land by mid-afternoon. I had no trouble finding my way back, though the ride seemed rougher, maybe because I was worrying about its effect on Chris. But she didn't seem to notice the absence of a road, other than to say, "Good heavens, we'll have to do something about this cow path." But then she had no way of knowing when we were trespassing on the Remacher place.

The day before, in looking around with Mister Chipman, I'd found a nice little flat knoll that I thought would make a good camping place. I pulled to there and we got out of the pickup.

Almost on all sides of us we could see mountains rising, some far, some near. The immediate place we were standing on was clear, it being an exposed rock ledge, but a hundred feet in any direction you ran into heavy forest. I stood watching Chris. "Well?" I asked her. "What do you think?"

"I haven't seen much," she said.

"Com'on." I led her down into a little draw, out of one side of which bubbled a spring. It issued from a fissure in the limestone rocks and fell down to a rocky shelf and then to the bottom of the gully. I filled my hands with some of the sweet, cool water and drank it. "Here," I said, "Try that. Just get some in your hands."

She got a palmful and took a tentative drink.

"Isn't that the best water you ever tasted?" I asked her.

"It's good," she said uncertainly. "Tastes like water."

"Listen," I said, "let's not try to look around too much today. Just make camp and relax. We couldn't see much anyway, before dark. Besides, from what I saw yesterday, it mostly looks like this. I understand there's more bottom land toward the west," I waved an arm, "down toward a dry creek bed. But we don't have to start picking cabin sites, we just want to get a feel of the place this evening and take it easy."

I unloaded the pickup and set up camp and made supper. We had the last of the several bottles of wine I'd brought along on the trip. "This is really something, isn't it," I asked Chris, "sitting here in this absolute wilderness drinking a very civilized bottle of wine. Makes an interesting contrast."

"It's all right," she said. She seemed distracted. I'd noticed her several times glancing quickly over her shoulder. We only had one lantern burning—I'd forgotten to buy fuel and it didn't make much dent in the gloom. The sun was down behind the mountains but not the horizon, and it was twilight.

There was no mistaking night when it did come, with great darkness and the sounds only a very deep and still forest can make. Unfortunately, there was little moon and that, with the surrounding trees and mountains, made it pitch black. Outside of our little circle of light, the darkness was like an impenetrable wall. I looked at Chris and laughed. "You can take the lantern when you go to make your ablutions in the salon I've fixed you."

"I'm all right," she said quickly.

There was no comparing the two places we'd camped in. At the national forest we'd simply been camping, but here there was something primordial, primitive, as if we were totally removed from any world we'd ever known. In a way, we were lost, alone amidst nothing but wilderness and nothing familiar to remind us of anything or anyone we'd ever been.

We went to bed early. Wrapped in the huge sleeping bag I caressed and kissed Chris, but she was unresponsive and I finally turned on my back to sleep. I thought she wasn't in the mood, though she lay huddled very close to me. I had banked the fire down and it was just a dim glow. I lay on my back trying to see through the trees and find a star, anything to look at in that overwhelming black. And then the lantern, which had been growing dim, sputtered and went out. I felt Chris shift beside me. "Franklin?"

"Yeah, Baby?"

"I want to go sleep in the truck."

"Oh, don't be silly. We're perfectly comfortable right here."

"I don't care. I want to go sleep in the truck."

I worked my way around until our faces were very close. "Are you kidding?"

"No," she said. I could feel her breath though I couldn't see her face.

"Well, what's the matter? Aren't you warm enough?"

"It's not any of that. I just want to sleep in the truck. Where's the flashlight?"

"Say, what's the matter? You've got to tell me."

"I just don't like it out here," she answered. "To be truthful, it scares me. I don't want to have to explain it. Give me the flashlight."

"You can't sleep in the truck. Why—"

But she was sitting up and unzipping her side of the sleeping bag. "Where's the flashlight?"

"Here," I said. "Here. But you can't sleep in that pickup. There's no blankets. You'll freeze to death."

"I'll be all right." She was up and had the flashlight on.

"Oh, hell," I said. I heaved myself out of bed and followed her, trailing the sleeping bag over my shoulder.

There was very little room for two people to lie down in the cab. I tried to persuade Chris that we should at least sleep in the bed of the truck, but she wouldn't do it. I didn't argue with her; I understood. She wanted something familiar and civilized and safe around in all that primordial blackness. Her feeling that way disturbed me very much, but I didn't know what to say about it.

Chris was glad to get back home. I was too, in a way, though I dreaded going back to the drudgery of correspondence, sales calls, telephone calls, and the endless haggling and positioning that goes on in my particular business. While in the little towns in Arkansas, we'd gotten out of touch with the news. The first day or two home we were a trifle overwhelmed with what had been happening. It wasn't any more than normal, but it seemed so, coming all at once like that. There weren't any new wars and the riots had cooled, but every expert in the country seemed to be predicting a critical shortage in everything from food and gas to potato chips and cement. Surprisingly, there was a sudden shortage in soybeans. It seemed that only the day before soybeans had finally gained acceptance as a substitute for meat, and now it too was threatened.

Chris and I had talked all the way home about the land and money and things in general. I'd made up my mind, during the night we tried to sleep in the pickup cab, that I was not going to force anything on Chris. I was betting on the long run, purely on intuition, and that wasn't a solid enough reason to make my wife unhappy. I thought tract 12 was perfect for my purposes, but I wasn't going to insist. Chris had changed her thinking also. "I want you to do what you think is best," she'd said. "After all, you've got to slay the dragons. What do I know about it, anyway?"

"I'd asked her what had scared her so badly in the mountains.

"Nothing," she confessed. "I don't really know. It was like anything could be out there. I don't know, it just scared me. But I've got to stop being that way, and I will. Go ahead and buy that land if you want to."

I'd finally told her about the landlocked business and how the tract would be useful to us for just the one purpose; that we'd probably never be able to sell it. She frowned as she understood. "Well, I don't know, Franklin. I mean, that's sort of putting your eggs all in one broken basket, isn't it? Shouldn't we look around some more, find something not so final?"

"That's just it," I insisted, "the very features that make tract twelve unsalable are what make it perfect for what we want it for. I mean, I don't know that we'll get it, but if we do I think we better not worry about resale. Every move a man makes doesn't have to be for the purposes of making money, does it?"

"I suppose not," she'd admitted.

"It's only paper," I'd said, "with a barter value. We could see the day when that tract would be worth all the money in the world."

"What the hell," she'd said, and laughed.

But I wanted her to understand it clearly. "Now wait a minute," I said carefully. "Buying the land is just the beginning of it. We'll have to spend more money."

"How much more?"

"Well, we'd have to build a cabin. And stock it. We'll need some farming essentials. The sort of things you need to survive. Maybe a few thousand dollars more. I'll have to build the cabin myself."

"You don't know how to build a cabin."

"I might surprise you," I told her. "You might truly be surprised at the number of things I can do that you don't know about."

Back home I was interested to see that I'd lost twelve pounds— a good loss in the right places. Importantly, I could feel my stamina increasing. I hadn't been able to do much about the smoking, but I'd cut down on liquor until it was no longer an everyday affair.

Before we'd left I'd given Mister Chipman a check for a

thousand dollars earnest money and he'd said he'd get off an offer of fifty dollars per acre. "I tell you, if it was mine," he'd said, "I'd sell it damn quick for that price. Or any price. But I can't guarantee what that yahoo is liable to do. He's as crazy as you are. Maybe you both know something I don't know. Well, we'll see." He'd promised to write at the first word he had. I'd asked him to call, but he'd said the only way to make things clear was to put it in a letter.

While we waited, we fell back into our normal way of life. One day we had a letter from Chris's parents. "Oh, lordy," she said, looking up from reading it, "they're coming for a visit."

"When?" We were sitting in the den. Chris had been working a crossword puzzle and I was busy with some government pamphlets on farming.

"Doesn't give an exact date. Daddy has to go to the Pentagon on some sort of business. Probably," she looked up and grinned, "about the cost of living in Colombia. He'll probably want to call in an air strike if they don't lower prices on London gin. Anyway, mother's coming and they'll let us know once they get in the States." She read some more and then frowned and looked up at me. "What does this mean? He makes some reference to Australia and then says, 'so is imperative I have your cooperation in talking sense to your husband.' What does he mean by that? Did you upset Daddy while you were over there?"

"Not any more than he upset me," I answered, and then I told her what I remembered.

"Oh, Franklin," she said reproachfully, "Why? Why in the world?"

"Listen, don't jump on me. Obviously, I'm about to be punished in full. Does he say how long they intend to stay?"

"No," she answered. "Probably until you become sensible."

"In that case let's just meet them at the airport and I'll agree with everything he's got to say and they can get right back on the plane."

"I'd like to see mother," Chris said. "Oh, hell, I'd like to see them both. Impossible as it sounds, I do miss Daddy sometimes."

I looked over at her, wondering if my wife was feeling a touch lonely and afraid and if I'd caused it by my attitude and premonitions of doom.

"Well, we'll try and give them a good time," I said.

She glanced suspiciously at me. "That doesn't sound like you, Franklin. Really, don't expect Daddy to understand your viewpoints. He can't and won't. So don't fight with him."

"I promise," I said.

Morton Dowd was a friend to both Chris and myself. When you wanted to describe Morton you first thought of charming, then funny and witty, and then undependable. He was a big, bluff, out-of-shape Irishman who drank too much and ate too much and didn't often concern himself with what his antics did to those who loved him. He'd been spoiled all his life. His wife spoiled him, as well as any other women he was around. For a man who wasn't particularly handsome or manly, he was certainly popular with women. The men liked him too. He could flirt with wives in a way that had no threat in it. We all recognized that and were glad to see our wives charmed and pleased. At some dim past point he'd been an actor and had the voice and mannerisms of the profession. He could still walk into a crowded room and have every eye in a matter of seconds. I suppose all that charm was a mixed blessing for his wife. He displayed it as much for her as other people; it was no act. But to go with it, she also had the worry and insecurity of his irresponsibility. She called us one night, late, and wanted to know if we had any idea where Morton might be. Chris took the call. We were lying in bed, not quite ready for sleep. I knew immediately what it was about. When she hung up, she turned to me. "Well, Morton's off on another one. Poor Ivy is getting worried. He hasn't been home in thirty-six hours. She said since you were his best friend you might know something."

"All the world's Morton's best friend," I answered. "That's just a little trick of Ivy's. She'll call six guys and tell them the same thing, hoping the implied compliment will stir them to go out and hunt our fat friend down. I ain't falling for the old best friend trick."

Chris frowned. "Where do you suppose he is?"

"Drunk somewhere."

"You don't suppose he's with a woman, do you?"

"If there's one within a mile, he's with her."

At that moment the phone rang again. Chris picked it up and

handed it over to me. "Here, you talk to her this time."

But it wasn't Ivy. It was Morton.

"What do you want?" he said as soon as I said hello. "What do you mean calling me at this hour? Don't you know I'm busy?" Then he laughed.

I could tell from the sound of his voice that he was pretty drunk. His beautiful enunciation would never allow him to slur words, but there was a little pitch that gave him away.

"All right," I said, "What are you selling fellow. Office is closed. Call back tomorrow."

The teasing went out of his voice. "Hey, this is Mort. How about coming down and getting me."

"What for?"

"I'm drunk. Better not drive."

"Hell with that. Take a cab."

There was a pause. "No, com'on down, Franklin. Really." There was another pause. "I'm in a joint and I got a problem. I've lost my billfold somewhere and I got a bar tab I can't pay and I can't get home. Com'on buddy."

"Damn you, Mort," I swore. "I'm in bed."

He spoke rapidly and I could tell he was worried. "Listen, I could be in a little trouble if I don't get out of here pretty soon. And I don't think there's anyway I can walk the tab. You're my last chance, buddy. This is my last dime. I'm not kidding you."

I cussed and ranted for a moment but finally said I'd come. "If this is the old get-Franklin-out-for-a-wild-night trick I'm going to break his neck."

The place was called the Pigtail and it was about as dark as any of its type. I had to stand a long time just inside the door before my eyes would adjust. A cocktail waitress, shadowy and pale in her topless outfit, came up to seat me, but I told her I was looking for a friend.

I found Morton in a corner of the bar. He was sitting half slumped over a drink, very quiet and staring down at nothing. I got up on a stool beside him. "When are you going to learn you can't drink?"

"Last time," he said lowly. "I've learned my lesson, buddy. You're gonna see the new Morton Dowd."

"Sure," I said.

"And if you buy that," he announced with a touch of his normal nerve, "I got some used TVs I'd like to unload."

He looked pretty bad. His suit was rumpled and his tie was loose, and from stains on his shirt front, it looked as if he might have vomited on himself. The bartender came over and asked for my order. "Nothing," I gestured. "Just his check."

The bartender stared at me narrowly. He was a big, sloppy-looking man with a bullet head and heavily muscled forearms. "You paying his check?" He said it as if he weren't quite sure it'd be all right.

"Sure. Why not?"

He didn't answer, except to jerk his head at Morton. "Couldn't he paid it? He been drinkin' and couldn't pay his tab?"

"What the hell, I'm here now." I got out my billfold. "How much is it?"

He gave me a last suspicious glance and went off to get Mort's total. I looked around the shoddy little place. "You got a lot of class," I told Mort sarcastically. He said, "Let's have one more drink before we go."

"No chance," I told him flatly. "And don't give me any trouble. I'm taking you home." For some reason, I had an uneasy feeling about the bar. It was nothing except maybe the way the bartender had acted. I'd been in rougher places. As if he were thinking the same thing, Mort said, "Yeah, you're right. I don't like this place." He stared at a Lone Star beer sign hanging over the bar. "I almost got killed in here a while ago."

"What happened?" I asked. "You fall in some fat broad's pussy?"

"I'm not kidding," he said. "Listen, there's two guys that—"

But the bartender had come back. Mort's bill was $57. I looked first at the bartender, then Mort, then back to the bartender. "Are you kidding me? Nobody can drink that many drinks."

The man shrugged. "You just got here, fellah. What do you know?"

Mort was peering over my shoulder. "Listen, that's not right. This guy is padding my bill. I'm not—"

The bartender said steadily, "You guys starting trouble?"

"Never mind. Keep your mouth shut, Mort." I counted out the money and left it on the bar.

The bartender looked at it. "We usually tip around here."

The bad feeling was getting worse and worse. I felt like everyone in the place was staring at us. The room wasn't very big and, now that my eyes had adjusted, I could see shadowy forms sitting around at tables. "Listen," I said lowly, "what's your problem? Do I look that easy?" I didn't wait for an answer, but got Mort's shoulder and steered him off the bar stool and to his feet. "Let's go." I wanted out of there.

We were going down an aisle between the tables. There wasn't room to walk side by side and Mort was following me. All of a sudden two men stood up, blocking our path. One of them, nearest to me, said, "I don't like that sonofabitch."

I didn't understand for a second, didn't even realize he was talking to us. I kept walking until the man put out a hard hand and shoved me to a stop.

"I said I didn't like that sonofabitch," he repeated. There was venom in his voice, hate filled with the sound of a man who wants to smash something.

I was off balance. "What are you talking about?"

The man stabbed a finger over my shoulder at Morton. "Him! You a friend of his?"

"Sure," I said. I started around the man, but the second man, who hadn't spoken, stepped out and blocked the rest of the aisle. I could feel the trouble thick as rock. "What is this? Get out of our way." I wasn't scared, but I had that little surge of weak excitement like something bad was going to happen. Morton hadn't said a word, and I was hoping he wouldn't. The men weren't very big or particularly tough-looking. They were just ordinary-looking men. Neither was going to be mistaken for the president of a bank, but they didn't look like hoods, either.

The first man, who was the bigger, said, in that grating voice, "I'm gonna kill that sonofabitch. And I'll get a piece of your ass if you get in the way."

"Look," I said. I took a step backward, pushing Morton as I did. "Look, I don't know what this is."

The man immediately closed the distance. They were crowding us, pushing. I didn't know what to do; I didn't understand all that hate.

"I don't like that sonofabitch," the man said.

"Well, everybody else does."

"I'm gonna whip his ass!"

I don't know what might have happened. At that instant Morton decided to get brave. He said, loudly, "Well, you can get me, buddy! Just get you a handful!"

The man leaped forward; whether he was going for me or Morton I couldn't tell. I ducked and threw my side into him swinging instinctively. I felt my fist go home in his belly, heard a grunt in the whiskey-smelling breath on my face, twisted, swung again, and then gave ground as I felt another body thud into the pile. I was conscious of Morton just at my back, swinging wildly. Then something clipped me on the side of the head, and I stumbled into a table and went to my knees.

It was all one swirling mass, impossible to assimilate in the darkness and noise and confusion. The second man, smaller than the other, was on the floor beside me. He reared up, drawing back his arm. Somehow, in the gloom, I was able to see that he had bad teeth. I lashed out, punching him hard and solid in his bad mouth. He disappeared. Then a heavy body fell on me and I went to the floor, suddenly frightened. I was at the bottom of a heap of tangled arms and legs. I felt as if I were smothering and the thought came that these men, whom I didn't even know, were going to kill us for some reason of their own. I twisted and fought, swinging in every direction with my fists and feet. Something hit me in the side, and I knew it must be bad because it hurt even in the heat of all that fighting. I got to my knees again. The bartender was there, easy to see in his white T-shirt. He had a short piece of hoe handle in his hand. He swung at my head and hit me on the shoulder. From my knees, I punched him twice in the belly and he stumbled backward. Then I was hit in the back of the head and I went down. I felt the fright come strong and I heard my own voice yelling, "Help! Help!"

I got home a little after four in the morning. Chris was up, waiting for me in the den. When I came into the room she jumped up, her eyes getting big. "Franklin?" she said uncertainly. "Franklin? Honey? For God's sake!"

I knew I looked bad; my shirt was torn to pieces, I had scratches and cuts all over my arms and upper body, my mouth was cut, one of my eyes was swollen, and an ear was bleeding where some-one had hit me. I sat down. "I'll try to tell you about it," I said painfully. My tongue hurt; I think I'd bit it.

"Oh, my God! Look at you!" She came hurrying forward and knelt by the side of my chair. "Have you been in a car wreck?"

"I'll tell you about it in a second. Get an ice pack now. Maybe I can hold down the swelling."

She came back with a bowl of ice and water and cloths and a glass of straight bourbon. I took the whiskey and swished it around in my mouth and spit it out in a big ashtray. It hurt terribly. My mouth was all cut up inside. When I could I began, little by lit-tle, to tell Chris what had happened. I finished with, "And when I came to the bartender was taking a hundred dollars out of my billfold. He said it was for damage we'd caused. Then they threw us out. I guess I should be thankful the police weren't involved?"

"But why?" she cried. "Do you have any idea why they attacked you? What had Morton done to them?"

"He says nothing."

"Oh, that's impossible."

"No. I believe him. I've been thinking about it and I believe he doesn't really know he did anything. Chris, you couldn't be-lieve that hate. Those guys wanted to kill us. I mean, the hate was like a physical force. I can't quite explain it."

"Then what caused it, if Morton didn't do anything to them."

"Oh, he did something all right. He just doesn't realize it. He came in that bar his charming, witty self. I can imagine that in five minutes he had every woman in the place either actually or covertly in his company. He came in there in his three-hundred-dollar suit and all his charm and sophistication and seeming hap-piness, and those guys hated him for it. It wasn't that he took the women or the attention or any of that. It was just flatly that he had something that they wanted. Greed caused that hate. They wanted to be like Morton. And, failing that, they wanted to smash him up, get him out of the way so the comparison wouldn't be there. From what little he said, I think they must have already made a run at him but he held them off with his best defense, fast words. Besides, he was plenty drunk and there's a code in a place like that you don't punch out a real drunk. And he was wearing a suit. All these guys were laboring types. I bet not a one of them ever hit someone wearing a suit.

"But then along comes me. I'm fair game. And all that hate and greed has had time to build. I'm not wearing a suit and I'm not drunk. Look at the bartender. Driving home, I finally figured out why he'd reacted as he had. He'd been fooled, and he didn't like it. Here was Mort in there, big-timing it—you know how he can act. Like he's got a million dollars in his pocket and a chauffeur-driven limousine waiting outside. And then here *I* come to pay his *tab!* The bartender sees he's been fooled, that Mort's just another broke drunk. Bam! He'd like to have hit me right then and there because I was the one who made it obvious how fooled he'd been. He'd probably been paying real servility to Mort, sir-ing him and yes-ing and acting the way Mort always makes the hired help act. I tell you, now that I've figured it out, I'm surprised we got out of there as light as we did."

"Is Mort hurt very bad?"

"Morton?" I smiled in spite of my painful mouth. "Morton is the king of the survivalists. Compared to him I'm just an amateur. Morton never got hit once. He was on the floor, but I think he simply passed out. Never took a punch. You won't believe this, but *he* drove us home. I could barely see and he'd sobered up. He's probably home right now being babied by Ivy and entertaining her with some cock-and-bull story. And next week he'll be going around town telling people how he pulled me out of a fight and got me home." I shook my head and laughed. "I'm out a hundred and fifty-seven bucks, have a smashed up face and probably a broken rib, and Mort's the hero. I got to get that boy to give me lessons. Sliding Morton Dowd."

I'd met Chris almost eleven years previous in the Nicte Ha Bar of the Hotel Del Prado in Mexico City. I was just in from a dirty mining job deep in the interior and I was lonesome and happy to be in town and ready for a good time. I was at the bar when I saw her. She was sitting by herself at a nearby table, wearing a white linen suit and drinking a champagne cocktail as cool and unbelievably beautiful as it's possible for a woman to look. She was wearing her blond-brown hair in a helmet cut, as was the fashion of the day, and she was lounged gracefully back in her chair, coolly surveying the room, part of the crowd and yet completely removed. I watched her for a long time, certain there was a man about to come and yet wondering what man would be such a fool as to go off and leave a woman like that for over five minutes. She finished her drink and ordered another, and I decided that she was going to be out of my life in ten minutes if I didn't do something. I'd gone over to the table and made some silly opening remark. She'd stared back, not at all interested. I'd said, "Do you mind if I sit down?"

"Yes, I do," she'd answered.

I sat down anyway. "Look, I know I'm intruding, but I'm just in from the interior and I don't know a soul in town. And I've got the most beautiful love story to tell you've ever heard, and if I don't get to tell it, I'm going to die." I'd said all that very rapidly and then waited to see what effect it might have. It was no line; I really had just witnessed a love story and it had touched me and depressed me and I wanted to share it with this young woman because there was something in her face that told me she'd understand the story and understand why it had touched me.

She'd looked at me uncertainly for a moment, appraisingly.

"It won't take five minutes," I said.

She looked at me for another full five seconds. Then she said, "All right."

I began to tell her of my trip, how we'd gone deep into the interior to investigate a precious mineral claim that had been lying dormant for years. We'd been in Tahamarraun Indian country. This was a wretchedly poor tribe of mountain Indians who didn't speak true Spanish, but a mixed-up dialect that none of us in my party knew. Since we'd needed some of them for laborers and to clear away a large stretch of brush, we'd been delighted to find an intelligent young man among them who not only could speak good Spanish but knew a good deal of English as well. He was such a cut above the rest that we'd hired him as interpreter and general factotum and taken him into our camp with us. One night after we'd been there a couple of weeks, he began hesitantly telling me that he'd been in the United States. Some three years past he'd crossed the border illegally and gotten into California. With the wetbacks' instinct he'd worked his way north, knowing he'd be less subject to detection in that direction. He somehow got up into the state of Washington and there got a job in a lumber mill. In six months he'd fallen in love with the daughter of a Mexican–American that worked at the mill and they'd planned to get married. But the father had wanted more for his daughter, so he'd turned the boy in to the immigration authorities and they'd deported him. For the next year he'd spent his time on the border, making several unsuccessful attempts to get back to his love. The last time the border patrol had caught him they'd made it clear that he would be going to jail for a long time if he gave them any more trouble. Frantic and anguished he'd gone to Mexico City and found work. He'd been told that with a thousand dollars he could get into the States legally. So he'd worked at everything he could find to do, lived frugally, spent nothing, and in seventeen months had saved a thousand dollars. He'd taken it to an uncle in Urapan; an uncle who was considered the only successful man in the whole wretched tribe because he lived in the biggest city in the state and had a job that paid actual cash money. The boy had thought sure that a man such as his uncle could manage the affair and he knew no one else to go to. Unfortunately, the uncle took the money and got in a gambling game with a group of wealthy avocado farmers in a room in a hotel that fronted on the plaza in Urapan. Of course, he'd lost the money, but then he'd been shot dead in the fight that followed. The boy had been standing right there in the plaza when they'd carried the uncle out. No one had known anything about his money. Almost finished he'd gone back to his family in the little village of Tumbuscatio, to which we'd come. He'd been there for a year and hadn't seen his love for over two. But it was still on. The mail came to the village six times a year (when the road wasn't washed out), and he had a letter about every other time.

I'd stopped and looked at Chris. "What do you think of that?"

"What's he going to do?" she'd asked me.

I'd shrugged and gestured with my drink. "What can he do? He's outweighed and outclassed by forces and powers over which he has no control. I suppose it's the lack of realist in me that drives me crazy with the idea that here's a guy who just wants to be with a girl from a little lumber town in Washington. Wants to get married, have a family. Who's he hurting? Who would he be hurting? But they got this imaginary border he can't cross. So he sits up in the mountains and lives for three or four letters a year. I mean, these aren't the most important people you'll ever see. I read one of the girl's letters and it sounds like just about what you might expect from a love-sick, nearly illiterate seventeen-year-old."

Chris, the practical realist, had said, "Why can't they get married and live in Mexico?"

"Girl's not of age," I'd explained. "Needs her father's consent. But why should they have to? They're citizens of the world. Why can't they live where they want to? My God, look at what this boy's already overcome. You'd have to see that village to really understand. I don't mean they're Indians in the sense they wear loin cloths and shoot bows and arrows. They look about like any other poor country Mexican; they live in mud huts and grub a little living out of poor soil and skinny goats. About one in every five hundred can read and write a little. I don't know how this boy learned. And that ought to be enough of an accomplishment right there, never mind making it all the way to Washington, never mind somehow saving a thousand dollars. Do you have any idea how hard that is? It's impossible. Just flatly impossible. So I think the kid's done enough. I think he ought to have his chance. But he's not going to get it." I was cooling down from my rapid, fevered talk. "He'll sit up on that mountain until he forgets. And the girl'll forget. Already he says her letters are less romantic."

"He said romantic? The word romantic?"

"No," I'd admitted. "He probably said less friendly. This is not Romeo and Juliet or Tristan and Isolde. This is a grubby little Mexican boy and his equally grubby little girl friend."

"Why don't you do something about it?" she asked me. "I'm sure that's why the boy told you the story."

"Certainly," I'd agreed. "But I'm not going to do anything. I don't really care what happens to that boy."

"I thought you said the story had touched you."

"It did. But it's the idea of the thing. The frustration. The unrequited freedom." I'd smiled slowly. "The idea being that it could happen to me and then I *really* wouldn't like it. I'm sorry to disappoint you, but I'm not a humanist. I'm a survivalist."

She'd smiled then. "An honest idealist. My God!"

"I'm not an idealist. Furthest thing from it."

"Oh, yes you are."

I was in love with Chris before the night was out. But it was two years before I could get her to marry me. She was just off her brief, unsuccessful marriage and she wanted a period by herself. All her life there'd been her domineering father; then had come the weak husband that leaned on her. She'd never had a time when she could simply stand alone and be swayed by her own breeze. To be alone, she'd come to Mexico City by herself, and it was because of that that I'd happened to find her in that bar on that particular evening. I use to get little bolts of fright when I'd think of the immense odds that had to be overcome for us to be there and meet. I think it even took the novelty of the Mexican boy's love story to give me a chance with her. If I hadn't had that to win her initial interest I expect she'd have brushed me off and sent me back to the bar.

I told her, that night, that I loved her and wanted to marry her. "I'm thirty-three," I'd said. "I've done and seen just about everything I want to. I've never been really seriously interested in a woman because I never found one of that much interest. But you're different and I'm going to marry you."

She'd said, not at all shocked or rattled by the sudden proposal, "I don't want to get married. I want to be on my own."

"That's all right for now," I'd answered. "But I'm going to change your mind."

She'd smiled. "Nothing is impossible for the idealist."

"You're thinking about that Mexican boy. I don't know about the idealist part, but I do know about possible. They couldn't build a wall high enough to keep me away from you."

While we waited, waited for Chris's parents to come and for word from Mister Chipman, I went forward with some of the groundwork necessary for creating our retreat. I was neglecting my business, but I considered it in a good cause. Actually, I wasn't neglecting it that badly because there wasn't much to do. The diamond market was in such a chaotic state that a man was better off just sitting back and waiting. The demand for diamonds was growing every day and prices were rising faster than delivery could be made. A picture was gradually emerging. People were buying diamonds, individual people, as security. Of course, this was nothing new; people had been doing it for centuries in times of trouble and uncertainty. When it was over and the country was stable, they had their property ready to turn back into cash and usable possessions. It was interesting to note the same pattern in my own culture. One more omen in a steadily increasing list.

But I was finding something far more stable to put money in than diamonds. I was buying usable and useful goods. I bought more gasoline. I bought a hundred pounds of nails, all sizes. One day I came home with two crates each of hoes, rakes, shovels, axes, and mattocks. With 12 tools to each crate that made 120. Chris looked at the array in some amazement. "Are you going into the hardware business?"

"Listen, I don't want us ever to fail for want of a hoe or an axe."

"But all those?"

"There might come a day," I told her, "when these are worth a hundred dollars apiece."

With every day that passed I became more consumed to own that piece of land. I felt we had to have it. If he'd had a phone, I would have called Mister Chipman a half dozen times. I even considered calling some nearby business, a café or something—any place that had a phone—and having someone fetch him. But I held off because I knew he didn't have anything to tell me. There was nothing to do but wait.

I drew up some simple plans for the cabin I intended to build. Chris looked at it and asked what we'd call it. "The Fort," I answered. "What else? God, honey, can't you just see yourself in this little kitchen canning peaches and making jelly and baking bread."

"No," she answered truthfully. "I really can't."

I looked at her suspiciously. "Have you been studying those pamphlets I got you on canning and preserving?"

"Some," she said. "But, God, Franklin, they don't make the most interesting reading. I'm not really looking forward to this as a preferred way of life. It was my understanding it would be an emergency measure."

"Well, sure. . . ." I told her. "But we ought to be as ready as we can."

I finally felt as if I were refuting the common belief that nothing could be done. I was doing something. Maybe it wasn't the course everyone would have chosen, and maybe it would turn out to be ineffective and bad, but at least I was moving in a direction intended to counteract a threat. I felt good about myself, more whole than I had in many a year. Like a good general, I was summoning my logistics. If I got the land I would have my fort; meanwhile, I was proceeding with other efforts that would always be useful. I was getting my forces, me, in shape. I was able now to jog three miles without becoming seriously tired. I had more stamina than I could remember since my days of knocking around in the brush. I *felt* as if I could build a cabin and till a field and do the heavy labor necessary for self-sufficiency. It was a confident feeling, knowing I would not fail myself. I'd cut the drinking to a minimum and had lost weight down to 195 pounds. Looking in a mirror I could see the transformation in my face. It looked harder, more determined, capable. I'd joke by saying, "There's a man with a face you can trust." But the part I liked about it was that I felt it was true.

I really knew very little about farming, but I'd been reading voraciously on the subject, and if I didn't have much practical knowledge, I had a great deal of theory. I haunted the library, seeking old books that had information out-of-date for present-day, but in vogue for my uses. I was probably the only man in the city with a good working knowledge of how to build a corn sheller. I'd never made one, but I had the instructions and a picture and I knew I could do it. Sometimes I would dream my way through a typical day of the life we might expect. I would take it step-by-step, from the time I got up in the morning until I went to bed at night. Along the way I'd imagine every tool or article I might use during that day. If I didn't have it already, I'd write it down and plan to get it. By doing that during all the seasons, from corn planting to hog killing to building fence and piping water, I felt as if I'd cover the needs of all eventualities. I didn't want to get back in there and fail for want of the right kind of nail.

There were other areas that concerned me; medical and dental care and social company. I thought I could do without the last myself, but I wasn't sure it would be good for Chris. The medical and dental was something that had to be strongly considered. There were two ways to look at it; one, the country would be in such a chaotic state that there might not be any doctors and it would be too dangerous to try and slip out of our fort to find one, or, two, things might just be in a super-strained state with sporadic trouble and we could chance going out with some hope of returning safely. The best solution would be to have a doctor with you. I think it had been subconsciously on my mind from the very first. Nick. Nick Pfeiffer. He was no longer a practicing physician, but he'd once been and he'd be a lot better than nothing or a copy of *The Doctor's Helper*. And of course, Nick was on my mind because of so many of the things he'd said. A great deal of his personal philosophy agreed with mine, though I didn't present it as readily for public consumption as he did. He was a strong individualist, a violent anarchist, and selfish enough in his personal viewpoint to be interested in surviving first and saving his fellow man second. His wife was compatible with mine and with me, and he had enough money to contribute to the expenses of such a plan.

But I was hesitant about mentioning it to him because of his irritating sarcasm. In spite of anything he might personally believe, he could just as easily tear the whole plan to shreds on a whim. I didn't want to listen to that. Nick Pfeiffer had the best capacity of anyone I knew of getting me into an absolute rage.

And Morton Dowd. Of course Dowd's only contribution would be purely social and entertaining. But he was the best at that I knew. How Morton would feel about it was something I couldn't even guess. If the worst came and we had to use the fort, they would both have to do their part in getting it ready. I wanted a commitment now, when the whole idea might seem farfetched and silly.

But first I'd have to broach the subject, and I shrank from that. Just happily dreaming on it in the privacy of my own mind the idea seemed right and necessary. But to throw it out in front of a couple of other people, with the very solid effects of a working society all about you, is quite a different proposition. It's difficult to get someone to believe the roof is about to fall in when you're sitting in a restaurant having a cocktail while business as usual is all around you.

But that's what I finally did. I invited both Morton and Nick to lunch. They both liked an audience, so I thought I'd give them each other if they wanted to ridicule me.

We met at a downtown restaurant, and first, Morton had to tell Nick his story of our barroom fight. By the time he'd finished it, he was carrying me out with one hand while holding off a massed phalanx of armed hoods with the other. When he'd stopped laughing at his own humor I said, "You know, I don't think that was very funny."

"Oh, com'on, buddy. Just a little tussle. You and I need that sort of thing every once in a while. Keeps us young."

"I hate to tell you this," I answered, "but we're not young. We're middle-aged men. What I wanted to say was that we were in real trouble. You didn't realize it because you had passed out. But I was scared. Those men had half a mind to kill us. There was a very weak thread holding them back from going all the way."

"Aw, Franklin," Morton laughed, "it wasn't that bad."

"Yes it was," I insisted. "And you were scared, Mort. You were scared when you called me. I heard it in your voice."

"I just wanted some reinforcements, buddy. That's good thinking."

"Sure. Because subconsciously, when all the booze would let you think, you realized what a tight place you were in. I doubt it was on the top of your mind—even if you were sober—because such things don't happen to nice people like us. Getting killed in a saloon brawl. But way down deep inside you knew. You almost felt it strong enough to make a break for the door, didn't you? Run for your life. Didn't you?"

My hard analysis had taken the humor out of Mort. I'd spoiled a good story, that was all he saw. He didn't really see the correlation I was setting up.

Nick was looking at me with his hard, black eyes. "That's a very good point, Franklin. That such things don't happen to, quote, nice, unquote, people like us. Why not?"

"Because they're unthinkable," I said readily.

"My, my," he said.

"We've got too many governors, too many safeguards. We've built our defenses too well. All that sort of thing is long out of our life. Except Mort wandered into the wrong place and a whole new set of conditions came into play. The rules were different. But he went on being Mort, he didn't adapt. And he could have gotten killed for it."

Morton looked disturbed. "Aw, Christ, Franklin, stop that kind of talk. You'll have me scared in a moment. After all, I did save your life." He tried a laugh but it didn't come off.

"Am I making you uneasy? Pointing this out?"

"Hell, let's eat," he said. "Or have another drink."

Nick was still looking at me. "Franklin's not drinking, I notice. On the wagon?"

"Not entirely." I took a sip of tomato juice. I could feel Nick's analytical eye going over me. When I glanced up he said, "You look different, Franklin. I hadn't noticed before. Your face is thinner. You've lost weight. You look fit. What are you training for?"

I shrugged. "Any eventuality, my friend. Who knows?"

"Tell us," Nick prodded.

But Morton broke in. "*I'm* in training for the fat man's Olympics," he announced in one of his stage voices. "So let's eat." He pounded the table with his spoon. "Meat for me and my merry men and water for our horses. Where is that lady with the menus?"

I didn't plan to say anything until we were through eating. With food around, it's hard to get Morton's full attention. But Nick would not be put off. He instinctively knew something was different about me and he knew that I hadn't invited them both to lunch just because I needed their immediate society. He kept probing me, going, with that irritating intuition of his, toward the very heart of the matter. Morton was eating, oblivious of what we were talking about. I finally pushed my plate back and asked, "Nick, what's going to happen in this country? Say, the next five years."

"Martial law," he answered. "Or anarchy."

"No other alternatives?"

"Not with the present trend. It happens in every country that fails in the supply of basic goods and services. And then there are several valid philosophic reasons also. However, I don't expect to be agreed with."

"Oh, I agree with you," I said quickly.

Morton looked up and asked: "What's that?"

"Martial law or anarchy," I told him. But my concentration was on Nick. "But do you really believe that? I mean, do you believe it in actuality? That it can really happen? Isn't this just some more of your word games?"

He smiled thinly. "Why of course it can't happen," he answered. "You put it very well yourself. Such things don't happen to nice people like us. We wouldn't allow it. It would be unthinkable. Our lives have always gone along on a nice, pleasant norm. Therefore, they always will."

I leaned back in my chair. "You're saying a frightening thing," I told Nick slowly. "Do you realize that?"

"That would depend on what frightens you."

"I wish I knew what you two guys are so intense about," Morton said. He turned and signaled to the waiter to bring him a drink. "Tell your old dad. I'll put you straight."

We went on talking, drawing Morton into the conversation. We rehashed all the ground Nick and I had covered so many times before. "It'll start," Nick said, "with a riot in . . ." He thought a moment. "Albuquerque, New Mexico."

I felt a strange stirring.

"Thirty-three rioters and eight police will be killed," he went on. "The governor will panic and call out the National Guard. There'll be heavy street fighting and certain organized groups, who've been waiting for just such an opportunity, will attack the traditional controls of power—the communications centers, the transportation facilities, the utility centers. Normal life will be interrupted as effectively as if an atomic bomb had been dropped in the middle of town. And once that happens, once a new set of rules come into play . . ." He smiled thinly at me. "You said it. It's a whole new ball game."

"Aw, com'on," Morton broke in. "None of that's going to happen. Things are a little fucked up now, but they'll get it straightened out."

"Who is this *they*?" Nick asked him with distaste. "Who is this omnipotent *they* that wins your childlike trust? *They* might be a group of people just about like yourself."

Morton blinked at him.

"How'd you like to trust your future to someone like you?"

"Com'on Nick," I said, "lay off Morton. I got something I want to talk about."

I laid it out for them straight, with very little of the personal fire or fears or convictions. I cited the situation, trends, history, consequences, in some cases quoting Nick back to himself. For Morton's benefit I quoted what I thought were fair percentages. Without being specific about location and other particulars, I painted a realistic picture of the land and how it lay and what work would be required. I finished with, "So. That's the way I see things are and what precautions can be taken. Obviously, I'm being an alarmist and overreacting, but my point is—what have I got to lose? I don't think even the cost of the land. Some time, perhaps, in getting it ready. A few thousand more in tools and supplies and building materials. But that's inconsequential beside the value of such a place if it became necessary. But, as I said, if you two are interested I'm going to need a real and actual commitment from you. You've got to come in now and come in with work and money."

I leaned back in my chair and waited.

For a long moment neither spoke. I knew one thing in advance; they would each speak for themselves with no interest in what the other thought. Then Morton said, "Well, that ain't no decision for me. You can get me, baby, and right now. Damn right count me in. I'm like you, I see everything to gain and nothing to lose. I think it's a smart idea."

That was fine coming from Mort, but I would believe it a little stronger when I actually got him up in the mountains helping me build the cabin. I wasn't particularly interested in his getting out his checkbook and writing me a check; it would probably bounce depending on what day of the month it was.

Nick still hadn't said anything, just sat there, a little half smile on his face, looking as if he were stroking his beard without actually moving his hand. "Well?" I asked him.

"I'm just wondering," he answered, "about you. Wondering what it is you're really after."

"I told you," I said. That was just like Nick, having to overcomplicate everything.

"I don't think so," he answered. "Though I'm sure that what you say is part of it. No, I think you're flying a test balloon for your own benefit."

"How so?"

"Well," he told me comfortably, "you think you've either got a brilliant idea or a very ridiculous one. But you're not sure which. Our reaction will tell you."

"That's bullshit. I'm doing this either way. With or without either one or both of you."

Nick pounced. "Then why tell us? Why offer us a piece of the action?"

"I told you. Because of your contributions."

"And that's bullshit. You want this commitment from Morton and me. Can't you just see either one of us helping you build a house or raise a fence or plow a field. Morton might tell funny stories about building a house and I'm sure I could discuss it brilliantly in theory, but in actuality? Of course not. And you know that as well as I do. My idea of exercise is reading without my glasses."

Morton put in, "Well, I personally think it's a very good idea. And I appreciate Franklin thinking of me. Ivy will be thrilled to hear about this. She's been a little edgy about things."

"Living with you, I wonder why." Nick said. Then he added. "I didn't say I didn't think it was a good idea."

"I don't care whether it's a good idea or not," I snapped. "Just tell me where it can hurt."

Nick stopped to slowly light a cigarette off the end of the one he'd been smoking. "You made the remark a few moments ago— what have you got to lose? That's what I think you're overlooking. You do have something to lose. A great deal. You have your commitment to your present life to lose."

"What does that mean?" I was irritated and about half sorry I'd told Nick. I might have known he wouldn't be content until he'd picked it apart.

"I expect a great deal," he answered me. "You will be, once you take this step, selling out your faith in your life as it now is. How do you expect to be any longer interested in it or involved in it? Your whole attention is going to be on those mountains and you'll be impatient to start your new life. You can't play at this sort of game, my son. We're too old for that."

"That's bullshit, Nick," I said angrily. "And you know it."

"Is it? Listen, you're preparing for a war of sorts so it will have to come or you'll be left standing high and dry and feeling silly. World War I was fought because the Germans were ready for war. There was a reason at first, but it evaporated. But they were ready and they had to go to war. The German generals went to the Kaiser one night, got him out of bed, and said they had to go to war because they were ready and the people expected it. They didn't know what else to do. The Kaiser said he didn't care what they did and went back to bed. On such casual turns, my friend, is history decided."

"I think you're getting things out of proportion a little," I told him. "So let's get it down to this—are you saying you're not interested?"

"Not all all," Nick said surprisingly. "I'd be a fool to do that. I've already told you you're giving me virtually a free ride. *I* won't have the same kind of commitment you're making, my friend. Certainly. Count me in."

"I've already said what I think," Morton added. "Put me in the pot."

I had bought so many supplies and tools that I'd overflowed the garage. To handle them I'd erected one of those aluminum carports in the backyard. Chris didn't like it and I'm sure our neighbors appreciated it less. It was an eyesore, standing there beside the swimming pool.

"Oh, hell, Horn," she said violently. "You get that damn thing down right now! That thing looks like some backyard car mechanic is setting up shop."

"I need it baby," I said. I've got to protect those supplies from the weather."

"And that's another thing—how much damn money are you going to spend on all this? I'd like to get a look at your checkbook. You're buying stuff we couldn't use up in a hundred years."

"That's stuff we—"

"And another thing—are you working any? It doesn't seem as if you're tending to your business at all."

"Chris!" I fairly shouted at her. "Will you stop! My God," I said in a quieter voice. "Look, we're going through a little crash program right now, but it'll be over with shortly. The business doesn't need any looking after. There's nothing to do; I can't get any goods and if I could I wouldn't know what price to sell them for, things are changing so rapidly. And I'm not spending that much money. For God's sake, I haven't bought that land yet."

She came up and leaned her head on my chest. "Horn, sometimes I think you're crazy. You're getting so wrapped up in this fool project I expect to see you in a coonskin cap any day now. I'm surprised we haven't already moved up there."

"Honey, honey," I told her, patting her arm, "this is just a little vacation retreat we're diverting ourselves with. As soon as I get the land and get it all set I'll put the slowdown to the crash program." But I couldn't help being troubled by her words coming so close on the heels of what Nick had said. I had to admit there might be some justice in the idea, but, the problem with Nick, he made you so damn mad with his insulting manner that you couldn't let yourself think about anything he said. Anyway, I was able to control my own direction and I'd be my own arbiter.

We had a letter from Mister Chipman the next day. Enclosed was a copy of our accepted earnest money contract. The loon in Oklahoma had taken our offer. There was a terse note from Mister Chipman, written in ink in a spidery hand. "Come up and arrange to buy this land before you come to your senses."

"Well," I told Chris elatedly, "looks like we got it after all." I was smiling.

"I'm glad, honey," Chris said, though she wasn't anywhere near as pleased as I was. "I'm glad you got it. I know how important it was to you."

"Important to us," I said. "Us. Listen, I ought to get right up there and close this thing before something happens. Are you going?"

But she didn't want to and I didn't blame her. I intended a fast trip and there was no reason for her to go. I told Nick and Morton about it, not expecting either one of them to want to accompany me and neither did. Though Morton did say, as if he felt some sort of obligation, "Damn, Franklin, I'd like to go with you, but I don't see how I can get off right now." I assured him it wasn't necessary, that his turn was coming.

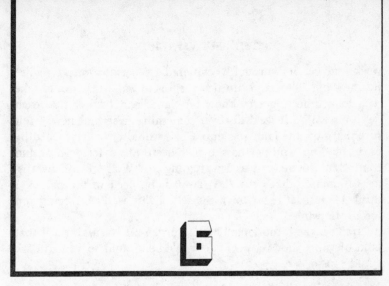

Just before I was to leave, Chris got a telegram from her father saying they'd be arriving the next day. "Oh, Franklin," she said, "what do we do now?"

"Oh, Franklin, hell," I told her. "I'm just unlucky, that's all. Hate it as I will, I'll be forced to miss your folks' visit."

"None of that! You told me you'd be back in two days. Franklin Horn, don't you dare go up there and stall. I mean it! You get back here."

Back in the southern lowlands where we lived, it was still humid summer; but there was just a touch of fall in the air as I stepped out of my car in Yellville. I stood a moment looking around, enjoying the appearance of the old town, so settled and sedate and looking as if nothing could change it. The world might cave in, but the granite mountains rising just in the distance would be there forever.

It was really a very short piece of business. I gave Mister Chipman a check and he gave me a deed. Then we stepped across the street and had it recorded and the thing was done. "Well," he said, "I hope you know what you're doing young man. I just hate to see that damn fool in Tulsa make a profit on this."

I really hated to leave. Somehow, I felt very secure and at home in that country, and I wanted very much to go up to the land that was now ours and just be there for a time. But I knew that Chris was serious about my coming right back. There'd be plenty of time for the land later. Chris and I could come up and stay a week and get it thoroughly explored. A person doesn't realize just how big 700 acres is until he begins to walk it. It would take us a long time to get to know our land, and I knew that each day we were on it we'd discover something fresh and new. I felt sure that now the land was ours Chris wouldn't be frightened by its forbidding wildness as she had been. She'd feel secure and comfortable there, just as I was going to. "Well," I said to Mister Chipman, "that's that." I slapped the deed in my palm. "I think I'll just let it lay for a time. Probably won't be seeing you for a little while."

"Don't make it too long," he said dryly. "If you wait until that land of yours shows a profit, I won't be around so you can say I told you so."

I got home and went in the house and kissed Chris and greeted her mother. "Where's the general?" I asked blithely. I was in a wonderful mood, feeling as I used to when I'd accomplished some difficult piece of business out in the back country.

"He's out by the pool," Chris answered dryly, "inspecting your aluminum *carport* and wondering what the hell is all this stuff you've bought. He's been driving me crazy with questions, but I've told him to just wait until you get home. Better prepare yourself."

"Oh, I'll handle the general," I said. I took the deed out of my coat pocket and put it on the table. We were alone in the kitchen. "There it is, babe," I said. "There's our fort. Signed and paid for and recorded. We have got our bastion when we need it."

She walked over and looked down at the piece of paper lying on the table. She picked it up, turned, and then hesitated. "Honey, don't say anything to Daddy about this. Or at least, don't give him the reason why you bought it. I just told him you were buying some land for speculation. All right?"

"Sure," I said. I was glad to see her. I put my arm around her and whispered an obscene suggestion in her ear.

"Franklin," she said, "stop that!" She blushed. "What did you do up there in Arkansas? Read pornography?"

"Listen, I missed you. How long are your folks going to stay?"

"Just a couple of days. You can be nice that long."

"Much longer. I'll go see dear old Dad now."

"Oh, by the way—Daddy was very glad to hear you were buy-ing speculation land. Said it shows you've gotten this nonsense about Australia out of your mind."

"Aaah." I stopped at the door. "Listen, while I take my tie off, fixed me a couple of bourbon and waters. I'll take the general a drink."

"It's near dinner time, and you know Daddy drinks martinis in the evening. I'll fix you a bourbon and water."

"No, fix two. He chooses my drinks at his house, I'll choose his at mine."

"Franklin, now you promised you'd be nice. Listen, don't start—"

"Chris, I'm being nice. My God. Fix the drinks."

I shucked my coat and tie, picked up the drinks from Chris—who was giving me a worried look—and went out in the back-yard. The general was sitting in a patio chair by the pool, smok-ing a long cigar and staring at my pile of material beneath the carport. I greeted him and handed over his drink. We never, neither one of us, wasted much time on the amenities.

"What's this?" he asked me, looking suspiciously at the drink. I told him.

"I don't drink bourbon and water," he said stiffly.

"Oh? I thought you did. Now where did I get that impression."

But I didn't fool him. He glared at me out from under his shaggy eyebrows and set the drink down with a final gesture. "What is all this?" He gave an impatient wave toward my alumi-num carport.

"Just stuff," I said.

"Just stuff!" He glared at me. "All those *hoes* and *rakes* and *shovels* and *barbed wire*? My God, you've got enough barbed wire to set up an obstacle course at an army training center. What do you mean, just stuff!"

"Stuff I might need." I was trying to be as offhand and even about it as I could. Actually I was rather enjoying myself. I was in such a good mood that I doubted the general's ability, consid-erable as it was, to get me angry. I intended to treat the whole situation very lightly.

"Need for what?"

"I'm speculating," I said, "in farm tools. I hear a shortage is coming. When it's at its height, I'm going to load my pickup and sell them door to door for an immense profit."

"And that pickup. What in hell do you want with that? Say, what are you up to, anyway? What are you planning for my daughter's future?"

However, my good intentions notwithstanding, that approach could always get my attention. "Well," I told him with a little edge in my voice, "whatever my plans are for *my wife's* future, you can bet they'll be for her best good."

"So you don't intend to go to Australia," he said, glaring at me.

"Never did. Just something to get your goat, general."

"And no apologies for all the worry it caused Chris's mother."

"Ha ha," I said dryly. "That's technique number three-oh-one, isn't it?"

"You're some specimen," he said, getting up and stalking off proudly to the house.

But even that grating encounter couldn't ruin my good humor, and I stayed out by the pool enjoying the day and the light drink I was permitting myself. After a time Chris called me to dinner. When I came in she asked me under her breath what I'd said to her father. "Nothing," I told her. "Why?"

"Well just don't. He's got that look on his face like he's going to call a general court martial."

Chris had given the general two martinis before dinner, and this had infused the maximum measure of good humor in him. He even loosened up enough to tell us how he'd gotten them straightened up at the Pentagon. "There's too damn much mixing into politics by this country's military men," he said. "A soldier's job is to fight when he's called upon, and when he's not fighting, his job is to be getting ready to fight. I tell you, I'm appalled, appalled, at the recruiting practices being followed by the armed services today. How *in hell* do they expect to make soldiers out of recruits when they've done everything but put 'em on a sugar tit to get 'em in? I know just how quick everybody wants an old soldier's advice, but the way they're treating the men in the ranks today is inviting wholesale mutiny. And if not that, at least gross inefficiency and dereliction of duty. No wonder we couldn't win in Vietnam. How in hell can you expect to win a war when you've got to discuss every order with the low-liest *private*. And not only discuss it, but *persuade* him to carry it out." He gave a disgusted look. "I'm glad my career tour was over and done with before such degrading practices entered the forces. They'd have had to court martial me because the first time some pimply-faced little private stood up and wanted to argue with *me* I'd of shot the little sonofabitch!"

"General," I asked, "are you actually criticizing the armed services of the United States?"

He gave me a sharp look. "Listen, young man, when you've given your life to a cause you have a right to criticize that cause in its own behalf."

"I thought criticism was the right of all citizens?"

"You don't know enough to criticize."

"Is that because of my lack of years or my lack of the military mind?"

"It's your lack of commitment," he said steadily. "Your talk of going to Australia."

"Maybe it's not such a bad idea after all," I said. Out of the corner of my eye, I could see Chris giving me little warning looks.

"Oh, you're not going to Australia," he announced. "But I see what you're doing."

"You do?"

Unexpectedly his wife said, "Harry . . ." warningly.

He didn't even glance at her. "Yes. You've been up in Arkansas buying raw land. And you've bought all these *farm* implements. And you've bought a pickup and a *gas generator*. I know what a gas generator is for. And I saw all this dehydrated food you've got stacked in the garage. I've been hearing about people like you. We get such news even over in Colombia. I've heard about some of these movements going on." He looked at me accusingly. "You're building a retreat. Aren't you?"

"I don't call it that," I told him.

"Harry . . ." his wife put in again. And Chris said, "Daddy, let's get off the subject."

But he was inflamed now at my obvious treason. "Oh, yes, I've heard all about fellows like you. I'm just a little startled to find my daughter *married* to one. When you pulling out for your hideout?"

"When the country goes to pieces," I said. "Which ought to be soon."

He straightened in his chair. "What's that?"

"You heard me. I said the country was going to pieces."

His face flushed and his eyes got hard and angry. He just sat for a moment, then he got up and walked stiffly over to my chair and slapped me in the face. He said to his wife, "Come on. Get packed. We're going to a hotel."

"Daddy!" Chris said. She jumped up and tried to stop him, but he was already out of the room. I heard her chasing him upstairs.

June got up and looked at me uncertainly. "Franklin, I don't know what to say. Good heavens." She looked worriedly toward the door the general had marched through. "He's upset. I don't think they paid much attention to him at the Pentagon. I think he's hurt."

"It's all right," I said. "I shouldn't have needled him. He takes these things very seriously."

"Well . . ." she said. "I guess I better go up. I am so sorry about this."

"Maybe he'll cool off," I offered. "It didn't bother me. Worthy of George S. Patton. Has he just seen the movie?"

She gave me a reproachful look. "I don't think he'll change his mind," she said. "You know how he is."

"Like granite," I said encouragingly.

"I'll go talk to him. I know how Chris must hate that this happened. I'll be embarrassed to face her."

"Do what you can. Tell him I don't feel particularly insulted. No," I added, "better not say that. I expect I'm supposed to feel insulted. But do tell him that I was referring only to the politicians when I said the country was going to pieces, not the generals."

They were upstairs with the general for quite a time. I expected any moment for him to come marching through on his way out—his wife bringing up the rear with the suitcases. But, in the end, he was mollified and agreed to spend the night. I expect the thought of spending twenty or thirty dollars for a hotel room was what carried the day. But he wasn't coming back downstairs. No indeed. Probably was killing him to be in the same house with such a treacherous dog, let alone the same room.

Later June went to bed, and Chris and I were alone downstairs.

"Franklin," she said reproachfully, "you shouldn't have done that. I warned you not to."

"Don't start on me, Chris. Your old man did all the doing. I just replied to some pretty open insults."

"But you shouldn't have paid any attention. He's an old man, Franklin. You should just have ignored it."

"He's an old man with a pretty sharp tongue and an overbearing manner," I told her dryly. "And this 'old man' excuse won't get it. If he'd shot me instead of merely slapping my face, would you still have excused him on the basis he's an old man?"

"Franklin, he's bewildered. And disappointed. He's been trained one way all his life. All his life he's thought just one way was right. And now it's all changing and he doesn't understand it. Everything he's ever believed in, been taught to believe in, is going under. It's killing him and he doesn't know any other way to react. He can't strike out at all the elements he hates and—"

"And I'm there," I finished for her, nodding my head. "I understand. But what the general doesn't understand is that I agree with a lot of the same things he does. God knows I hate what's happening in this country. We're just fighting it in different ways. I still believe very strongly in the principles this country was founded on, and I'm just exercising my right to those principles."

"Why don't you explain that to him," she urged. "Sit down and talk about it."

"Are you kidding? Talking with the general is purely a one-way street."

"Well you ought to try."

"I'll say one thing," I offered, rubbing my cheek. "That old bastard is still plenty sharp. Did you see the way he looked the situation over and came up with the right answer in nothing flat? He's got that military mind, that analytical mind, and he's plenty good. Didn't take him any time to figure out what I was up to. Listen, the old general wouldn't be a bad man to have along on such an operation as ours. He could be a lot of help."

"Franklin," Chris said in alarm, "don't you dare! Don't you even mention this to him."

"I'm not crazy," I said. "But if he wasn't so goddamn biased

I would. If he'd look at it with a clear mind, he'd see that I was right and the military man in him would have to approve."

We sat a moment in silence and then I said, "Chris, I feel absolutely wonderful about buying that land. If intuition counts for anything, we've made the exact right move. I feel more relieved in my mind than I have in months."

"I'm glad," she said.

"Listen, we ought to get back up there pretty soon and look the whole tract over. We want to know every foot of the place. What say we go up there and camp a week or ten days?"

"Franklin . . ." she said, her voice rising at the end of my name. "I don't want to go camp *anywhere* for ten days. Besides, can you afford that much time off from your business?"

I frowned at her. "Say, when did you get so concerned about my business? You let me worry about that. I've been able to handle our welfare so far. Trust me for five or ten minutes more at least."

"Well, you certainly don't seem to pay it much attention lately."

"Com'on, Chris," I said sharply. "You want to start making the living?"

"Don't get so touchy, Franklin." She stood up. "Com'on, let's go to bed and see if that nasty suggestion you whispered in my ear is physically possible."

"You know how to get me," I said. "How come you can handle me so easily?"

"I know your weakness," she answered dryly.

Chris's parents stayed the next day, though the general was very stiff and formal. Late in the morning I caught him out in the garage looking at my gas generator. "What's that thing put out?" he asked me.

"Hundred and ten volts."

"What's the volt to gas consumption ratio?"

"Why, I don't know," I said, staggered.

He grunted and gave me a pitying look and walked over to where the dehydrated food was stored. He kicked one of the boxes. "That stuff's not much good."

"Why not?" I asked, following him.

"Poor food value return. We did a study on it a few years back."

"I meant it only as an emergency supply," I said hesitantly, realizing what I was admitting.

"Better figure it for a damn short use period. It's insidious. Bulk fools you into believing you're getting proper nutrition and energy, but the long-term effect is physically debilitating. What other food sources you going to have?"

"Crops," I said.

"Not those," he said irritatedly, "that's two or three months minimum. I mean for the initial period, when you're logistically committed to on-hand supplies. *Before* you can raise food stuffs."

"Preserved foods," I answered. "Canned goods. Such as that."

He looked up at the ceiling as if he were pulling teeth to give such advice. "Better make up a nutritional chart. Don't you have any access to a military station where you could get proper field rations?"

"Well, no," I answered.

He cleared his throat. "Maybe I'll see what I can do."

"Well, thanks," I said, staggered again.

He glanced at me. "You ever drink whiskey in the morning?"

"No."

"Well, I do. Have you got any rum?"

I told him I thought we could find some. I was still off balance.

"Well, let's go in," he said. "I want a drink."

We went in with him complaining bitterly that you couldn't get any decent rum in Colombia. "Imagine that, if you will," he said. "Used to be able to get the Cuban stuff, but then that god-damn Castro henchman—what's his name? Che something—came in and started raising hell and the government cut it off. Hell of a note."

But I wasn't much fooled by the general's seeming interest. He hadn't changed his viewpoint; it was simply the military mind intrigued by a logistics problem. I'd tried, as Chris had suggested, to talk to him. I'd opened up by asking him if preparedness wasn't part of the military creed. He'd said that it was. "Then how," I'd asked him, "can you deny me the same right?" Peering out from under his eyebrows he'd told me I wasn't qualified to decide what and how to prepare. "Panic," he'd told me, "is the way amateurs prepare. Don't congratulate yourself into thinking that you're preparing."

I said to Chris one day, "Do you know I'm bothered by windmills."

She looked up slowly from the crossword puzzle she was doing. Her glasses had slipped down her nose and she took a second to push them back in place. "I can't tell you," she said, "what that does to me. Why don't you go out and fight them and then do a book about it."

"No. Not like that. I mean the problem of getting one. Did you know you can't buy a windmill anymore?"

"Can't Congress do something?"

"Listen, this is serious. We need a windmill for the fort. And they just don't make them anymore. I've been trying to buy one second-hand and have it dismantled, but it seems they've now become valuable as antiques. People are going out in the country and buying old broken down ones and putting them up in their yard for decoration. You can't believe what this has done to the price. I don't blame the farmer; I'd do the same thing in his place. But you can't convince one you want a functional windmill and want it for its functional purpose and that you're not some rich city slicker who can pay him two thousand dollars for something he paid two hundred for twenty years before. But we've damn near got to have a windmill."

"I thought you said there were springs. What do you want with a windmill?"

"To pump the water with. Oh, it's not absolutely necessary, but it'd be nice to have. Besides, I like windmills. They're very fundamental."

"And now they're lawn ornaments." Chris noted. "I'll bet that galls your soul."

"More than you can know. There's got to be a moral in there somewhere. I hope it's not that anachronisms like me and windmills have had our day, to be replaced with new and sophisticated machinery. You wouldn't replace me, would you, Chris?"

"I will always keep you as a lawn ornament, Franklin. Don't worry."

We were in the dog days at the tail end of the summer, the hurricane season in the Deep South. We were far enough away from the Gulf that there was no danger from the winds, but each tempest invariably spawned violent thunderstorms that became our share of the weather. Late one afternoon, a huge storm descended upon us. Chris and I sat in the den, looking out the patio door, enjoying it. The sky was black and purple, with high, scudding clouds, intermittently illuminated by terrific flashes of lightning. It was very dark outside, and when the lightning flashed, it gave an unreal quality to the day as if it were being illuminated by some sort of strobe light. We had the TV on, and they were interrupting regular programming every five minutes to give severe-weather alerts. It hardly seemed necessary. The thunder alone was enough to shake you. It roared and boomed like an artillery barrage. Sometimes an exceptionally loud clap would rattle the windows and almost lift you out of your chair. But Chris and I didn't mind it. We were comfortable in our secure house, looking out the glass door watching the rain fall. It was coming down in torrents. Already our backyard had flooded to the point where it was awash with the top of the water in the swimming pool.

"This is something," I said to Chris. We were drinking brandy because there's something very satisfying about drinking brandy while you watch a storm expend its fury. "I believe the wind is even getting up a little." It was blowing thirty or forty miles an hour. Nothing to cause us serious worry, but the little nursery trees in the backyard were whipping to and fro like weeds. The television announcer came on to say that flooding was occurring in certain parts of the city and that motorists were warned to be on the lookout for increasingly hazardous conditions.

All of a sudden, just before evening, the electricity went off. It was already so dark we had the lights on and, when they went out, the room descended into a deep gloom. The voice on the TV faded out and the picture went black. It became suddenly quiet with all the power off. "I've been expecting that," I said to Chris. "Storm like this had to get a wire or transmitter box somewhere. It'll be back on in a moment." I got up and went to the front door. The wind and rain roared in my face, but I was able to see enough up and down the street to tell that it had gotten the whole neighborhood and not just us. I went back in the den. "Transmitter box," I told Chris. "Probably. I'll turn on one of the portable radios."

"How am I going to fix supper?" she asked me. We had an all-electric house.

"Don't worry. They'll have it fixed in no time."

But they didn't. We sat in the dark for a half hour and then Chris wondered if we shouldn't light some candles. "I can do better than that," I said. I heaved myself out of my chair. "I'll fire up a couple of lanterns. Hate to do it because as soon as I get them going the electricity is going to come on."

I came back in the room with two lanterns. Chris was bending low over our portable radio. The batteries were weak and it was barely coming in. She looked up. "I think it might be very bad, Franklin. From what I can hear that sounds like what they're saying." I could just see her in glimpses, when the lightning struck. Even in the modern setting she looked like the dim subject of one of the old Dutch masters. I pumped the lantern up and lit it. It came on with a flaring glow, but I trimmed the wick until it was putting out a fullsome circle of light. With a piece of string I tied it to the light fixture suspended from the ceiling of the den. "There," I announced.

"That still doesn't tell me how I'm going to cook supper," Chris said.

"We'll cook in the fireplace. We've got charcoal don't we? Well, get out some steaks and I'll get the coals going. We can make a grill out of one of those things in the oven."

I got the charcoal and got it burning in the fireplace, unused through the summer. Noticing that the lanterns were smoking a little I opened the patio door for ventilation.

Chris came back in the room with a worried look on her face. "There's no water," she said.

"No water?"

"No. I turned on the faucets and it drizzled for a few seconds and then stopped."

"You don't suppose the electricity is out all over this side of town, do you? If it is, it got the water power station, knocked out the electric pumps. That's a hell of a note, but that must be what happened. Let's phone and see what we can find out."

"I've tried that. Phone is dead."

"Maybe I better get in the pickup and go see what's happening."

"You better look out the door first. The street is flooded and I mean flooded."

I went to the side door and looked. The street had disappeared and water was halfway up our lawn and the lawns of the houses across the street. "Jesus Christ!" I turned to Chris. "Kid, we're cut off," I grinned.

"You may think this is humorous," Chris said, peering over my shoulder at the storm, "but I don't. I'd like to know how we're going to get by with no water and no phone and no electricity. Especially the water. What are we going to drink, or cook with? Not to mention bathing. And the commodes won't even work will they? Now *that* will be pleasant."

"God will provide," I told her. I got my raincoat and went out the patio door into the slashing rain. It was heavy going. There was about a foot of water on the back lawn and the wind was blowing hard enough to knock a man off his feet. Also, I wasn't too keen about the lightning flashes. The storm was right on top of us and walking in water is not the best lightning protection. I made it to my aluminum carport, glad for the chance to wipe the rain out of my eyes. I'd bought several galvanized tubs and a quantity of buckets. I got a tub out and set it under the drain spillway coming off the roof. It would be clean, I thought, since aluminum is nonreactive and the top of the roof had had a good washing for several hours with pure rainwater.

The tub was full in nothing flat and I dipped two buckets up and carried them back in the house. Chris scolded me for dripping water all over the house, but I carried one in the kitchen and left it for cooking. I carried the other into the bathroom and showed Chris how to pour it in the top of the commode to make that work. "See," I said, "we're able to make out."

I made half a dozen more trips until I had all the water we could conceivably want for the next twenty-four hours. I let one bucket fill up with rain straight from the sky. We'd use that for drinking.

After I'd dried off and changed clothes, I set up a makeshift grill over my charcoal coals and put the steaks on. "There," I said, sitting back and putting my feet up on the hearth, "this isn't too bad."

But Chris was looking around. "Franklin, those lanterns are smoking up the ceiling."

"The kerosene lantern is not the most efficient machine in the world."

"And I'm afraid the floor is going to be ruined from all this water." She was down on her knees mopping the floor with a towel. We had one of those phony antique wooden puncheon floors that you see featured in the home-of-the-month section of the Sunday paper. I hated it. I knew that the pegs were pure decoration, that the floor was put together with very modern glue and screws and that the "solid oak" look was pure veneer. I had not the slightest doubt that the water would warp hell out of the veneer overlay.

"Leave that alone," I ordered her, "and get a pot of beans going over the fire. We've got to have something to go with the steaks."

She frowned at the fireplace. "Franklin, that would just ruin the bottom of any pan I've got. They'll get all black."

"Say," I asked her, "what good is a pot if you can't cook in it?"

"They're for an electric range. They've got ceramic bottoms to spread the heat."

I made a disgusted sound. "Use one anyway. If it'll work."

Dinner was coming along in fine fashion when Chris came walking in from the kitchen and sat down in a chair and watched me busy at the fireplace. The room had a rosy glow from the lantern, and outside the rain was still beating down and the wind and thunder and lightning were hard at work. I winked at her. "We can handle this, can't we?"

"I don't know," she said. "I'm having trouble seeing inside the refrigerator."

"What's that mean? Bulb burned out? Use your lantern."

"Noooooo," she said. "I think it's a little more serious than that. When I noticed the bulb wasn't on it occurred to me the refrigerator is electric and we don't have any electricity."

"Uh, oh," I said, sitting back on my heels. "I hadn't thought of that. And that means the freezer is off too."

"Right, Horn. You're really sharp tonight. And we've got about three hundred pounds of beef in there, choice steaks and such. At today's prices I'd say roughly equivalent to the cost of the Kohinoor."

"Hmmmmm," I put down the fork I'd been using to turn the steaks and went in the kitchen and opened the refrigerator door. Then I checked the freezer. "Well," I said to Chris, "they're off all right. How long before the stuff starts ruining?"

"The stuff in the refrigerator not too long. The meat will start defrosting in twelve hours."

"Maybe the power will be back on," I said hopefully.

She cocked her head to one side. "How about that most wonderful generator of yours? Isn't it intended to do more than gather dust?"

"It's on my mind, dear," I admitted. I touched my forehead. "Right here. I'm just not sure. Couple of problems. One, I think it might be illegal."

"Illegal? Explain that, please."

"Well, the electric company is a public utility, and I think when you take from them you're not allowed to take from anyone else, yourself included. Like the phone company. You can't furnish your own receivers, you know."

"Horn, you amaze me. I don't care if it's illegal or not. You hook that thing up if it'll actually work and let's save that meat. Illegal, my God! You pick the oddest times to become law abiding. No wonder you're always raving against city hall. You're scared to death of them."

"Well, there's another reason. I'm not sure I know how to hook it up. I've been thinking about it. Hooking it up to a simple little system in a mountain cabin is one thing, but you ought to see that switch box out there. I'm afraid if I were to get it hooked up wrong I'd short the entire house out. Might even wreck the system and we'd have to have it rewired."

"I'll be goddamn," Chris said flatly, giving me a look. "If you're not *really* something. Where is all this talk I've been hearing, Horn? *You* are going to sustain us in the wilderness?"

"Now just a damn minute," I said with some heat. "You're carrying me a little hard, sport. I never claimed to be any master electrician. And anyway, I haven't said I couldn't do it. I just don't want to take the chance until it seems absolutely necessary. Now how about getting off my ass. Who the hell elected you team captain, anyway?"

We ate dinner and then sat around trying to hear a weather report on the portable radio. But the batteries were fading so badly that nothing much would come in and what would was mostly drowned out by the static produced by the continuous thunder and lightning. The lanterns were smoking too much so Chris turned them off and lit a couple of candles. We went to bed early, and it should have been an ideal night to make love; but there was still a little strain between us so we just kissed good night and turned to sleep.

It was still raining the next day. Chris was the first out of bed. She went hopefully to the wall switch and turned on the lights. Nothing happened. "That does it," I said. I swung around on the edge of the bed and yawned and lit a cigarette. "I'll try and hook up the generator first thing after breakfast."

"How am I going to cook breakfast?" Chris asked me. "I can't fry eggs in the fireplace."

"You can at least make some coffee."

"In an electric percolator?"

"Oh, hell, Chris," I said irritably, "you're not even trying. For God's sake, just boil some water in a pan and throw a handful of coffee in it. People made coffee a hell of a long time before they had electric percolators. I'll get some charcoal started." I dressed and went downstairs.

The house was stuffy from the air-conditioners being off for a day. The kind of house we lived in wasn't built to be opened up to the fresh air. If the mechanical gadgets failed, it too began to fail. I could tell the house was going to be awfully hot before the day was out. I opened the patio door and looked at the sky. The storm was still with us though in a different form. The thunder and lightning had ceased even though the rain was falling steadily. The sky was dull and leaden and there was a stale calmness in the air. Apparently, we weren't going to wash away; the water was about a foot deep in the lower parts of the yard and holding. I figured it would be three or four feet deep in the street. Driving would still be impossible.

Breakfast didn't come off too well. I ended up eating some

warmed over beans and drinking a lukewarm Coke out of the useless refrigerator. Chris ruined the coffee. She put too much in the boiling water and it was strong as black strap molasses and damn near as thick. In addition, it boiled over and stained the white limestone hearth. That didn't bother me, but it did Chris. I watched her scrubbing at it with ammonia. "Why don't you let that go," I asked in some annoyance. "So it got a little coffee on it. So what?"

"Listen," she said, her voice sounding as if she was blaming the whole mess on me, "listen, why don't you go and fix your goddamn generator! I'm tired of this and I'm tired of you playing pioneer in our house. I don't want to cook in this goddamn fireplace! And I don't want to make coffee like some hobo!"

"Okay, okay," I said, backing off because I could see she was really getting upset. "Just take it easy. I'll see what I can do with this generator."

I went out in the garage and looked at it. The connection from the generator was easy enough; the hard part would be wiring in to the fuse box. I had bought plenty of wire, but it was #10 Romex and I wasn't sure it'd carry the load required. I turned the main switch off, just in case the power company decided to get efficient at the wrong time, and opened the switch box and removed the rear panel. There were more wires than seemed necessary to power just a simple house. Two, however, appeared to be the lead-ins. I disconnected these, having a great deal of trouble with the stiff, heavy wire, and connected in the wire I'd prepared. I ran that over to my generator and wired into the terminals. The door from the kitchen opened and Chris leaned against the jamb watching me.

"It's not as hard as I thought," I told her.

"Everything in the refrigerator is spoiled. Have you ever smelled the combination of spoiled milk and bacon?"

I was busy drawing some gas out of one of my fifty-gallon drums.

I filled the tank of the generator and went around to the hand crank. "Better get out of the way," I advised Chris. "This sonofabitch is liable to blow up for all I know."

She stepped back in the kitchen and shut the door.

I spun the crank. The generator, being new, was stiff and unresponsive. I spun the crank and spun it until my arm was about to fall off and I was completely winded. Giving up for the moment I went in the kitchen and drank another lukewarm Coke. Chris was busy cleaning out the refrigerator. "We've got to get rid of this mess," she said, "before it smells up the whole house. I guess I can't run this down the garbage disposal until you get the electricity on."

"You can't then," I told her. "You need water pressure to wash it well down into the pipes. You just pour a bucket of water in on top of it and it'll stop the drain up."

"Well, for God's sake!" she said disgustedly.

"And I'm not even sure about the electricity." I finished my Coke and went back in the garage. The first spin the generator caught and sputtered and coughed and then set up a steady hum. "Hot damn!" I said loudly.

I went over to the switch box and looked at the main switch arm. The generator was going full blast. I reached out and threw the switch arm on. For an instant the lights in the garage came on and then the circuit breaker popped out and the lights went out. The generator wasn't putting out enough current to carry the load. I turned the breakers off to the whole upstairs and tried it again. Chris opened the door and looked out just as I did. I could see the lights in the kitchen shining behind her. "Eureka!" she shouted at me over the noise of the generator, "You're a genius."

Then the lights went off.

Chris asked: "What's the matter?"

"Nothing." I turned off the breakers to the air-conditioning system. That was the main load. This time the power stayed on. I shut the fuse box door, stopped to check the generator, and went in the kitchen. Chris was standing with the refrigerator door open. "It works," she announced, "the light is on."

I stepped into the pantry. The freezer was humming nicely. "Looks like we're all right," I said.

"Let's see what's happening," she said. She rushed into the den and switched on the TV. All the power immediately went off. She looked around at me. "Now what's the matter?"

"I'm afraid it's carrying all the load it'll handle," I explained. "The generator doesn't put out enough current to handle but a few things. The downstairs lights and the stuff in the kitchen. If you overload it the whole system fails."

"Goddamnit, Horn," she exclaimed, "what good's the damn thing!"

"It's good enough," I told her, "to get by with. It wasn't intended to power a modern house."

I went back out and threw the main switch after turning off the breaker to the circuit the TV was on. Again things came on humming nicely. I went back in the house and told Chris, before she asked, that the air-conditioning couldn't be turned on. "How about the stove?" she asked.

"Yes, but you've got to turn something equivalent off. Such as two or three lights. I'm sorry, honey, but that's the way it's got to be. But I'll bet we're a whole hell of a lot better off than our neighbors. Let's turn on the radio and see what's going on. I'll turn off a light to compensate."

We came in right in the middle of a newscast. The announcer said, "Repeating again, lightning struck the main computer switching terminal of the power and light company. Crews are working around the clock, but officials hesitate to speculate when power will be resumed. Most of the city is affected, and normal business and school activities have been suspended." He went on to explain that the banks of computers responsible for switching power to the various parts of the city had been severely damaged by the bolt of lightning that had reversed the electric flow.

"God is finally striking back," I said.

"It's not funny, Franklin," Chris said.

"I think it is," I challenged her. "Those goddamn computers are supposed to be infallible. Do the work of a thousand men. Well, a thousand men wouldn't have all been wired together. I'll bet that computer room looks like the black hole of Calcutta. I hope every goddamn one of them is burned to a crisp."

"And meanwhile the toilets don't work and we're sweltering and we can't even get the news on TV. But old Horn is getting his jollies because some electrical gadget he obviously feels is a threat to his manhood is out of commission. You're a strange man, Horn. I think I never realized how strange."

"Well, well," I drawled at her, "little Chrissy is all upset because she might be called upon to make do and to think for herself. My God, do you realize you might have to go all day without the air-conditioning? And you've got to actually pick up a bucket of water and pour it in the top of the commode. Listen, that's really tough. And the really bad stuff hasn't even started. Have you thought that the washer and dryer are also out? What will you do if you have to wash some clothes out by hand? And the central vacuuming system isn't working either. I'd put some records on the phonograph to soothe you except it isn't working. I know what's got you down—you had to open that can of beans by hand last night because the electric can opener wouldn't work."

"Oh, shut up, Horn," she said angrily.

"Bah, Chris. Bah. You're as adaptable as that skillet of yours with the ceramic bottom. Neither one of you can stand the heat."

"Fuck you, Horn," she said furiously. "Fuck you!"

"Not a chance," I yelled after her as she went stalking out of the room. I followed her to the foot of the stairs and yelled up after her. "You're really great in a crisis, Chris."

I wandered back in the den and sat down, already feeling ashamed. I knew I really ought to stop expecting Chris to react differently to such things. She was what she was, and I was going to have to accept it. There was no philosophy connected with a power failure for her; it was just as she said, an inconvenience that made her uncomfortable.

As if she'd been reading my mind, she suddenly came walking back in to the room. "I know what you're thinking," she announced, "and you're probably right. But when things are supposed to work, I want them to work." Her eyes were a little red as if she'd been crying. She had a sort of chagrined smile on her face. "And I bought that skillet to work on an electric range. *Not* in a fireplace. And if you say another word to me about it, I'm going to hit you over the head with it."

"Okay," I said, willing to let the whole thing go, "but how about not dragging my manhood in like you did. That's roughly equivalent to calling someone a communist just because he disagrees with you."

"I'm sorry, dear. That was unfair. Let's have a bottle of wine and a can of tunafish for lunch and hope the goddamn power company gets their goddamn computers fixed."

While Chris was fixing lunch I went out in the garage to check on the generator. It was humming along, but I thought I noticed the smell of carbon monoxide from the exhaust fumes so I opened one of the huge garage doors. Outside it looked like a lake. Every view that wasn't obstructed by a house or fence or hedge was solid water. The rain was still pouring down from the leaden skies and the air continued stale and humid. Even though the sun wasn't shining, there was a sweltering feeling to the day, as if one were standing in steam. I went back in the house, leaving the garage door open.

We had a pretty good lunch. Chris had fixed a tuna salad on lettuce leaves and we had that along with French bread and a bottle of rosé wine.

"We're on the Left Bank in Paris," I told her, "and right after this typical artist's lunch, I'm going back up to my studio in the loft with the fantastic skylight and paint great art and you're going out on the streets and sell your body to rich American tourists because I can't sell my great art."

"Okay," she said.

"Is that all? Just okay? Aren't you going to shed a little tear as you turn your face bravely toward a life of sin?"

"No. I like it. You'd be surprised how jazzy some of those rich American tourists can be."

"Jesus Christ, Chris, you're not reading the script. This is supposed to be a sacrifice. You're supposed to turn to the wall and see my face in your mind even while you're in the cruel embrace."

"Can't do it. We're balling all over the bed."

"Well I'll be damned. Listen, how can I paint if I don't suffer from your sufferings, the despicable life I've driven you to? Didn't you ever read any—"

There was a knock on the door leading from the kitchen to the garage. I looked at it, surprised. It was a funny direction for someone to come calling from. Then I remembered I'd left the garage door open. I got up and answered the knock just as it sounded again. It was our next-door neighbor. "Hello, Jansen," I said. "What are you doing out?"

"I got a problem, Horn," he said. He stepped back, giving me room to move into the garage and shut the door behind me. He was wearing rubber boots and a raincoat, and I knew Chris wouldn't want him coming in the kitchen and dripping all over the floor.

"What's up?"

He gestured at the generator. "Where'd you get that?"

"Had it," I said. Jansen and I had never been too friendly. As a matter of fact, he'd had a few words to say about my aluminum carport when I'd put it up.

"You get electricity." He said it almost as if he were accusing me of holding illicit goods.

I waited for him to go on.

"Listen, I need a favor." But he didn't sound as if he were requesting a favor. "My electricity is out and we've got food defrosting in the freezer. I'd like to bring it over and put it in yours."

I shook my head. "I don't have room, Jansen. Our freezer is full."

He looked as if he didn't believe me. "You must have a little room."

"Come look for yourself," I offered. "There's not room for a single pork chop."

He studied me steadily. "All right," he said, "then how about my running a line from your generator over to my house." He pointed at the box of Romex on the floor. "You got plenty of wire."

I shook my head again. "I can't do that, Jansen. This little generator will barely supply what we need. Any more and it'd just overload."

"Well, I'll be goddamn," he said flatly. "You're refusing to help me, aren't you?"

"Not refusing," I told him, not liking his attitude at all, "I just can't. There's a difference."

"What the hell are you doing with electricity, Horn? Nobody else on the street's got it. What are you doing with that thing, anyway?"

"I told you I had it."

"Well, you're some neighbor. I guess I'm supposed to lose a freezer full of food while you sit over here burning lights and watching TV and God knows what else. You know, there's a lot of people been wondering about you. Look at all that stuff over there." He gestured to my supplies stacked against the wall. "And that stuff you got stored under that goddamn carport in the backyard. What are you, some kind of hoarder or something?"

I could see how frustrated he was, and for that reason, I let him run his temper a little. But I was getting tired of it. "No," I said, "just doing a little advance planning. Never know what you might need."

"I'm asking you one more time to run a line over to my house. You got no business with that thing if—" He started to say "—if nobody else has one," but stopped, realizing how silly it would sound. But that's what he was thinking anyway. "I mean," he finished lamely, "who the hell do you think you are?"

"I don't know, cowboy, but I'm getting a little tired of you standing in my garage and insulting me. I'd help you if I could, but I can't. Now how about you just pick it up and get along."

"Yeah?"

"Yeah."

"Okay, Horn," he said, backing up a few steps. "But your ass is gonna be mud on this street when I tell people a few things about you."

"Go on, get out of here, Jansen."

When I was back in the house, Chris was standing in the middle of the kitchen floor with an incredulous look on her face. "That *was* Clifford Jansen, our next-door neighbor, wasn't it?"

I told her it was.

"Talking like *that*. My God, was he drunk?"

I shook my head. "Just frustrated. Unable to cope. So he couldn't stand to see us coping."

"Well, I can understand his being upset about a freezer full of food. But, my God! Will he be embarrassed when this is all over! Wow!"

"I'm sure he will be," I answered. I went in the den and sat down and looked out at the rain. I felt frightened and I didn't know how to explain it to Chris. She thought she'd just witnessed a man losing his temper. But I knew better.

Z

They got the power back on the fourth day. It stopped raining, but it was almost a week before the water receded enough to make normal driving possible. The first thing Chris did was take a two-hour bath in hot water and wash her hair. And, when she could, the first trip she made was to the hairdresser. We got things back to normal with very little damage except to the stained hearth and the warped puncheon floor and a few blackened pots and pans. I got the generator disconnected and the regular service wired back in without too much trouble—conscious though I was that a licensed electrician was supposed to be doing the work. The first thing I did was go out and buy a newspaper. Of course, its major headlines were devoted to the storm, but there was quite a bit about some new troubles that disturbed me greatly. The dollar had been devalued again. One story, by a noted international money expert, was frightening. He cited the example of a private banker who'd used three billion dollars in leverage to drive down the dollar and make a 450-million-dollar profit. The columnist used it as an example of just how dependent we were on the good will of international bankers in Japan and Switzerland and France and England. "What the private banker did," the column said, "is just a drop in the bucket to what the international banks could do if they were of a mind. So far they are supporting our fiscal situation either through gratitude for past American services and dollars and fighting men or self-interest, but the day may come when greed or fear or both might force them into a hell-with-the-USA attitude. Neither are they reassured by what they consider wishy-washy fiscal policies by the American president and government. They feel there's too much free-handed spending, too much waste, and they seem to be taking a wait and see position."

I showed it to Chris. "I get more scared every day," I said. "I'm going to get rid of our cash as fast as I can. What I'm going to put it in, I don't know. But this is serious."

"I don't see how it could affect us too badly, could it? I mean what can happen to the dollar!"

I told her thoughtfully, "I remember seeing a picture in a newsmagazine many years ago of a German workman taking his week's pay home in a wheelbarrow. That was the economic situation that allowed something like Hitler to come into power. If that can happen, anything's possible. A sound barter system, which is what currency is, is one of the channels that keeps life normal. You break that down and you've got trouble."

"Well, don't do anything hasty."

I decided it was time to have a meeting of what I was calling the Home Defense Committee, so I invited Mort and Nick, along with their wives, over for dinner. "Now don't make a production out of dinner," I advised Chris. "The main business of this evening is talk and conclusions, and I don't want any ceremony getting in the way."

"I have a hard time," Chris said, "seeing Nick as part of this game."

I frowned at her. "I don't think it's a game, exactly."

"I'm sorry, dear. This backwoods thing, outdoors and log cabins."

"It's not that either."

"Well, whatever it is, it's outside the city and I can't see Nick in anything but a suit with a vest and some high-powered book in his hand. You actually told him about this and he actually wants to be a part?"

"And why not?"

She shrugged. "Well, well. That impresses me. If Nick thinks you're right, maybe you're not as crazy as I thought, Horn."

It angered me. "Listen, I don't like that kind of talk even in kidding. I get a little sick of hearing about Nick's super-intellect from Nick himself. I don't think I need hear it from you."

"I'm sorry, dear," she said again. "I didn't mean intellect so much. It's just that Nick's really not the type, you understand. And if he's willing to go to such lengths, maybe it really is necessary."

"I don't like the explanation a hell of a lot better than the insult," I told her, not kidding.

"Oh, don't be so touchy, Horn. Come and help me plan dinner. We've got to have lots if Morton is coming. How come you never mind when Morton kisses me?"

"He hasn't got any taste," I answered, insulting her in kind. I followed her out to the kitchen. "Listen, why don't you bake some bread for tonight. Sort of keynote the purpose of the dinner."

She turned around and gave me an amused look. "You're really not very hip, are you, Horn?"

"Why? I think it's a good idea."

"Oh, it's a good idea, all right. It's just not possible. Bread takes at least eight hours to rise. Do you think we have time?"

"Well," I said, sliding off the hook, "I'm glad to see you've been reading that material I got you."

Ivy, Mort's wife, and Florence, Nick's, were interesting adjutants to their husbands, though Florence seemed more like an aide-de-camp and Ivy like a camp follower. Being married to such an intellectual, sarcastic, somewhat bitter man, you might have expected Florence to be bowed by the load. But that wasn't the case at all. Rather, she shared most of Nick's interests and all of his views. When he was off on some lengthy dissertation, she'd sit by nodding her head vigorously and injecting, "That's right, that's right," at appropriate points. She wore a handsome pair of Benjamin Franklin glasses down on her nose and always seemed to have a sweater thrown over her shoulders, even in the summer.

Ivy just doted on Mort, in a fairly silly way, I thought. She was an attractive woman, about the same age as Chris but without Chris's flair or class, and by being silly about Mort I mean things such as insisting on being seated by him at a dinner party or holding his hand while we were all sitting talking in the den. And you didn't mix Mort's drinks, either; Ivy did because, she said, she knew exactly how he wanted them. Sometimes, watching Ivy in action, I couldn't much blame Mort for his womanizing. God knows, he had to feel as if he were smothering.

After telling Chris what I had about not doing anything special for dinner, I ended up going down to the fish market and buying some rainbow trout, they being caught in the White River and the White River being near the fort. Chris broiled them in a butter sauce and they were very good. Ivy, in her faintly idiotic way asked me if I'd caught them myself. "Oh, yes," I assured her, "this very afternoon."

"Well, I think that's lovely," Ivy told Chris. "The way meat is today, so expensive and so hard to get, it's wonderful that your husband can be such a good provider with his own two hands." Ivy didn't have a Deep South southern accent, she just always sounded as if she ought to.

Chris was going to tell her, but Morton jumped in. "Now, honey, Franklin didn't catch these fish. These are rainbow trout and they don't grow down here. He's just taking advantage of your trusting innocence, the crook."

Ivy sighed. "Well, I only know what Morton tells me. But they are so good."

Mort said, "My baby's got the right idea about fish and the cost of meat. Did you people see where five major, I mean *major*, meat packers closed up today? Just shut their doors. They can't get any meat. The ranchers won't sell their cattle because they say they'll lose money at what they can get under the price ceiling. And I read where the people who make feed say *they're* losing money. Where in hell's it all going?"

Florence put in, "Nick can name thirty other commodities that are all, as he calls them, crumbling girders in the economic structure."

Ivy said, "It's the President. He's just crazy as a bissy bug and we're not smart enough to see it. Did you know our next-door neighbors want to build a new house, but they can't because they can't get any bricks. *Bricks*, if you will, my dear. Of course I'm just as glad about them not moving, because they're the sweetest people. She can just sew up a storm, and my, that's handy in a neighbor."

I said to Nick and Morton, "I take it you've told Ivy and Florence about our plan?"

Florence said, "Oh, yes," and Ivy exclaimed. "Yes, and I just think it's wonderful. I don't know what this old crazy world is coming to and I've been just worried to death, but I can always count on my Mort to look after me." She covered Mort's hand with hers on the top of the table and smiled at the rest of us.

"Well," I said, "the basic idea is a sound one, I think. But now we've got to get down to the real work of actually building this retreat. And as I explained to Mort and Nick, it's us that's got to do it. We can't have workmen in because the whole idea is to keep the place a secret. Be hidden away. So the thing is we've got to get up there and build a cabin. At least one to start with. If we have that and we all have to take off in earnest we can at least have a roof over our collective heads while we build a cabin for everyone."

"Isn't this exciting?" Ivy asked Chris.

Chris ignored her, watching Nick's reaction. "The thing I was thinking," I went on, "was that we ought to get some plans laid for going up there and getting busy. What might be fun would be if we could all go, wives and all. If the women didn't want to stay in the woods there's several towns nearby that have hotels and motels."

Nobody said anything. Finally Chris offered, "Won't it be hard for everyone to be able to take off at the same time?"

"Why?" I asked her, as if we were alone. "There's no children problem." Nick's two sons were both in college and away for the summer. Ivy was Morton's third wife and they had no children together. "People take vacations together all the time," I added.

"I've taken mine already," Mort said. He was an executive salesman for a clothing chain.

I made an annoyed gesture with my head. "I'll bet you could get a few days off if you wanted to." I almost added, "Christ, you've gone off on enough unscheduled drunks for that long."

To Nick I said, "And you ought to give your associate pastor a chance, Nick. Your understudy could fill the pulpit for one week, couldn't he?" I felt uneasy about Nick. I'd felt uneasy about him all the way. I kept feeling he might laugh, now, at the whole idea, now when I was actually getting down to the real work.

He didn't answer me, just shrugged and looked over at Chris and smiled.

Florence said, "When are you talking about, Franklin? Nick has a vestry seminary in a week or ten days. And besides, what kind of work are you talking about? Isn't building a cabin awfully heavy work? I'm not sure that'd be good for Nick."

"What are you, Florence, his booking agent?" Then I looked at Nick and Mort, frowning a little. "What's the matter with you guys? Can't you talk for yourselves? I thought we had all this discussed. Let's get down to some concrete dates. I'm wide open."

Mort looked over at Nick, but the preacher was sitting there with a slight smile on his lips. Mort said, "Isn't it awfully hot right now? Shouldn't we wait a month or two until it's good and cool."

"Wait? Listen, if you can tell me the exact date we might need this place, I'd be willing to wait. But I don't think you can. I think we better get it ready just as quickly as we can. There's one hell of a lot to do. Not only building a cabin, but buying supplies, storing them up there. Maybe buying some cattle and turning them loose. Water system. Quite a lot."

"Goddamn, Franklin," Mort said, "this is my heavy season. The winter line is ready to hit the market right now."

I stared at him. "Don't give me that bull. Your winter line was sold months ago. If anything this is your *slack* season." I looked slowly from him to Nick and then at their wives.

Nick took a drink of the cognac we were having and said, "Mort's attitude is pretty well mine, Franklin. Though I'll be pleased to say mine direct rather than talking about my winter line." He gave Mort an amused glance. "The thing is, we agree with your idea in principal, we just don't want to get involved in a lot of hard work. Something like the fort is marvelous to sit around and talk about in the comfort of a bar, but that's a long way from the business of actually going out in the hot sun and sawing boards or some such. Isn't that what you mean, Mort?"

"Uh . . ." Mort said, flushing a little, "well, not exactly. I mean, I'm not backing out. I still think it's a darn good idea and one we've got to do something about—"

"Sometime," Nick prompted him.

"No, damnit, Nick," Mort said, "stop that. I'm not hedging. Hell, Franklin, this is a pretty grand idea. One doesn't just take it all in like you down a cold beer. This is large, man; you've got to worry it around in your mind a little. Plan."

"That's what I'm trying to do here, Mort," I said patiently. "I'm not proposing we all get in the car and go up tonight."

"Then let's do a little realistic planning," Nick said. He smiled at me, then at Chris and the other two wives. "I want to say quite frankly, for the record as the politicians love to put it as if they don't plan to change their minds later, that I am absolutely for Franklin's concept. I think Franklin will agree that some of his thinking has come from a few things I've said."

"That's right," Florence put in, her eyes bright, "about your idea. Nick came home after your lunch and said you had amazed him."

"Not too well put, Florence," Nick said, cutting her off. "I did want to make that point very clear, however. I sincerely believe that we will soon enough be facing some sort of social crises in this country. I expect it to be brought on by an economic failure since that's really what sends people to war in spite of all the fine talk about ideology and philosophy. Franklin's idea is a good one, a good way for handling the trouble."

Chris suddenly broke in. "Let me interject one point. I don't want it lost sight of that we planned and bought this place as a just-in-case type of thing. I mean, it still has the main function as a vacation retreat. I want to make that clear because I'm not sure that I go along with this disaster-around-the-corner talk."

I gave her an appraising look. "That wasn't necessary to say. Everyone understands that and everyone feels the same way." I was interested in where Nick was heading.

But Mort put in, "What is this, Franklin, some clever idea to get you a vacation house built? I'm beginning to see through the whole scheme. Ho ho ho, what a trick."

In a loud voice, Nick said, "However!"

"Go ahead, Nick," I told him. "I've been expecting the 'however' or the 'but.' The qualifier."

"Oh, not a qualifier on the idea. That's fine. I'm just concerned why you feel it necessary that we all go up in the mountains and take off our shirts and sweat."

"No other way," I said. "I've explained about the need for secrecy."

"Oh, I agree. But, I still believe it would be possible to have this retreat built by professional workmen and keep it a secret."

"You hire a crew up there and everyone in the county would know about it."

"I'm not suggesting you hire a crew from up there. Why couldn't you take some men from here? A simple cabin shouldn't take long. And if this place is as remote as you say, they'd have the devil's own time finding it again. Even if it would occur to them. And they wouldn't be around to talk to the neighbors. I fail to see why that wouldn't be perfectly safe. It would be for me."

"That makes sense," Morton said, nodding at Nick.

I was irritated. "It'd be too expensive for one reason. Taking a crew all that way."

"Oh, baloney!" Nick said. "To build a simple cabin? A crew could do it in two days. No good, Franklin. And Morton and I are certainly willing to come in on the cost. Split three ways it couldn't amount to much."

"I knew it," I said. "You want to make your commitment in paper. Money. Goddamnit, I told you I didn't want that. I want you involved, part of it. Hell, anybody could lay out a little cash."

"Well, what difference so long as the place gets built?"

"Oh, hell, Nick! I don't want to do it. So you lay out a thousand or two dollars. So what!"

"You're not making sense, Franklin," Nick insisted. "You're sitting there in the best condition I've seen you in in the ten years I've known you. That's fine for you. But Morton and I aren't ready for that sort of thing. We're city people, armchair people. Morton has to go lay down after a good laugh, and it's an Olympic feat for me to make love to my wife." He smiled. "Well, maybe I exaggerated the last part."

In the little silence that followed Ivy asked me, "Franklin, what type of cabin are ya'll thinking about?"

I blinked at her. "What?"

"I mean, I have a *Home Beautiful* book that has some of the loveliest cabin plans you ever saw. One of them has a bedroom loft and one whole wall is practically all glass. It's very striking."

Morton laughed and patted Ivy's hand. "My baby," he said. "She doesn't understand."

Ivy looked bewildered. "Well, you've got to have plans! My goodness."

I stood up. "Let's go in the den and sit. I'm tired of this dining room table. Everyone fix his own drinks."

Nick was right behind me. When I sat down, he was looking at me with an amused expression on his face. "You're not making sense, Franklin. You're not being logical."

"Maybe not," I conceded. "Not by your lights. But I know what *feels* right. And hiring a contractor and crew doesn't feel right. Building it ourselves does *feel* right. That's all I can say."

Nick didn't answer for a moment. The thread of a smile was on his face as he watched Chris and the company come into the room and seat themselves. I knew that he was waiting for his audience. He said, "The word 'metastasis' comes to mind, listening to you." He was still standing in the middle of the room.

I wasn't going to go for it, but Chris asked, "What does that word mean, Nick? Meta-something. That's one I don't know."

"Well," Nick said, "let's be specific." One wall of the den was a bookcase and Nick strode over to it and reached for a medical dictionary. For a second he turned pages. "All right." He cleared his throat. "Metastasis. I'll extrapolate from the biological meaning. Obsolescent traits and artifacts that once had survival value and that passed out of a society's culture by taking on a recreational function and holding sentimental value."

"I still don't understand," Chris said.

"Tools and weapons that have become toys. The *Queen Mary* is a good example. A passenger liner costing fifty million dollars that can transport fewer people across the ocean than a five-million-dollar jet plane. Why take the liner? Because it's fun. I was in a store the other day, a department store. And I saw an electric range that was almost twice as expensive as the other ranges sitting with it. Why? Because its marvelously modern parts were encased in a replica of an old wood-burning cook stove. The bow and arrow is another example. Who shoots bows and arrows? People who want to play at some role only they understand. The rifle is much more efficient. Do you understand now?"

"I understand," I said distinctly.

"Franklin's desire to build the cabin himself, to have us built it with him is metastatic. Isn't it Franklin?"

"I don't know," I answered slowly.

Nick sat down across from me.

"And how much more of the whole plan, Franklin, is metastatic?"

I got out a cigarette and lit it, thinking. Finally, I said again, "I don't know, Nick." I closed my lighter and put it in my pocket. "I only know I'm going through with it."

"What if it doesn't become necessary, Franklin?"

"I mean the preparations," I said. "I'm going through with them."

"Are you sure that's what you meant, Franklin?"

"Yes, Nick. I'm sure. You're my authority for when the actual retreat becomes necessary." I looked at him and he laughed. I said, "I've been expecting this. For you to take the other side. Are you out?"

"Oh, no, no, no. I was simply illustrating what I warned you about the other day."

"I don't remember," I lied.

Morton broke in and I was grateful. He said, "Well, what's the deal? God, you and Nick get off on all that dictionary talk and I don't know what's going on. Are we going to hire the cabin built or not? I'm with Nick on that!"

"Well," I said carefully, "there's one little factor being overlooked. I'm not proposing a democracy. The fort is still my idea and my land, and I'm going to make the decisions about certain things. I invited you two in under specific conditions. As far as I'm concerned that part hasn't changed, and neither are we going to put it to a vote." I sat back in my chair and looked around the room. Mort and Ivy were shocked. Nick still wore his little amused smile.

Ivy said, "Well, goodness, Franklin, that's not a very friendly thing to say. And it's not so fair either, if you ask me."

Mort patted her arm. "Hush, baby. Let us men talk about

this." He started to speak to me, but Nick shook his head at him. "Not now, Morton. Your timing would be very bad."

There didn't seem to be much else to say, I hadn't left them much to say. I wasn't angry, but I was very disgusted with Nick's attitude and with a few things Chris had said. Probably I wasn't being logical. But then neither was Nick with his inconsistent attitudes. The sonofabitch was a voyeur among human aspirations and ideals, and I was just goddamn if I was going to let him run barefoot through mine. The fort was as much a philosophical concept as a survival technique and I saw nothing wrong with that. Metastasis? I admitted to it to a certain degree, but that didn't mean I'd gone Amish. It was my belief that every move we made at the fort should be to prepare us for a life that might be more rigorous and demanding than we'd ever dreamed. If we had to use it for real, there'd be no crew of workmen to do our chores for us; it'd be us and our muscle and our sweat. Better to begin in the right way so we'd be conditioned and mentally ready. Of course, I had no intention of explaining any of this to Nick. I didn't see why I should have to. After all, I was offering them something of limitless value if the right set of conditions came to be, and I didn't see their privilege to quibble—not if they held it in the same light as I did.

There was another reason for my attitude as well. And it wasn't such a minor one. We were going to have to have a leader, a boss. If we got back in there and someone wanted to do something to the danger of the others—go into town, say—there'd have to be someone to say no and make it stick. I chose myself because I was the best qualified. And I thought it important that the others get used to the idea.

Chris mixed another round of drinks and got the conversation going. But it was strained. I think everyone had the idea, with the exception of Nick, that I'd just offered to deprive them of some sort of executive clemency. Ivy was almost hostile toward me. Strangely enough I believed she felt the need for such a plan as strongly as I did, and I wasn't a bit complimented by the comparison.

They left after a time. It was an amicable enough parting and Nick stood at the door smiling at me for a moment. He said he was still willing to have his check ready to pay for the workmen.

"No, Nick," I said. "I'm going to force you to take a stand on something and believe in it to the point of personal commitment. No switching. I don't know what you really value. I thought maybe your own life."

He smiled that infuriating mask at me. "Look at the sky some night, my friend. Huge stars crash into each other and die and are no more. What's one puny human life to all that."

"Bull shit," I breathed at him. "If you believed that you wouldn't make an effort about anything."

"Oh, I'm interested in my comfort," he said. "I value that."

"You better quit reading those decadent French philosophers, Nick," I told him.

When we were getting ready for bed Chris said to me, "I almost hope now that something does happen. For your sake. You're going to feel awfully silly if it doesn't. After what you said."

For Chris, even though I was still a little put out with her, I tried to justify my thinking. I told her about the need for a leader and the necessity of my taking a stand now.

But she was too presently practical to see what I was talking about. "That doesn't sound like a very good reason to embarrass and alienate some of our best friends."

"The general would understand."

"Daddy? You certainly seem to be taking a different view toward him than you always have."

"Maybe that's because I'm beginning to understand why generals have to think and act the way they do."

Next day I asked my wife, "Chris, do you think the real issue was us building the cabin ourselves, or do you think it was really disagreement with the whole plan?"

"I don't think there's any underlying motives," she answered. "Why should there be? We all think your plan is a good one. I just truly don't believe you're going to get Mort and Nick to go off up in the woods and build a cabin."

She was in the bathroom, soaking in the tub, and I was sitting in the bedroom polishing my shoes. "Well, that's the point. You realize we're actually talking about a survival plan. How then, if they believe in the necessity, can they be unwilling to do a little carpentry work in order to protect their lives? That doesn't make any sense. Hell, Nick is supposed to see more trouble in the signs than I do. How can he make such a big magilla out of building a cabin?"

"Well," she called to me, "you know Nick. I don't think you're going to get anywhere trying to figure Nick's reasons by the way a person ought to think."

"And what about Morton?"

"Com'on, Franklin. Morton's going to do whatever appeals to him at that moment. Morton never thought *anything* all the way through."

"Well, I'll tell you, Chris. You aren't helping anything by your attitude. Especially in front of people. You keep insisting it's a vacation cabin. It's not a vacation cabin. I wouldn't want to go up and build a vacation cabin either. But I'd drive the nails for a fort with my bare fists. You've got to stop that. You influence people, even Nick."

"Franklin," she said dryly, "you keep wanting to circle the wagons and we haven't seen any Indians yet."

"Maybe not Indians," I argued, "but plenty of signs. Like this." I was using a sheet out of the morning paper to protect the rug from my shoe-shining operation. Framed between my feet was a news item announcing the end of the government's Plentiful Foods Program. "Twenty-eight years ago," I told Chris, "the Agricultural Department started the Plentiful Foods Program as an aid to people on tight budgets. The idea being that these foods would be cheaper. Well, they've just announced that there ain't no more plentiful foods—of any kind."

"So? Will that start rioting?"

I could hear her getting out of the tub, the water splashing and dripping.

"Chris, use your head. It's all part of an overall picture. You know what's on the front page."

"I still can't get too excited about it," she said, the last part coming out muffled as she dried her face.

"The dollar is being devalued every day," I explained patiently, "and prices are rising. And commodities are becoming scarce. People are feeling the pinch already. It's going to reach a crisis—it has to."

She came out of the bathroom naked. I loved her body when there was the contrast between her golden tan and the milk-white of the tiny areas covered by her bikini bathing suit. Her pubic hairs fascinated me. She was a natural blond, but for some reason, there was a reddish-golden tint to the hair between her legs. It looked marvelous shining and still a little wet. I grabbed her as she walked past me and pressed my face against her crotch. "Hmmmm," I said, "fresh pussy. I want some."

"You can't have any. I don't like your attitude."

"All right," I said, letting her go. "See if I care."

"We don't have time, anyway," she claimed. "I've got to get dressed and go downtown."

I told her. "Listen, when *you* want to you've always got time. Don't kid me."

She walked on over to her dresser and began slipping into her lingerie. "Listen, Chris," I said seriously. "I really want you to change your attitude. This thing could turn bad any day now, and I want you to begin mentally preparing yourself. This see no evil and it won't happen is dangerous. And unrealistic."

"Well, what do you want me to do, Franklin? We're not flee-ing today, are we? I mean, why worry until we have to do some-thing."

"That's just what I'm talking about, Chris. You don't wait to make your plans until the enemy's at the door. You've got to be ready well in advance of that."

"I thought that's what we'd done—made plans."

She was frustrating and irritating me and I couldn't exactly explain why. I just didn't feel that she was serious enough about the project, committed enough. I couldn't seem to impress the danger on her, the necessity of being ready.

"Okay," I said, "go ahead. But please, do me the favor of not interfering when I'm talking sense with anyone else."

"You're getting angry, Franklin. And I don't understand why. What exactly is it you want me to be doing? I've done every-thing you've asked; read all those booklets. I've got recipes and nutrition charts coming out my ears. I could can green beans right now if I had to, God forbid."

"What about the dental work? I told you we'd need to have our teeth in perfect shape and keep them that way. We won't be able to get out and see a dentist, you know. I'll bet you've forgotten all about that."

"We've got appointments next week," she said. "Now, what else?"

"Listen, Chris, don't be funny with me. You may think this whole thing is a joke, but I don't."

She faced me from her dressing table. "That's obvious, Franklin. Very obvious."

I told her, "Look, I want you to get an assortment of clothes ready for us. The kind of clothes we'll need at the fort. Pack them away in boxes, ready to go. We might have to leave at a moment's notice."

"Franklin . . ." she answered. She went over to the bed and sat on the edge. "Come here a minute." She patted the place beside her. "Come sit by me a minute. I want to talk to you."

I sat beside her and lit a cigarette. "What?"

"Franklin, you're not thinking of pulling out anytime soon, are you?"

"I don't know," I told her. "It appears to me that things are getting pretty tense."

"What about the cabin?"

"We might have to make do with a tent until we could get a cabin up."

"Listen, are you sure you're not overreacting?"

"We haven't left yet, Chris."

"Yes, but all you think about is those mountains and that fort, as you call it. I wish you'd get something else on your mind."

"You just be ready," I told her. "I'll let you know."

She gave me a funny look. "I'm not too sure I'm crazy about that kind of talk."

"Nevertheless."

And now I was ready to go; I mean really ready to go. I got up one morning a few weeks after our dinner with Nick and Mort, and all I could think of was to get away, flee, run to the fort. All I was looking for now was an excuse. I won't even call it a reason, just an excuse would do. I wanted away from the city, away from my treacherous fellow man, away from systems and civilization and dependency of any kind. I wanted to eat bread from the wheat I'd grown, plow my own fields, drink my own water, kill my own game, be totally the man I was intended to be. It was like a pain, that need to be away, to be gone from it all. Each day now I brought home some new story to persuade Chris. I knew I must make it logical and necessary. To be sure, there were enough things happening, but none of them seemed final and necessary enough. A man went berserk in a restaurant where Mort and I were having lunch and began grabbing up coats and hats and throwing them on the floor; there was a riot started by a march on city hall; a man even came and tried to sell me some stolen diamonds. None of these incidents were forceful enough to affect Chris to any great degree. She continued to see all that was happening as isolated incidents.

It was very frustrating to me that I couldn't just say to my wife, "Here is a new life I've chosen. We're going."

One of our standard arguments started one evening during supper and continued until I went into the library and got out my lists and checked over my supplies and materials. Chris looked in on me after about an hour.

"What are you doing, Horn?"

"Nothing," I told her savagely, "nothing, according to your view."

"Listen," she said. She leaned against the door jamb. "Listen, hadn't we better talk? It seems to me we've let this whole situation come a long way between us. I don't understand what's happening, Horn."

I glanced up at her. "What's happening is that you're taking a position on a situation that is not yours to handle. You're out of your territory, sport. And not only are you wrong, you're giving me a lot of trouble besides."

"Can't we disagree," she asked, a note in her voice, "without it coming between us like this? Do you realize how many fights we've had over this fort thing?"

"That's it right there," I told her heatedly. "This fort thing attitude. You seem to believe this is an ordinary issue like what kind of car we should own. There's your mistake. Listen, on something like this we don't argue. We do it my way because I'm better at this. If we were indeed building a vacation retreat we could do all the mutual conferring you wanted."

All the time I was talking, I knew I was letting a really important opportunity pass and it made my heart ache to see Chris slowly withdrawing from me. I didn't know what to do, what to say. I felt I was doing the right thing and I had to press forward, for her sake as well as mine. But I also knew I wasn't handling her right. I suppose, that evening, if I hadn't been so frantic I could have taken advantage of the opportunity she offered me. But I didn't.

"All right," she said uncertainly. She sighed. "Whatever you say, Horn. Maybe you're right."

We were in bed at about eleven o'clock that night when the phone rang. I answered it and an operator said, "Please hold for an overseas call."

"A what?" But the operator had already gone. I heard a succession of whirrs and snaps and a sound like wind blowing. I sat up straighter in bed. Then another operator said, "This is Bogotá, Colombia, calling. Mister Franklin Horn."

I said to Chris. "It's your daddy." I handed her the phone.

She took it, listened, spoke a second, and then handed it back to me. "It's for you," she said.

"It is?" I was surprised. I put the receiver to my ear in time to hear the operator say, "Go ahead, sir, your party is on the line."

"Hello? Hello?"

The connection was bad and the wind noises were swirling in and out. "This is Franklin," I said loudly.

The general said, "Now pay attention. I want to tell you something and I . . ."

Then his voice faded out slightly. I yelled "What?" into the mouthpiece.

He suddenly came in strong, sounding a little irritated. "I said pay attention because I'm going to be brief. These overseas calls are very expensive."

I wanted to laugh.

He said, "On that matter you and I have been discussing . . ."

"What matter?" I thought his voice had faded again, but he was still there.

"That strategic matter. I can't talk very well. This line might be tapped."

I did laugh then. "You mean the operation concerning the gas generator?"

"Yes," he said. "That plan." There was a pause and the wind noises swirled in. "Understand," he said after a second, "I don't agree with what you want to do. But I believe, for my daughter's safety, that you should act on it very soon."

"What?"

"I said you should put . . ." But his voice faded.

"What?" I shouted.

". . . should put the plan in effect. I have information that certain dissident elements are going to take advantage of the . . ." he groped for a word that would satisfy all his requirements, ". . . the temporary confusion. It doesn't . . . it doesn't look good. I think you should go to the country for a time."

"When?" I shouted. "What date?"

"I can't be that definite," he said. "We don't have that information. But soon. You should go on standby alert right away. Have your logistics in order and be ready to move at the first overt sign."

"General," I said loudly, "is this reliable? Are you certain?"

"Fairly," he said.

"What else? Anything concrete? Any signs to look for?"

"That's all I can tell you now. Use your own judgment."

There was a click and then the wind noises came in stronger. I hung the phone up slowly. For a moment I didn't say anything. Then I turned to Chris.

"Did you understand much of that conversation?"

"No." She shook her head. "Except from the way you were acting it must be serious. What was it all about?"

"It's serious," I said. I punched the pillow and lay back. I stared at the ceiling.

"Well?" she asked me again.

"I'm thinking," I told her. "I'm trying to find the right words so you'll understand them. So you'll feel their impact."

She sat up beside me, staring down in my face. "Franklin, what is it? For God's sake, tell me! Is something wrong with Daddy or Mother?"

"No, no," I said quickly. "Nothing like that. That was an official call from the general."

"Goddamnit! What is this all about?"

"It was a starting bell," I said. "We're going. We're leaving for the fort."

Her face went blank. "When?"

"Right now," I said it softly, definitely. "Tomorrow, the next day. As soon as we can get ready. But we're leaving as of this moment."

She didn't say anything for a long time. I let her sit in silence. There are some times you have to let Chris alone and I knew that this was one of them. Finally she roused herself and got out of bed. She looked around. "Where are your cigarettes?"

"Here," I said. I raised up on one elbow, opened the nightstand drawer, and got out the pack and a lighter. I lit hers and took one for myself. Then I lay there and watched her moving restlessly around the room while she puffed amateurishly on the cigarette.

At length I told her, firmly, "Chris, I mean this. It's not open to discussion. It's what we're going to do." Then I told her what the general had said.

She turned around and looked at me quizzically. "I assumed that was what it was," she said, "but I want you to tell me one thing . . ."

"What?"

"You've never respected my father at all on anything. Why now does what he has to say make our minds up for us?"

"You're wrong," I said calmly. "I have always said I thought your daddy was a hell of a soldier. I respect that part of him. And I think anything he has to say on that score is valid. Listen, this is a war."

"And that tipped the scales, huh? Just that one phone call?"

"It didn't take much. I've been ready to go for some time now."

"All right, answer me one other thing—that cloak and dagger sound to what he said. 'We have reason to believe that dissident elements are,' are going to what? What'd he say? Well, whatever— But this, now do you want me to believe that you seriously paid attention to that? Daddy's not in the CIA."

I just shrugged. "He's supposed to know. I don't know what he's into and neither do you. But I don't believe he'd make such a call if he didn't really know something."

"Oh, bah!" she said. She turned away and took a quick puff on her cigarette.

I stared at her back. "Chris?"

She finally turned around. She looked unhappy. "What?"

"Please don't argue with me about this, dear. We've got to do it. That's all. My mind is made up."

"Goddamn!" she said violently. She went to an ash tray and snubbed her cigarette out. Then she leaned back against the dresser and crossed her arms. "All right, Franklin," she said, "I'll go. I guess there's no other way. You've apparently got to get this out of your system. And I don't know what else to do. It's all you think about. It's all you talk about." She turned her head and looked away from me, a strained expression apparent on her profile. "I don't understand it," she said, coming back. "I can't even pretend to understand it. But it's so goddamn important to you. I understand that. So I don't see any other way to get you over it."

I asked her, "You don't see the need?"

She shook her head. "No I don't, Franklin. I really don't. I'm going to do it because you apparently have to. But I'm not going to pretend I like it."

"Well, that just makes me feel great," I told her.

"But—" she pronounced.

"But what?"

"I've got a few conditions. One at least."

I turned away from her and lit another cigarette. "I hate to see this happening," I told her. "I hate to see you acting like this. Talking to me like this."

"Nevertheless," she said. She was tense and some inner strain was showing in her face. "We don't sell the house," she said.

I just looked at her.

"I mean that, Franklin. You go down to the bank and make six months of payments. When we come back I want our house here. I won't do it otherwise. And I want nothing else sold. We leave as if we were leaving on a long vacation. I don't know how long it's going to take you to get over this, how long before you get tired of it, but I'm not willing to throw everything away in the experiment. It's the only way I'll go."

I went to the bathroom and washed my face, and brushed my teeth from the taste the cigarettes had put in my mouth. When I came back in the room she was still in the same position, still leaning up against the dresser. Tensed up.

I got back in bed. "All right," I said. "I agree. And thanks for the confidence." I punched up the pillow again. "We'll start getting ready in the morning. I'll go and see Nick and Morton."

"No," she said it distinctly, finally.

"What?"

"I don't want you to involve anyone else. If we have to go, let's just go. I don't even want anyone to know."

"Well, the hell with you," I said. I reached over and turned off the light. "You have the most marvelous ability to make me feel about as big as a six-year-old child. But that doesn't matter. I don't care what your reasons for agreeing to go are. You can suit yourself on that."

I lay there in the dark for a long time, unable to sleep, unable to even shut my eyes. At length I reached up and snapped on the bedside lamp. I looked over at Chris; she was lying stiffly on her back, her eyes open, staring at the ceiling.

"You keep," I said, "talking about what this is doing to me, this fort thing, as you call it. Well, have you ever stopped to think what this life, this phony twisted life we call normal has been doing to me?"

She turned her head, slowly. "I don't know what you mean."

I told her about the thief who'd come by to sell me the paper of diamonds. "And I was actually considering it," I said. "I was actually thinking about doing it. The situation has gotten so out of focus, values have become so distorted, that I was actually thinking of stealing!"

She frowned, a tiny furrow appearing between her eyes. "I don't understand. What's that got to do with this?"

"Just that it must be time to go. It must be time to do something, if I can let myself slip that far. To actually consider such a proposition!"

"I don't follow that, Franklin," she answered, the little frown mark still between her eyes. "And I don't think you do either. I think you'd use any reason, any rationale you could, and fit it to your own purpose. I think you want to do this so badly that you would do that without even realizing."

"God, thanks for your understanding. I sometimes wonder how it is possible for you to live with me for this long and know so little about me."

Her face suddenly flamed. She reared up on an elbow. "Goddamnit, don't you dare say that to me! Have you ever seen *me*! *Me*. Me, Chris Whatever-My-Last-Name-Is. Not as your wife or your woman or however you think of me, but as myself? As a person? Have you ever looked at me like that, Franklin?"

"You're good, Chris, very good."

"You're not thinking this project is best for me, me the person. You're dragging me along like something that belongs to you, your horse or your leg or that goddamn gas generator. If you would just stop for one minute and—"

"You stop!" I ordered her. "It's decided. You hear me? It's decided. Now go to sleep. We're going to be moving fast tomorrow."

I reached up and turned out the light. It was time to go. God, was it time to go.

The next day I was tremendously excited. I kept wanting to hurry, to rush, to flash out the door and be gone. I wanted to pack the pickup and leave right then, that second. Chris, on the other hand, went about her preparations like someone who's said she'd go but hadn't really made up her mind yet. There was a distance and a coolness between us. I made no attempt to bridge it and neither did she.

There were a number of things to be done, mundane things like stopping the paper and having the gas and water and telephone disconnected. In the afternoon, I went down to the bank and made a year's house payments in advance. I also drew out a large amount of cash. I was thinking of taking it all, but I finally took the balance and put it in our safe deposit box. After that I went by a lawyer I sometimes used and made arrangements to have my office sublet if possible. He was curious, but I wouldn't tell him anything.

There was a certain dreamlike quality about the whole affair. I felt like a man who'd hit his head against a rock and was being swept downstream by a swift current. I felt disembodied and only about half conscious of what was going on around me.

We spent that night packing clothes. I loaded a few articles in the pickup, but I left most of it for the next evening. I wasn't going to try and take the gas generator or some of the other heavy equipment. I wanted to get up and get settled; get Chris settled before she changed her mind. We wouldn't need the generator for a time anyway and I could always slip back and pick it up. I just wanted to be gone.

The distance was still between us that night. I went to sleep with Chris's even breathing coming from the furthest part of her side of the bed.

I was not going to talk to Morton. I had decided that the night before. But I was going over to see Nick. Nick, at least, was decisive. I didn't want to listen to any of Morton's phony enthusiasm.

I got up very early, not waking Chris. While I was having breakfast she came down. She got a cup of coffee and sat down at the table with me. "I would have gotten up and fixed your breakfast," she said.

"No," I told her, "I'm going over to see Nick and I didn't want to argue with you about it."

"So you're telling me now."

"Why not?"

I looked down, eating. It was amazing me just how easy it was to pull up all your roots. I'd expected an overwhelming amount of detail to attend to, but there'd been surprisingly little. We were really almost ready to go.

Then Chris said, "Franklin, let's wait a month."

"No," I said. "And I don't want to argue about it. We've decided."

"It's that important?"

"It's not important, it's necessary." I got up. "I'll be back in an hour. Hurry with anything you've got left to do."

Outside I drew in a breath of the cold air. I suddenly felt very good. I was excited, like I used to be when I was going off on a mining trip or back into the bush. A new adventure, a new test. I felt new and I felt clean.

The drive to Nick's house was a route I'd followed many times, but now, all of a sudden, things looked unfamiliar, strange, as if I were in another town. And, if you considered where my home was now, I was.

It was not quite seven o'clock and the sun was just up. Through the haze I could see it rising off in the east, its rays a dirty yellow. I was driving through a residential district. I slowed as a man came out of his house and went out to pick up his newspaper. He was wearing pajamas and he stopped and looked up at the sky and yawned and beat the paper against his leg and then trudged back in the house. I suddenly envied the man. No, that wasn't right. I envied him his illusion that God was in his heavens and all was right with the world.

I knew Nick was an early riser, so I wasn't worried about his being up. At the front door Florence said he was in the back in his greenhouse. She stared at me curiously, but I expected that was mostly surprise at seeing me so early in the morning.

I walked around the house, watching my breath steam in the frosty morning air. It had warmed up a little, but there was still a heavy chill in the air.

Horticulture was Nick's consuming passion. And it, as much as anything, illustrated the basic differences between us. He grew ornamentals, plants grown for the pure pleasure of looking at them; while I, if I'd been a gardener, would have grown nothing that couldn't be eaten. We'd had many deadly serious arguments on the subject. He'd tried to convince me of the hunger of the soul for beauty, for sensuality, while I'd doggedly insisted that a stalk of corn or a cucumber vine could be just as beautiful as an oleander or a pyracantha or whatever. He always ended up calling me a clod and my view of him was that he was a spoiled, unrealistic sensualist. "If you had to grow your own food," I'd always told him, "you'd change your opinion damn quick. I'd like to see which you valued most, one of those ferns or a tomato plant, if you were starving."

I opened the door and stepped inside. The greenhouse was warm and humid after the chill of the late winter morning. Nick was at his potting table, transplanting some kind of fernlike plants out of the piles of dirt and humus and moss he had on the table. He was wearing the thin, black shirt and the turned-around collar of his profession. He had his sleeves rolled up, exposing his skinny, white arms. He glanced up at me. "Hello, Franklin," he said, seeming not at all surprised to see me so early in the morning. But that was Nick; even if he was he wouldn't let on. He never showed his emotions, thinking it gave him a moral superiority.

"Hi." I sat on a nearby stool and watched him. I didn't know what to say or where to begin.

With his back to me he went on working and said, "Just helping out mother nature here. Poor raped old bitch. Though I'm not sure she's raped as much as she allows herself to get fucked. Otherwise it would seem she'd rise up in a wrath of titanic destruction and turn on her persecutors with fire and famine and flood. Or at least a damn good earthquake. Right through the industrial district, for instance. And how are you this morning?"

I didn't answer. Instead, I got out a cigarette and lit it. Nick turned around and looked at me.

"You appear bemused, Franklin."

"We're going, Nick. Pulling out for the fort."

He raised his eyebrows. "Really? Who is we and when?"

"Chris and I. I've come over to tell you."

He turned back to his potting. With his back to me he asked, "Are you sure you're doing the right thing, Franklin?"

I was suddenly irritated. "You've agreed all along it's the right thing."

"No. I mean this suddenly."

"Suddenly? What's suddenly? We've been talking about this for six months. I guess anything's sudden when you finally do it."

"But now. Why now?"

I told him about the general's call.

He turned around and faced me, sitting on the high stool he had for use at his table. "I was under the impression you didn't think much of the general's opinions."

I shrugged. "The general knows about war. This is a kind of war. I respect his opinion on that."

"And he said to leave today."

My lethargy left long enough for a wave of irritation to sweep through me. "Of course not. Quit treating me like a fool, Nick."

He turned back to his potting table. For a long moment he kept his back to me without speaking. Then he said, "So you've made the final commitment. No turning back now."

"What the hell does that mean?"

"Just what you think it does, buddy boy. Now you've got to go to the mountains, to the fort. I told you you'd have to cast the dice once you took them up."

"Oh fuck you," I said, "you prophetic bastard. You're full of shit." I got up off my stool. Stiffly, I said, "I came by to tell you what we're doing. I still want you along. I'll draw you a map of the place and you can come up when you feel it's right."

He didn't say anything, just went on working on his plants.

"Do you want me to draw the map?"

And then he said, "You know, Franklin, the house plant is a peculiar creature. Totally out of its environment. The house plant was once a wild thing growing in the forest. But we came along, ripped it up, introduced it to an unnatural environment and forced it to like it. Now it likes the careful watering, the careful feeding, the regulated sunlight, the pampering, the nurturing. Likes it? Actually, it has to have it. Raising house plants you have to be so very, very careful. Not too much, but not too little. There's a very thin line of life-sustaining care necessary. It's the artificial environment, you know. But there's one other important characteristic. Even though it is an unnatural environment you're producing for the fragile little plant, it comes to need it. Its adaption span becomes very limited. For that reason, you can't take a house plant and return it to the wild. It will die. It's no longer the plant it was with all the adaptive facilities. No, no, it likes its comfort too well now to fight for survival in the alien forest."

"Do you want me to draw the map?" I asked carefully.

"No, Franklin, I don't. We won't be coming."

"Mind telling me why?"

"Not at all." He turned around on his stool. "In one word. Comfort."

"I see," I said.

"I doubt it. You're an absolutist, Franklin. That's why I knew you'd have to follow your plan, your course of action once you settled on it."

I looked at him.

"You're a moralist, Franklin, whether you know it or not. A prude. An idealist. You still believe in the guys in the white hats against the guys in the black hats; that the good guys always win; that your heart is pure; that you're the arbiter of your own fate; that country folk are better than city folk; that life is really very simple. You believe that civilization has gone wrong, so you want to simply sweep it out of the way and go be a lion in a mountain lair. You—"

"Listen, I'm not interested in—"

"You think that all the choices are yours. That you can challenge and win. But I know better. It's a very difficult life, Franklin. Very complex, very hard to understand and to handle. I don't even try. I enjoy it in my own warped way, and that, Franklin, is the reason we're not going. I don't think I'd enjoy it. I may or may not be right about what's going to happen, but I have no intention of going off and squatting in some shanty in the mountains. I wouldn't like that life, Franklin. It would be uncomfortable. You don't seem to know how to use modern life. I do. And while you deplore and battle, I take what I want of it. It's that simple."

I lit a cigarette and looked at him.

He said, "You know I don't like you to smoke in the greenhouse. The little plants are very delicate."

I ignored that and went on smoking. "You know," I told him, "I knew you'd finally have to put your dirty foot on this. I knew you wouldn't be able to keep your mouth out of it. I didn't want to tell you about it at first because I knew how it would finally end up. Well—" I dropped my cigarette deliberately on the greenhouse floor and ground it out with my foot. "I feel sorry for you, Nick. You voyeurs never really find out what it's all about, do you? You can make me angry, Nick. You could always do that. But, then, so can any other fool."

"Let me give you some advice, my friend," he said. He swung around on his stool. "And you are my friend, in spite of what you might think. I advise you not to go, Franklin. Forget all this business and go on back to your life."

"You're a sonofabitch, Nick, did you know that? Don't you have any scruples, any morals at all. Can you remember all you have told me, how you talked, how you agreed with this?"

"Listen to me, Franklin. Listen to me carefully. You have a very thin veneer of civilization. I beg you not to go off to that life because I don't believe you could survive it. You would revert, Franklin. For once in my life, I don't know exactly what I mean, but I have a very strong feeling about this. Franklin, you're just not civilized enough for such an experiment. You haven't learned to make the compromises the rest of us have. You take a thing too totally into your head. You become that thing. I beg you, man, forget this idea. You're just not civilized enough to handle it."

I looked at him. "So long, Nick." I tried to keep my voice light, but I couldn't in the end. "I'll be so goddamn glad to get away from you and sharpshooters like you. Do something real, Nick, sometime, just for the novelty of the thing."

He called to me as I opened the door, but I just waved a hand behind me and kept going.

I was racing by the time I got home, driving faster and faster. I wanted to go, to go, to go, to go. I couldn't wait any longer. I felt as if I were smothering, strangling. I skidded to a stop in the driveway and jumped out and ran in the house. Chris was in the den, packing a box. She straightened up as I came rushing in.

"Are you packed?"

"What? Well, yes. Just about, I guess. It's impossible to tell because I really don't know what to take. I mean, my God, have you got any idea what—"

"Never mind," I said. "We're going now." I picked up two suitcases and started for the door.

"Now! But you said tomorrow. Good God, Franklin!"

"Never mind. We'll take what we've got now and come back for what we've missed later."

She followed me outside. I set the suitcases down. I'd load in the supplies first. With her standing in the driveway, I jumped in the pickup and backed it up to the carport, threading my way between trees and by the swimming pool. She followed along.

I would not stop to talk to her. I was frantic to go. I didn't want to waste a minute.

Finally, she said, "You're determined to go now?"

"Yes," I said, throwing boxes in the back of the pickup.

She shook her head. "My God," she said. Then she turned away and went back in the house.

I couldn't get ready fast enough. It was all frantic and wild and dreamlike. I pushed Chris and shoved her and threw supplies in the pickup and did a thousand last-minute details. When it was done I came outside and Chris was standing by her Mercedes.

"You can't take that," I told her.

"I want to," she said.

"We don't need it. You can't drive that in the mountains. It wouldn't make it over that trail."

"Yes it will. Listen, Franklin, I'm going to take it."

I stared at her, level-eyed. "You sound like someone keeping one foot on the shore."

"I'm taking my car."

Suddenly I didn't care. I just wanted to go. I whirled and jumped in the pickup. "Try and stay up," I yelled at her. Then I threw the truck in reverse and backed up furiously, spinning the tires.

I don't remember much about the first part of the drive. I know that I drove furiously, like a man possessed by a demon. Little by little, I began to calm down. Seventy or eighty miles down the road I pulled over to the side and stopped. I'd loaded the whiskey in the back, and I got out and rummaged in the bed of the pickup until I found a bottle. As I was opening it Chris pulled in behind me and got out. She came up, looking splendid and beautiful in the brisk sunshine. "What are you doing?"

"I'm having a drink," I answered, not looking at her. Chris wasn't real, just as none of it could be real. Surely this wasn't my wife standing by the side of a highway watching a mad man rummaging for a bottle of whiskey in the back of a pickup.

"Let's go back, Franklin."

I shook my head. "We can't." I turned the bottle up and took a long pull, feeling its effect almost immediately.

"Franklin, this is all wrong. You know it's all wrong."

I shook my head again. "No. This is the right thing to do. Just trust me, Chris. It'll work out."

I got back in the cab, taking the bottle with me. As we drove away I wondered, dimly, what she must be thinking. I could see her in the rearview mirror, following me as faithfully as a trailer.

We drove hard for most of the day, stopping only for gas. We stopped to eat once also, and I wouldn't have done that if Chris hadn't driven alongside of me and made frantic signals. But, then, we only went to a quick-order hamburger joint where there was little time to talk. I didn't want to talk to Chris; didn't even want to think about her. I just wanted to drive and drive and to get to the mountains and the fort.

We continued to drive hard, fleeing. Late in the evening, just as it was becoming dark, we came into Texarkana. I intended to go straight on through and not stop for gas until we came to Little Rock, but as we were on the highway leading out of town, Chris suddenly speeded up, passed me, and then pulled into a little roadside café.

I pulled in beside her. She got out and stood by her Mercedes. I rolled my window down, leaving the motor running. "Let's go, Chris. We can't stop here."

But she shook her head. "No, I'm going to stop here." Her face was set and calm. "Go on if you have to, but I'm going to stop. We've been driving for nearly twelve hours straight and I've got to stop. I don't even know what the rush is." She turned around and walked into the café, putting the strap of her purse over her shoulder as she went.

I sighed and turned off the engine and got out. I was surprised at how stiff I was.

It was just an ordinary roadside café, like a thousand others of an older vintage. Not the chain types that had grown up on the huge interstate highways, but the kind that advertised home cooking and prided itself on attracting the truck driver trade. Chris was in one of the booths, though she could have chosen any place since the café was deserted except for a tired-looking waitress leaning against the counter.

I slid in opposite her and the waitress came over and took our order. We both ordered hamburgers and coffee, and the waitress went away chewing her gum and shuffling her feet. For a moment I stared up at a beer sign that had some kind of a bubble effect in its neon lights. I instinctively felt that something was coming.

Chris said, picking at the paper napkin under her silverware, "Franklin, what's going on? This is crazy and you know it."

I didn't say anything.

She said, "I don't see any people running wild—except us."

"It's below the surface."

Then we both sat staring off at nothing for a time. The waitress brought our food. "Ya'll want anything else?"

"Just the check," I told her. She wrote it out and laid it on the tabletop. The top was vinyl and a generation of knife carriers had carved their initials there. It was, I thought, as good a way as any to leave a record of your passing.

We ate in silence. The hamburger tasted like so much cardboard to me. I could barely get it down my throat was so tight. After a bite I gave it up and fiddled with the coffee.

"Let's go back, Franklin," Chris said.

I told her simply, "I can't."

She said, "Let's go back."

I told her again that I couldn't.

She picked up a spoon, looked at it, put it back down; picked up her coffee cup, made rings on the tabletop with it, then set it back in the saucer. She looked at me. She said, "I'm going home, Franklin."

I was not too surprised. The air of unreality that had accompanied me made it seem a perfectly natural thing for her to say.

I nodded my head slowly.

"Are you coming?"

"No," I said.

She put her hand on mine. "Will you listen and let me tell you how I feel?"

I nodded. "Of course."

"I followed you this morning, Franklin, blindly. I did whatever you told me. But you ask too much, Franklin. You ask too much of me." She stopped, her eyes blinking furiously as if she were about to cry. Then she seemed to gain control of herself. "This is not for me, Franklin. None of this. I'm not going to give up my right to live where I want to and do what I want to. And nothing's going to scare me into it. I'm not going to run off and hide."

I looked down at the table. "Then you think I'm a coward for running. Do you think I'm afraid, Chris?"

"No," she answered after a moment.

"Yet, I'm running. I'm not a coward, Chris. And it's not cowardice to retreat from a situation that you can't handle.

There are other reasons, perhaps, but we've talked all this over before. We both know what the other thinks."

"Yes," she agreed, "we do." She hesitated. "I'm going back home, Franklin. Are you coming?"

I looked up at her. "You going to run out on me, Chris?"

"I guess that depends on how you look at it, doesn't it. I think you're running out on me."

"You said you'd come, Chris. I didn't like your reasons, but you said you would."

She was silent for a long moment.

"Didn't you?" I asked her again.

"Yes," she answered.

We weren't either one looking at the other. Her eyes were directed far off on the other side of the café. I was staring at the paper napkin container.

"Well?" I asked her.

"It's difficult to explain," she said. "I—I just can't, Franklin." She shook her head. "I just can't. I know you won't see how you've been today. This wild running. This frantic dash. I don't understand you. I don't understand any of this. You're not like yourself, Franklin." She put her hand on mine again. "Please let's go back. Please, dear."

I took my hand away. "You're like Nick. You've talked a good game, but you won't follow through. That's all it is, talk. A game."

"Please don't say that. Please try and understand how I feel. I'm frightened, Franklin. Absolutely afraid. This is nothing like what we discussed. I can't even pretend to understand this. I've only got one weapon to control you with. And if that doesn't work . . . well . . ." She sat back.

"Is that what you're doing now, Chris? Trying to control me?"

She pressed her lips together.

"Is it?"

Her voice trembled. "If you really believe what you say, then I don't see how you can let me go back alone. I don't—" She broke off and lapsed into silence.

Hell, what did it matter. What did any of it matter.

I leaned back in the booth also. We were now as far apart as we could get. "You do what you want to, Chris."

Several moments passed. We were both still. Then, very slowly, she took her purse up from the seat and pulled the long strap over her shoulder. "Then I guess I'd better start back." She looked at me. "I'll stay here tonight. At a hotel. At a downtown hotel. There shouldn't be many."

I nodded slowly. "Yes, you ought not to try and drive at night." She got up. I didn't look at her.

"Come home, Franklin."

I still didn't look at her. I let her get to the door and then I turned in my seat. "Chris?"

She stopped, her hand on the knob.

"Are you sure you know what you're doing?"

"No," she said, still standing there holding the door knob.

"Do you realize how serious this is?"

She looked tired, drained, worn out. She said, in an uncertain voice, "I think so."

"And you're still going out that door?"

"Yes."

I nodded slowly and turned back around in my seat. "You know where I'll be. You can find it."

She opened the door. "And you know where I'll be, Franklin." She went out.

The waitress came over. "Everything all right?"

"Oh, yes," I assured her. "Everything's fine."

It seemed, after a moment, that I heard the engine of the Mercedes start up and then pull away, the sound fading. She was truly gone, but it took a little while for it to sink in, for the loneliness to come.

And so I was finally there—on the mountain, on my land, in my fort. I was very much alone and very much aware of how alone I was. With the night and eerie stillness of the mountain forest came doubt and fear and the compulsion to race away from this place, back to the city and the lights and Chris.

It was raining and I sat in the mouth of the big tent I'd put up and listened to the rain spattering off the leaves with that solitary sound a slow rain makes in a forest of dried, fall leaves. It wasn't cold enough to freeze yet, but I knew it would be before the night was out. Dark hadn't come fully, but I could follow the retreat of the light, see the trees getting bigger in the darkness, and see the ridges and hills taking on that deep brown cast they get just after sundown. I sat there and watched and thought and worried.

There really wasn't much danger of my suddenly jumping in the pickup and breaking for home, no matter how depressed or afraid I might get. I'd fixed it so I couldn't do that.

I knew I ought to get up and bring in some firewood before it got really dark, but I was tired from setting up the two tents and from unloading the pickup. I had the tent I was in, the tent we were to live in while I built the house, and I had another one, the supply tent where I'd stored all the equipment and tools and such I'd brought along.

I wasn't feeling the cold very much because of the bottle of whiskey I had at my feet. I was sitting on a camp stool, and every once in a while, I'd have a pull at the bottle. The whiskey was keeping away the illusion of the cold, but that didn't mean it was any less cold. A man does that—creates artificial sensations and situations and then makes himself believe they're real. But he can only do that as long as the whiskey holds out. Or until he can't stomach it anymore. Then the cold comes in.

I decided the hell with the firewood. A big fire makes a nice circle of light in a dark forest, but right then I just didn't give a damn. I had kerosene lanterns and kerosene stoves aplenty and I didn't even need them, for I'd set up my cot and spread it with my big sleeping bag and in that I'd be warm in any kind of cold. Any kind, that is, that rides on the wind and comes from the north pole.

So I just sat there and watched the night come and listened to the rain. The darkness comes differently in the mountains than it does on the plains or the desert. On flat land it gets dark much quicker once the sun sets. But in the mountains the sun goes down behind a broken hill line and the light just seems to hang. The sun isn't actually down, not below the horizon; it's just hidden, just giving the illusion of being down. And the light lingers, throwing your whole world into deep shadow. I guess if you're feeling all right that mellow, dying glow will make you feel good, tranquil and at peace. If you're not, then it's just going to make you more depressed.

But it had become night and the black was like an impenetrable wall just at the end of my vision. I could hear the rain falling on the tent roof, but I really couldn't see the tent, nor make out the shapes of the trees or the lines of the mountains that moments before had been so distinct. And of course, my first thought was to remember how Chris had been frightened by the alien mountain night so that we'd had to hide in the truck. I had expected it, as I expected to be reminded of her every time I turned around or drew a breath. Even sitting so drunkenly in the tent mouth, not doing the chores I should to make a camp, I couldn't keep from remembering the trip we'd taken and the pains and diligence I'd used to persuade her how easy it was to live in the woods and how comfortable we could be. But I wasn't feeling at one with my great mountain at that moment; I was feeling rather lost and afraid and unsure of what I'd done and of about what I was going to do. I'd known that this was the way I'd be feeling; I'd known that ever since Chris had walked out on me in the café in Texarkana. Or I'd walked out on her; I wasn't really sure which it was. The whiskey was numbing my mind, which was what I intended. I didn't want to think for a time. I wanted to let things slide, let my avalanche instincts settle, let things fall in place, let some perspective grow. I was still consumed with that disembodied feeling that I was a third-party witness to all that had happened. But the thought that kept forcing its way through my mind was: What the hell am I doing on this mountain without my wife?

A little wind had come up. Through the sound of the rain, I could hear it making the walls of the tent bow and thump. I took a drink of whiskey, spilling some down my front because I couldn't see where the level was in the bottle when I tilted it. I took another drink and then set the bottle down carefully on the uneven ground. I all of a sudden wanted some light. I was afraid of that dark; afraid to look sideways, afraid to turn my head and look over my shoulder behind me. There was a flashlight in the truck, but it was several yards away and that seemed miles in that inky blackness. I decided I would go in the tent, find a lantern, and light it. When I got up I stumbled, from the whiskey and the tiredness and the uneven ground. I knew I'd piled the lanterns in a far corner and I groped my way there, stumbling over sharp-cornered boxes and bags and bundles that seemed insurmountable. I found a lantern and then I found the fuel. But of course, I couldn't see to pour the fuel in the lantern. I lit my lighter; its weak flicker was just enough to work by.

When I had filled the lantern I pumped it up, and then I lit it and trimmed the wick. The brown canvas walls suddenly came jumping out of the black and the littered floor took on the reality of just a littered floor. When I had the lantern going like I wanted, I hung it on the ridge pole of the tent and then stumbled backward and sat down on my cot. I was suddenly very tired. I remembered then how little sleep I'd had and the pace I'd been going at for the last forty-eight hours. I looked over to the mouth of the tent, wishing I had the bottle of whiskey I'd left there, but unwilling or unable to cross and get it.

The night sounds of the forest were commencing, audible in

Concord High School Library
2331 East Mishawaka Road
Elkhart, Indiana 46514

the quiet I'd made after rummaging through the bales and boxes. There came a noise like a man walking through dried leaves and such a fright sent through me that I half started off the cot toward a rifle propped in the corner. Then the walker turned into the quick, scurrying run of some small varmint, and I settled back again.

Even though I was becoming aware of the cold, I decided not to light a heater. The hell with it, I thought. If I was going to feel bad, I'd just go ahead and make a good job of it. I wasn't going to eat either. I had a huge variety of canned goods, some that could have been eaten cold, but I didn't feel like opening a can. I knew I was drunk and not thinking good, but there wasn't anything I could do about that.

After a little I got up to get the bottle of whiskey and made ready for bed. I just took my shoes off, folded my sleeping bag top back, and slid in, not bothering with the rest of my clothes. I was going to let the lantern burn. I hoped it contained enough fuel to last all night. I didn't want to wake up sometime during the night and find myself in this strange place in the dark.

It was hard to drink out of the bottle lying on my back, but I managed it, only spilling a little on me and the sleeping bag. But how the hell had things gone so wrong, I wondered. How did the place I'd started for turn into the place where I was at? Should I have gone back with Chris? Hell, there wouldn't have been a lot of point to all the plans I'd made if I had. Of course, it was so difficult to feel the social hysteria here in the seclusion of the mountains.

But I wanted to stop all that sort of thinking. I wanted to stop all thinking. I was drunk and about half out of my mind with loneliness and anguish for Chris, and that was no time to be thinking of anything. I wanted the light of day for that. I wanted to sit in these mountains, get myself back in shape, and think all of it through. I was here now, and I'd better make the best of it; just shut my mind, just stop thinking.

What I wanted to do most was go to sleep. But I couldn't seem to. I could feel the tiredness, like ropes, all through me, but my mind wouldn't turn off and take the darkness behind my eyes. Just as I'd start to relax a wave of anguish would cut through the whiskey haze and seize me with such force that I'd almost start off the cot. I saw, vividly, Chris going out the door of that café a hundred times, saw her small and alone and deserted. I saw her standing by the side of the road, a helpless look on her face, while her idiot husband rummaged in the back of the pickup truck for the bottle of whiskey, and her saying, "Please, Franklin, let's go back. Let's go home."

Oh yes, oh yes, I was really taking care of her.

In desperation I finally heaved myself up on an elbow, tilted the bottle straight up, and drug on the straight whiskey until I gagged. I did that three times, until the bottle was empty, then dropped it off the side of the cot and determinedly buried my face in the pillow. The wind was blowing through the tent very strongly because I'd forgotten to tie the flaps. The tent was sitting all wrong, facing to the north. But I was determined to forget it and go to sleep. I heard the leaves rustling again, but this time I didn't react. I didn't care. The last thing I remembered thinking about was wondering what someone would think if he were to come stumbling upon me in the dark.

When I awoke in the morning, it took me a second or two to realize where I was. For an instant I had a good feeling, then I remembered and it quickly went away. My head was bad from all the whiskey, and I had to lie still a moment to let a wave of nausea pass before I could heave myself up. I couldn't tell from the light what time it was, except I knew it was late. I looked at my watch. It was almost noon. My body and my mind had been played out; they'd needed a long rest. When I could I swung myself up and around to the edge of the cot. The ground was cold to my feet and I felt around until I'd located my moccasins and slipped them on.

I didn't want to move. I didn't feel like getting up and doing anything. The empty whiskey bottle was at my feet. I looked down and rolled it around with one toe. I knew there was plenty more in a case over in a corner of the tent, but I didn't think I could take any more whiskey. I felt sick. My head hurt and I wanted to throw up and there was a bad taste in my mouth. I looked down at my hand. It was shaking. It wasn't just a hangover, not really; if anything it was that plus an emotional shakedown. I'd been beat up pretty badly emotionally in the past couple of days and the toll was starting to be felt. It was hard to believe, really, that all this had come about in the way that it had and that I now found myself where I was and in the shape I was.

What was it Nick or I or someone had said about such things not happening to nice people like us? Well, a hell of a lot had happened, how much of it was my fault or due to my misplanning I couldn't tell, not right then.

I reached over and pulled on my heavy coat. It was no good sitting on the side of the cot. I had to get moving, do something, make some plans, figure out something. Considering the shape I was in, I knew I was going to need a little more whiskey to get me started. I wasn't ready just to tough a day through.

I went over and pulled a bottle out of the case. My head was pounding, and when I got it opened, the vapor smell almost made me vomit. But I choked that down and put the bottle to my lips and took several frantic pulls. When I took the bottle away, there was a dangerous pause. I stood there like a statue, not moving, not even breathing. Finally, I could tell it was going to stay down. I took two more quick gulps and then stumbled back over to the cot and sat down and lit a cigarette. The whiskey made my mouth feel coated. I wanted to brush my teeth, but I knew I'd have to sit quietly for a few moments and let the stuff do its work.

It was a cold, dismal day when I finally parted the tent flaps and stepped outside. Scattered around on the ground were little patches of thin, sheet ice that crunched under my moccasins as I stumbled around looking for firewood. There was plenty of down wood lying about, and with an effort, I gathered up several armloads and made a pile in front of the tent.

I started to feel better once I got the fire going. Its bright head seemed to drive off some of the dismalness of the morning. I piled on the wood, knowing I was making it too big to cook on for any time soon, but content just to listen to it roar and crackle. I wasn't feeling hungry, anyway.

For a long time, I sat and watched the fire, letting its warmth drive the cold out of my bones. Eventually, I wanted some coffee and I roused myself and got the pot and filled it with water.

I just put the coffee grounds straight in the water, intending on boiling it in the traditional way. That, of course, made me think of Chris and the argument we'd had about cooking in the fireplace the week the electricity had gone out. She'd been so worried about the stain on the hearth. Well, maybe Chris never was cut out for this kind of life. Maybe I'd been asking too much of her. But what was I to do? I'd seen a path that I'd thought was the right one. I had to take it. She'd even agreed with me at first. Or maybe she'd been like Nick, just agreed with me in principle, never expecting it to come to practical application. Something fun to discuss over the after-dinner brandy. Well, the hell with all that.

The terrain around me was more broken and hilly than mountainous in the strict sense. It was actually in the foothills of the Ozarks. Of course, I hadn't wanted to be right in the mountains. You can't farm that kind of land. I looked it over, what I could see, from the warmth of my fire, drinking coffee. It was covered all over with scrub oak and beech and hickory. The underbrush was negligible, which would be an aid in clearing the land for farming. I reached over and took a handful of the soil. It was crumbly and good feeling. Fescue and lespideza, good stock grasses, grew naturally on my land. A man could turn his cows and horses loose and they'd have an abundance of natural fodder the year round. In the spring and summer, the grass would be green and filling; then, come fall, it would cure off and they'd get the kind of nutrition they'd need for the hard winter months.

I got up to get the whiskey and poured a good slug in my coffee. Some of the physical bad feeling was going away, but that lost, everything-is-wrong sensation was still there, a little stronger than I was ready to handle. The light of day hadn't really changed that nor made the knife cut any less cruelly.

But I never liked whiskey in coffee, so after drinking half a cup, I poured the mixture out and put in straight bourbon. I didn't plan to get drunk again, but I couldn't seem to make myself get up and get busy. I kept telling myself that I had to make a start. It was late. But with the whiskey and my mood, I couldn't seem to think what it was that needed doing so urgently. I couldn't decide what was pressing. I was in the mountains, all right, now where was all the work I was going to do? Build a cabin? Hell, the rate I was going the tent would probably out-last me. Plant crops? I had enough food to last me months. The drunker I got, the less point there seemed to be to doing anything. So I just sat and drank whiskey. I was hurting; I was hurting bad. This was one factor, in all my planning, I hadn't expected and hadn't allowed for. I didn't know what to do about it either.

It was three days before I could summon strength or resolve enough to do anything. For those three days, I just sat around, eating very little, drinking whiskey, and staring into the fire. I did manage to collect quite a bit of firewood, but that was just primordial instinct, not an indication of growing life. That fire was my only interest. I'd sit and stare into it, drinking whiskey, for all of the day and half the night. I didn't think much; I was in kind of a stupor, a half awake–half dreaming state that made it sometimes difficult to know what was real and what was not.

On the fourth day, for some reason, I got up knowing I was going to have to collect myself and push out in some direction. I think the survival instinct had reasserted itself. There is a place where self-preservation takes over and will not let you go too far down the road of destruction. I could feel this reflex working in me.

I tried to make myself eat a good breakfast, but my stomach just wouldn't take it. I started out ambitiously to fix bacon and eggs, but ended up eating half a can of cold beans and some saltine crackers. But it was better than nothing, and in a little, I could feel it having an effect. I thought I would walk; I thought I would just walk and look my property over. I knew that I couldn't go far, as weak and sick as I was from all the whiskey and lack of food, but it would be a start in the right direction. I took one long drink of whiskey and then determinedly corked the bottle and shoved it inside my sleeping bag. Then I put on my hunting boots and my heavy coat, and took my rifle and started out.

It was mid-morning. The rain had stopped and a hard, cold sun gave the woods a harsh starkness. All the trees were bare. They looked cold and brittle in their winter bleakness. The dried, brown leaves crunched under my boots as I walked. The rifle was heavy and I constantly shifted it from hand to hand. I was walking west, half planning to walk to the dry creek bed just at the open edge of my land. I knew it to be a little over two miles. It would tire me, but it was the right distance not to tire me too much and yet let me feel I'd accomplished something. While walking I thought what a farce I really was. Such a strong, self-reliant man—I'd managed to undo months of conditioning with one brief emotional, drunken spasm. Oh, yes, I was a man for Chris to put her faith and trust in. I was going to outflank an insane society—out with the system—and prove that one man, so determined, could live on his own terms. And here was this same man, straining to walk a mile. I half idly wondered if Chris might not have sensed this subconsciously and decided to get the hell out while the going was good.

There were squirrels in the trees all around me. Each step would set a new batch to chattering out the news that there was a stranger loose in the woods. Off in the distance I could hear the occasional caw of a crow. Laboring up the side of a gully, I saw a coon staring at me through the bushes. I had just a glimpse of his wise-looking, bright-eyed face before he turned with a flick of his bushy tail and was gone. Somehow his face made me think of Nick.

I didn't walk as far as I'd intended. Partly I was too tired and partly I was too confused just to go on walking aimlessly. I sat on a downed tree trunk and lit a cigarette. The rifle I laid carefully at my feet. For a moment, I admired its lethal beauty, from the shiny mahogany stock to the oiled blue of the barrel and firing mechanism. It was a wonderful instrument for doing one thing—throwing a bullet a long ways on a very straight, fast trajectory. But, all parts of life examined, it seemed a very specialized talent to be used as often and for as many purposes as it was.

And there I sat, launched on my own very straight, very fast trajectory and wondering why I'd pulled my own trigger at the instant I had and if it had really been a good thing to do. Or necessary, or as necessary as I'd insisted it was. It all looked much different now, here in the quiet and lonely woods. It was a long way from the city, a long way from the feeling of the city, and I began to wonder if I hadn't been inventing a crisis for motives that weren't clear to me nor clear to those I'd tried to involve.

Certainly, it was hard to sit in the woods—hearing only the birds and the chattering of the squirrels, feeling the brisk air, aware of the space and the trees and solidness of things—and envision people running amok in the streets, raping and burning and looting. The breakdown of the economic structure, as I'd put it, seemed very far away and very unlikely.

I sat there a long time thinking about it. The more I thought, the nearer I came to the conclusion that I'd used very bad reasoning and a very bad method to achieve something worthwhile. Unfortunately, I feared, the method didn't justify the end. There was nothing unusual about what I'd been feeling; I suppose ninety percent of the men, especially of my age and general generation, were feeling it. Too many buildings, too much pressure, too much civilization, too much system. I'd heard it talked about from one end of the country to the other—get a little farm somewhere; start walking more; quit watching so damn much television; man wasn't made to live in one of those damn highrise skyscrapers; get back to the basics.

Back to the basics. But what were those?

Anyway, what were my motives? Exactly? And what was I going to do?

Now that running-amok-in-the-streets business. Did I really believe that? Down deep in my heart, had I really believed that? That was something the general might come up with. The ever present threat, the need for a standing army, the enemy within, the clear and present danger.

One thing, if I did believe it, then it appeared that I had deserted my wife in the midst of what I considered a serious danger. And I just wasn't that kind of a man.

I lit another cigarette and stared off into space, deeply troubled and confused by all the cross purposes that were running through my mind.

Still, it could be said that she'd deserted me, made her own choice.

But that was an unlikely conclusion, given the relationship between us and the sure certainty that Chris knew me better than I knew myself. It was not hard to know that Chris hadn't believed that I'd believed any of the things I was saying, any of the danger or crisis I was presenting as imminent. So there'd been no reason for her to go, and looked at like that, there was no desertion either way. She was simply letting me go off to play isolationist.

So why didn't I go on home? I dropped my cigarette down on the rocky soil, ground it out with my boot, and stood up. My sudden movement sent the squirrels off into fresh spasms of rage, and far off, the crow sentinel let off an urgent caw. I picked my rifle up and held it, being somehow comforted by its weight and purpose in all that alien bigness.

I started walking for camp. No, I didn't think I was going home, not just yet. There were many things still to be thought out. Nothing that had been wrong before had been much changed by my flight. It would still be there, in all its menacing sameness. I would stay awhile and spend the time looking deeper into myself. If I couldn't really change our physical environment, then maybe I could find some way to change Chris and myself so that we could handle it and ourselves better.

I went out often in the next few days, not going any particular way or very far, just wandering and looking at the land and thinking. The weather had abated and settled in to a succession of clear cold days with wind in the evening and freezing temperatures at night.

I liked my land, though I could see why it had instinctively frightened Chris. There truly was something primordial about it. Sometimes I could feel its instincts running through me: earthiness, baseness, a certain kind of brutalness, pride, arogance, power. It was very difficult to pinpoint, but I thought, several times, that a man could almost do anything in such a fastness. And I did; I felt capable of anything.

One morning, after my breakfast and coffee, I decided to walk to the western boundary of my land, the little creek bed that I'd started out for before. I'd just been wandering, but this would be a trip with a goal and that would be good for me.

I took my rifle and a sandwich. Before I left, I had a long pull of the whiskey bottle, but I deliberately left that behind. I was still drinking far too much, the proof was the serious inroad I'd made into the huge stock I'd brought along. I was getting myself under better physical control, but I was still lonely and depressed and the whiskey seemed to fill some of the voids. But I knew I was going to have to slow down; it was too debilitating.

I walked briskly at first, not having much trouble with the direction. I had a little pocket compass along, but I didn't consult it. The creek bed ran south to north and I had to strike it if I just kept generally to the west.

I could tell I was walking toward a valley of some kind because the terrain, in general, began to be less rough and broken. The birds and squirrels were, as usual, upset at my presence.

Finally, I broke out of the woods and started down the long, grassy slope that led to the creek bed. I started to feel better, out in the full sunshine, and I walked along, thinking what a nice piece of land the slope would be to farm if a man didn't have to hide.

The creek bed was about twenty feet across, floored with dry, fine-grained sand. The banks were not deep, only a couple of feet high, but you could tell the water ran swiftly by the severe way it had shaped the cut of the bed. I sat down on the side of the bank and put my boots flat against the sand. It was hard-packed. I supposed it to be granite and quartz sand, made by erosion, rather than a volcanic type.

After I'd rested, I stood up and looked around. The woods on the other side were much closer, almost right to the bank. The land rose immediately, climbing sharply toward a line of rounded high hills that strode off in the distance like the backs of elephants. I didn't care though; I wasn't going across. But I did think I'd walk north up the creek bed before I turned back to my camp.

After a little the creek bed turned sharply to the right. I rounded it, took a few steps, and then stopped. Up ahead I could see a trodden path across the creek bed. It could be cattle, but that meant people coming to look for them. I hurried forward.

It was not a path; it was where a crossing had been made during the recent rains. And it was not made by cattle. After a moment, I was able to tell that the sign had been left by a man wearing big, square-toed boots. And he must have been big, because, in one or two places the imprint was half an inch deep. Of course, the sand might have been really soggy, but I didn't think it had rained that much.

I was a good deal surprised and a little frightened. I sat down on the bank and studied the footprints. Very few of them were clear and distinct. It looked, or so it seemed to my untrained eye, as if whoever had made them had crossed several times. I tried to think, but all that would come to my mind was how Robinson Crusoe must have felt when he saw Friday's footprint. Or whoever it was.

After a moment I got up and looked further up the creek bed. I wanted to see if the man might have left some sign that he'd crossed since the rains stopped. I didn't see anything, but that meant nothing.

Well, I got to suddenly feeling very panicky. I looked quickly around to see if someone were watching me. There was no one on my clear, grassy slope, but the woods were thick on the other side and there could have been a hundred eyes concealed there. With the panic rising, I quickly climbed up the bank and started toward the woods. I wanted out of the open, and I wanted to get back to my camp. For all I knew whoever it was might be in the middle of my camp at the very moment. Sitting in my tent, drinking my whiskey, and looking through my supplies and provisions.

I was winded and tired when I finally arrived at the camp. I paused, just outside my camping circle, and squatted down behind a tree to watch. For several long moments I watched and listened, trying to quiet my own heaving breath so that I could hear better. My two tents, one in a line behind the other, seemed undisturbed. Below them ten yards away, my pickup stood squat and powerful. My fire had burned down, but I could see an occasional tongue of flame lick up over the rocks surrounding it. For long moments I crouched motionless. I was breathing easier and my heart was not pounding in my ears so terribly loud. There was nothing more to hear other than the usual sounds of the forest. Nothing moved. All seemed as I'd left it.

I looked in my living tent first. At a glance, I could tell it was empty. Then I went around to my supply tent. The flap was still tied securely, just as I'd left it. I looked inside, though. It was dim and I had to wait a moment before my eyes would adjust. It was a tumbled mass of crates and boxes and packages and sacks. I assured myself it was empty. Then I checked the pickup; it was as I'd left it. Finally I circled my camp, looking for any sign of visitors. There were none.

In my living tent I sat down on my cot, heaved a breath, and took a long pull of whiskey. I kept the rifle lying across my knees.

Gradually, my nerves began to subside, and I felt a little silly about my panicky flight back to camp. I took another drink and laughed at myself. I supposed it was the feeling of the mountains, all that wildness, all that savage fastness, that had spooked me. It had been nothing more than the boot print of another man, yet, somehow, it gave one the sensation of being hunted. One thing you could say for the city, at least you didn't spook at the sign of another human being. But there were a lot of people in the city; here there should have been no one else. So, really, it had been the surprise as much as anything else. That and the way I'd been feeling about a man being capable of the most primitive actions, like a savage in the woods.

Of course, the next question was who was he? And what was he doing on my land? According to Mister Chipman the area was deserted for miles around. He could possibly be some squatter that had been overlooked, but the prospect was more likely that he was just some passing hunter.

And I would have left it at that except I couldn't shake my mind of the conviction that the tracks showed the man had come and gone several times. And that right in the middle of the rainy spell where a hunter, or some transient, would have quit the area and gone back to where he came from.

But then, what did I really care what he was doing or what his business was. My plans for the secret fort seemed to have gone up in disagreement so I didn't really mind if my unknown trespasser knew about me or not. Probably I wouldn't even be on hand too much longer myself.

I frowned to myself, however, thinking about his coming around my camp. A man could kill you out here and no one might ever know. Or he might come around and clean me out. If I left, it was going to be on my own and not by force. Hell, that guy could be an escaped con or a crazy or goddamn near anything. I thought about what I'd heard about these mountain folk who lived off in the solitude. He might think I was an enemy, an intruder.

I forced myself to stop thinking like that. My mind was running away with itself.

But that night, as I fixed myself a steak and a baked potato, I couldn't help staring out into the blackness and wondering who might be out there and what they might be planning. And later, in bed, it was a long time before I could go to sleep since my nerves were jumping so. I resolved, since I had nothing better to do, to find out something more about whoever had made the tracks. Probably, I was being an old woman. Probably, the man was miles away and growing smaller in the distance.

I owed my visitor a debt of gratitude for shaking me out of my lethargy. Despair is not a natural human emotion, and though I still despaired, I no longer sat in front of the fire in a drunken stupor. Nick had said that even those with nothing to lose are cautious. I think he was right in that.

My first act was to try and get some order back in my life. I still needed a little whiskey, but not the two bottles a day I'd been drinking. I began eating again and cleaning myself and shaving. Next, I inventoried my supplies and provisions. I'd tried to bring all the things a man would need to sustain himself. But it had been such a hectic time, so rushed and frenzied, that I might have brought up nothing but sacks of cement for all I knew.

I discovered, on inventory, that I'd done a pretty good job of loading that last hellish day—though where I got the presence of mind I'll never know. I didn't have much fresh meat or fresh fruit, but I had a large stock of canned and preserved foods. I had plenty of condiments, sugar, salt, pepper, coffee, and even several tins of an English breakfast tea. For a long moment, I stood looking at the tea trying to think why I had brought it or where I'd got it. I didn't drink tea. Then I remembered that Chris did and that I'd provisioned it for her. It made me suddenly sad to see it there in the tent.

I had bought quite a quantity of guns. I had two rifles: a 30.30 lever-action Winchester and a Weatherby .375 with a scope. I'd brought two shotguns, including my prize, my Browning 12-gauge superimposed. For handguns I had a Browning 9mm automatic and a Colt 357 magnum revolver. There was plenty of ammunition, boxes of it.

One thing I immediately recognized was the need to cache some of my supplies away from my camp. I couldn't be there all the time, and I wanted to insure myself against a total loss in case my visitor turned up and cleaned me out.

Before proceeding I knocked off my work long enough to fry some bacon along with a can of beans. I fried the bacon in a big skillet, poured off the grease, and then emptied in the beans. When that had heated I got a big Bermuda onion, sliced it, and sat there, drinking coffee and eating the bacon and beans right out of the skillet. It was very good in the cold air and I felt better than I had in days.

Of course, I still didn't know exactly what I was going to do. Initially I'd have built a house with lumber, which I would have hauled in gradually, a pickup load at a time. Now there didn't seem much point to building a house. The tents would last as long as I would.

Not to say that I had given up. Not yet; not altogether. I just knew that there were certain things it would be worthwhile to do, and certain things there were no point to. And since I couldn't know what might be coming my way in the next day, let alone the next month, a house seemed a shade ambitious.

After I finished eating, I scouted around until I'd found a likely looking spot to hide my emergency supplies. It was a wide crevice between some big rocks down in a gully. It lay about a half mile from my camp and I spent a hard two hours lugging over what I'd chosen. Along with food and tools and extra clothing, I put in one of the rifles and the Browning automatic pistol. I covered the supplies with an extra tarpaulin, and then spent another hour covering that, in a natural-looking way, with dirt and leaves. Then I worked to eradicate any sign I'd made. When I was finished my cache was practically invisible.

I turned in that night feeling fairly comfortable. I was tired from the work, but it was a good tiredness, and I was much refreshed in my body from eating again. I drank some whiskey, but not much. I even extinguished the lantern and lay there in the dark. I didn't do it so much for the purposes of secrecy—my camp would not be that hard to spot if you were in the area—but more toward hardening myself and building up my self-confidence. I know how odd that may sound, that a forty-four-year-old man should be proud of sleeping in the dark, but you must remember that I was very alone, both in the dark forest and in my own heart. It was an unprotected loneliness, one that I'd not had years in which to build up the habit of handling. There had been that time, actually for most of my life, when I did not feel the loneliness in being alone. I was a good deal tougher then, because I hadn't opened up. But after I met Chris, I threw away my anchor and set out to drift with her. There had been other women in my life, but that's all they'd been, just women, just people, just others that I was also an other to. I'd forgotten how to handle loneliness, I'd forgotten how to be just the one with motives and plans structured and made just for the one. It was a whole new feeling, strange and terrifying. It was another skill that I'd forgotten.

I lay there in the dark, hearing the faint rustle of the trees and the little billowing murmurs the tent made in the wind. I don't care how light the wind, or how well-secured your tent, it is going to make little noises in the night. Not that you mind such noises for they're friendly sounds. The ones you don't like are those far off, the cry of an animal, the sudden rustle of brush. Those will frighten you, as the unknown and unseen and unthought can frighten you.

Before I went to sleep I had a bad few moments thinking about Chris and our life and where we were. If I'd given in, I think my mood would have turned swiftly to gut-wrenching anguish, but I wouldn't let it. I fought all the bad feelings that were coming at me. What I had to do was think of this as a fight, a fight I could win if I were smart enough and brave enough and determined enough. I knew about fighting, and I had to keep on thinking of myself as a fighter. I had to make survival my goal and let there be a measure of happiness in just reaching that goal at the end of every day.

I had said there would be chaos; well, chaos had come, though not quite in the way I'd predicted.

For several days, I watched the crossing at the creek bed. I would go over at first light and stay a couple of hours and then go back in the evening. I did it this way on the theory that the tracks had looked regular, as a man bent on a daily errand, and our habits being what they are, I thought he'd be going in the morning and coming in the evening. I lay up on my land, just inside the tree line, amidst some rocks and underbrush. I had the scoped .375 with me and the magnum revolver. In the middle of the day I'd go back to my camp and piddle around and eat.

Thus far, my watching had been in vain, and on the fourth morning, I decided I'd stay all day, in case my theory about the man's coming and going was all wrong. I made myself a lunch out of canned meat sandwiches and some slices of onion, wrapped them in a paper sack and stuck the package in one of the pockets of my big coat. I put a half bottle of whiskey in the other.

I knew the walk so well by now that it seemed much shorter. I walked along, smoking a cigarette, and enjoying the crisp coldness of the morning. Cigarettes weren't something I'd run out of for a time—I'd brought four cases—but they were something I'd originally planned to give up on the theory that I couldn't haul in enough to last me a lifetime, and certainly, it was doubtful that I could learn tobacco culture. I didn't even know if you could grow tobacco in the cold mountains.

I got to my lookout point and settled down, burrowing into the dried grass to wait. It was boring work, just lying there and waiting for God knows what.

I think maybe I slept a little. It wasn't a good, sound sleep, because of the cold and the uncomfortableness of my position. Anyway, I suddenly came awake with a start. For a moment, I wasn't sure if I'd been asleep or just dozing and dreaming. But something had brought me to attention. It was not a sound, nothing perceptible, just something felt. I looked over the creek bed and saw nothing. All was as it had been, dull and silent.

But I kept bringing my attention back to the woods on the far side of the creek. Without knowing why I felt as if someone or something were coming. I wasn't being forewarned by animal sounds, nor was there the sign or sound of moving brush. But there was something. I felt it.

And even as I watched I saw the slightest movement deep in

the brush. Then came faint rustling sounds that grew louder. I raised my head, peering just over a rock, and saw a man abruptly step out of the woods. He came walking across the creek bed. I could see his face but I couldn't tell from that distance if he were old or young. I could see his face was weather-beaten and seamed, but he could have been thirty or sixty.

He walked purposefully across the creek, looking neither to the left nor the right. I noticed that though he didn't cross exactly at his ruts, he was only a few feet upstream from them. He looked to be a fair-sized man. He was dressed in old, blue overalls, and a faded blue shirt. He wasn't wearing a jacket, even as cold as it was, but he did have some kind of slouchy, wide-brimmed hat pulled down low on his head. He had a sack thrown over one shoulder, and he was carrying a shotgun in the other. I could tell he was probably cold from the hunched over way he walked.

He strode across the creek, climbed the bank, and then began quartering off to the north toward the forest. I watched him until he'd reached the first line of trees, and then arose myself and went slipping back through the forest.

I was going to follow him, but I didn't want to take a chance on his seeing me. I would lay well back. As I moved as swiftly, but softly as I could, I glanced down at my watch. It was almost eleven of the morning. My friend wasn't an early-riser, early-to-work type. If, indeed, he was going somewhere rather than coming back. But he proved he was a creature of habit in the way he took the same route.

I did not walk very far because I realized how easy it would be for him to change directions and for us to suddenly meet. And I wasn't ready for an introduction yet. I wanted to know a little more about my trespasser so that I could know what type of action might best suit our first encounter.

Once I stopped and listened for a full five minutes. I thought I heard some sounds to the north, but I couldn't be sure. Finally, I turned around and retraced my steps back to my lookout point.

It was necessary, I felt, that I assure myself that this was the same man. So after carefully searching the open country, I went back down the long slope to the creek bed. I'd carefully marked

the place he'd crossed because I knew I'd have a hard time finding a print in the hard sand. Finally, though, at the side of the
far bank, I found a faint indentation where he'd rose up on his
toe and heaved all his weight to climb the steep bank. It was not
a full footprint, but the square toe, matching the others, was
plainly obvious. I shouldered my rifle and went back to camp,
satisfied with what I'd accomplished for the day. What I was
going to do about it, I wasn't sure, but I was certain I had my
man.

In a way, I was glad for the diversion the man presented. At least I didn't have to think about what I was going to do. How could I go home? How could I simply go walking back in as if nothing had happened and Chris and I take up where we'd left off. Our life had changed; for better or worse, it was not the same, nor could I see it ever being what it was. We'd gotten into some fire and the temper of our steel had changed. All that, let alone the physical change from the things I'd done such as buying the land and selling all our assets. Good God, sometimes the enormous forces that had reshaped our lives would come over me like a wave. So I had to figure something out. Hell, maybe Chris, for all I knew, was through with me. Maybe she was gone from our home.

I went out and started the engine in my pickup truck to make sure the battery didn't get down. It made an amazingly loud noise in the quiet woods and I immediately got out and looked around, leaving the engine chugging. It irritated me, being jumpy like that about simply starting a pickup engine. Good God, I'd bought this land so I'd have some privacy, and here I was worrying about the least little move. That didn't seem right. I resolved, right then and there, to settle the problem of my visitor. I was going to find out who he was and what he was and what he was doing in my part of the country. Then I was going to deal with him. The whole situation was starting to make me angry. I was getting tired of everybody fucking around with my life.

The next day, about noon, I set off from the creek bed in approximately the direction the man had taken. I didn't have much hope of finding anything, didn't even know what I was looking for for that matter, but it was something to do. I thought I'd walk about three miles, keeping to the general direction, but zigging and zagging along the main course. From the purposeful way my man had walked, I somehow felt sure that he was heading straight for wherever he was going. I was allowing myself thirty minutes for each mile. After an hour, I considered turning back. I felt sure I'd left my land and I didn't want to take the chance of getting lost. Of course, I knew I could always walk due west and find the creek bed, then follow that back to known ground.

I decided I'd go on for another mile. The land, surprisingly, had turned flatter. From everything I'd seen to the north it had appeared to be rougher, much more mountainous. I decided I was coming to a broad valley. It was no less forested, nor the ground any less rocky, but you weren't forever stumbling into some little gully or having to climb a sharp hummock.

The farther I walked, the more cautious I got. For all I knew, I might suddenly walk up on some farm or a sawmill or something. I rather doubted it, on account of the silence, but I didn't want to take any chances.

After another half hour, I resolved to walk for fifteen more minutes and then turn back. I was probably way off his trail, anyway. Next day I'd do the same thing, only vary my route by a few degrees. Certainly, if I did that long enough, I ought to stumble onto something.

I had stopped and was picking a route back when I heard a sound. It was very faint, very distant. I squatted down and listened intently. It was a thunk, thunk, thunk kind of sound. It sounded a little like someone far off chopping down a tree. And yet it didn't. But there was that kind of rhythm to it. After a moment the sound stopped. I squatted there, thinking and listening. In a couple of minutes the sound started again. I couldn't identify it, could barely place its direction.

I walked on slowly and softly. The sound didn't seem to be

getting any stronger. After a time I veered off to the right. There was still that same indistinct, distant quality to the sound. I veered to the left, and the sound seemed to increase in volume. For some reason, it didn't seem so far off. The forest had grown thicker, and I was having trouble walking quietly through the heavy underbrush.

All of a sudden, the tree line thinned and I almost stepped out into a clearing. I stopped just in time. As quietly as I could, I eased my body behind a tree trunk and peered out. Out before me was a little clearing, maybe half an acre. Right in the middle, working away with a hoe, was my man. He had a little vegetable garden, and he appeared to be hoeing new ground, getting it ready for planting.

Frozen behind the tree, I looked him and his work over. I could see cabbage and winter turnips and lettuce and what looked to be dried-out potato vines. I thought to myself that he'd probably had a bunch of seed potatoes in his sack and he was replanting since his fall crop seemed finished.

Even as I watched he stopped and stood a moment breathing heavily. I'm sure it was hard work in that rocky soil. Not that there were any rocks in his garden. The plot looked as if it had been worked for several years, for all around the edges I could see piles of rocks he'd removed and stacked. His shotgun was leaning up against one of the piles.

Well, well, I thought to myself. So my boy was doing a little farming. That made him pretty permanent.

I watched a moment or two more and then faded as silently as I could back into the forest. I moved very cautiously until I was sure I was out of earshot and then moved off at a rapid pace for my camp. I felt encouraged. At least, now, I knew where it was he was going. And if this was his work then he had to be coming from where he lived. I'd done enough for one day, but next day I was going to find his cabin or shack or cave or whatever he had.

To celebrate my success I decided to treat myself to the last of the fresh meat. I let the fire burn down to just coals and then broiled a big steak to go with a potato I had stuck down in the ashes to bake.

When the food was done, I built the fire back up and then

sat out there, in the night coldness, eating and drinking a little whiskey. I only had about six fifths left so I'd been rationing myself. But, this night, I let myself go a little, even though I was cutting the whiskey with water to make it last longer.

It was a delicious feeling, that good food and the whiskey and the knowledge that I'd accomplished something. Looked at critically, I'd done nothing more than trail a hillbilly to a poor-land garden plot in the vastness of some second-rate mountains. But accomplishment, like beauty, is in the jaundiced eye of the beholder, and I felt that I'd made good progress toward strengthening my safety from an unknown enemy. Anyway, given the despairing lethargy I'd been in just a couple of weeks ago, anything would have been progress. I think it was even progress that I could sit there and forget what had been and take pleasure in the night air and a partial, if not basic, sense of well-being.

The night was a black void outside the circle of my camp light, but I felt secure in my strength and courage and the arms and supplies I had. Not that I wasn't fully aware that that hillbilly, or anyone for that matter, could have picked me off my camp stool from fifteen feet away and I'd be none the wiser until the bullet went home. But I wasn't worrying, and it wasn't just the whiskey giving me false courage either. I could sense a hardening taking place within me. Not just in my body, which was certainly so, but in my courage and will and determination. I'd made two weeks and that was something to be encouraged about. True, I'd have to begin thinking over a little longer range soon, but I had my squatter to contend with and that was purpose enough for the time being.

I wondered what he was doing just at that moment. I doubted that he was eating and drinking as well as I. Probably having boiled turnips and potatoes and some meat off a wild hog he might have killed with that rusty-looking shotgun. No, that wasn't right. The shotgun wasn't rusty, it had a well-used, but a well-kept look to it. I imagined that my visitor was pretty good with his weapon. Probably had it loaded with Double-O buckshot.

That wasn't a bad garden he had either. He was certainly much advanced over me. I shrank from the thought of clearing the rough land and trying to till the winter-hardened soil to where it would produce nourishment. Without heavy equipment, it would be some job, and there'd be many a shovelful of dirt to turn and many a rock to stack up. I had winter vegetable seeds such as lettuce and turnip and cabbage, but it takes a long time to produce from seed planted right in the ground. They needed to be started in a cold frame planter and then transferred.

That was something I could do, I thought, that wouldn't be too much work and would still be progress. I had enough crates and boxes to make a hundred planters, and next day, I'd refine some good soil and get started. The thought made me envision myself working away at a potting table, planting the delicate little seeds. It made me grin wryly, reminding me of Nick. Well, Nick wouldn't have thought too well of the planting of cabbage and turnips; that wasn't his style.

All that thinking about fresh vegetables got me hungry. I hadn't had any for some time. Vegetables out of a can just aren't the same, and right then, I wanted a turnip. I thought about what it would taste like, tangy and sweet with the white flesh still cool from coming out of the cold ground. I would have liked to have been sitting there peeling a turnip with my knife, watching the long strips of peel come off my knife and fall to the ground. It'd been a long time since I'd done that, and the whole idea made me very hungry. A raw turnip, if you're hungry for one, is better than an apple. I'd salt it lightly, of course, and it'd taste very good with the watered-down whiskey.

Well, maybe I was going to have to pay a visit to my neighbor's garden some time when he wasn't there. That'd be a laugh, I thought, me raiding him instead of just the opposite. Nick would have approved; the man had something I wanted, so I ought to go and take it. But do it honestly, he'd have advised, do it sneakily and slyly, but don't lie to yourself. Be honest with yourself. Tell yourself you're taking what you're taking because you want to and nothing's important anyway, so what difference does it make? That way it won't be stealing.

I was glad to be able to think of Nick that way and to know that such impressions were truly of him. It kept me from feeling bad.

I had good luck the next day. Figuring my man would want to be well on his way home before dark, I got to my roost over the creek bed about four in the afternoon. I'd barely settled down when he came popping out of the tree line, heading across the creek and home. I watched him stride across the creek and then ascend the bank and start into his own woods. He was carrying the shotgun, but he'd left his sack. I was surprised that he didn't fetch his tools back and forth with him. It didn't look to me as if he could afford to lose even a single hoe. Probably he had them well-hidden somewhere around his garden site.

He disappeared from view rather quickly in the dense, first line of trees. But I was able to follow his progress from my higher vantage point by the movement of the brush he was disturbing. I wasn't going to track him; that would have been dangerous. Instead, I was going to use the same method I'd employed to find his garden; get a bearing on his direction and then cast along the line until I came up with something.

But I'd do that the next day, when I'd satisfied myself he was gone to farm and there'd be no likelihood of running up on him. I wanted to do it in broad daylight, anyway. It was getting late and I didn't relish the idea of wandering through strange woods in the pitch black.

It had been another good day, and I went to bed with that tiredness that comes from satisfaction. I'd even cold-framed some turnip seeds, planting them in a long wooden box that had once held axes. It had been a lot of work, refining such an amount of soil and taking the necessary pains with it. But I'd wanted good clean soil that would give the little seeds room to sprout with no obstructions. For lack of moss or sphagnum, I'd mixed in a quantity of hay and dried grass to give the potting soil body and help it retain moisture.

To make an ideal cold frame, I needed a piece of glass to put over the top. Since I didn't have any, I'd be forced to move the box outside in the daytime, so it could get sun, and then back inside at night so that the tender little plants, when they sprouted, would not be killed by the cold. In the next few days, I planned to plant frames of my other seeds. In a month I'd have sprouts ready to transplant to a garden.

But then I wasn't even sure I was going to be there in a month. I made the cold frames because it was something to do and because it seemed to keep all my options open. But I could feel my options diminishing inside myself with every day that passed. I was missing Chris terribly. Every time I'd turn around, every vagrant thought that passed through my head reminded me of her. I was worrying about her, too. What was she doing, how was she making out? She needed me around to protect her, whether she realized it or no. God, I felt like I was letting her down terribly. Often I would look at the pickup and consider loading it and leaving and just saying the hell with it. Just pick up and leave and go on back to the city and try to get it back up.

Something wouldn't let me. I don't know if it was stubbornness or pride or just what, but I couldn't quite bring myself to leave.

So I did things like making cold frames and tracking hillbillies.

He crossed the next morning at about ten o'clock. This time, besides his shotgun, he was carrying a little paper sack that I supposed contained a lunch of some kind. But that paper sack told me something else, it told me he must have been in town fairly recently. A paper sack is just not going to hold up for very long, no matter how careful you are in using it.

I had some lunch along myself, a couple of salami and onion sandwiches. I had been disturbed to find that I'd left a big sack of onions laying on the damp ground and some rot had started amongst them. That was careless of me for I'm particularly fond of onions. I didn't lose too many, I didn't think, and I'd immediately hung the sack from a nearby tree to let the onions air and dry.

I gave it thirty minutes before I started back-tracking my man. The direction seemed plain to me, and since I knew he kept to a pretty straight course, I felt confident I'd have no trouble finding his lair. I didn't even expect it to be far, perhaps a mile. He was already walking some two or three miles from the creek, and I didn't think he could allow too great a distance between his home and his garden else he'd be too tired to work.

I felt a little nervous crossing the creek, out in the open like that. My man might have been far wilier than I'd given him credit for, and he could have turned back and been waiting, just inside the tree line, for me to step out where he could get a clean shot.

But once in the woods I felt better, and I walked along with a good measure of confidence, expecting to see his cabin at any moment. I'd almost expected, from my roost, to spot smoke hanging over the trees from his breakfast fire. Finding none, I'd assumed it was hidden by a ridge or a hummock. The day was a little gray, anyway, and if he were using a good hardwood, there wouldn't have been much smoke to see.

I walked for an hour and a half and saw nothing. Finally, I turned back and took a path a few hundred yards north of my original course. I walked until I was almost to the creek. I had seen nothing, yet I couldn't believe my man's cabin could be more than an hour and a half from the creek. It just didn't make sense. And I would have had to have seen it if I'd been within two hundred yards. A cabin is a fairly large thing to try and hide from someone on foot. I didn't think he could be living in a cave; I'd seen no caves in these mountains. A tree house? I doubted it. I just felt he had some reasonably comfortable mode of living.

I took the time to eat lunch. The walking had warmed me and started a little perspiration. Sitting under a tree, I once again became aware of the cold and I ate quickly, so as not to get too chilled.

The only path left was one a couple of hundred yards south of my original line. Once I'd followed that I would have surveyed a swath some six or seven hundred yards wide and three miles deep.

Once again I walked in a westerly direction for an hour and a half and again I found nothing. I was totally perplexed. My reasoning was faulty somewhere, that was evident, though I couldn't figure out why. But it was getting late, almost three o'clock, and if I didn't want to meet my man when he crossed the creek at four I was going to have to hurry.

I'd done quite a bit of walking that day and I could feel the fatigue heavy up my thighs and in my calf muscles. The rough terrain was particularly hard on your legs because you couldn't just strike a rhythm and swing along; you were constantly climbing up and down and jumping over rocks and downed logs, even forcing your way through heavy underbrush. But I walked swiftly toward the creek for fifteen minutes or so. Finally, I felt that I just had to have a short rest and I slumped down under a tree and put my back up against the trunk and got out a cigarette and lit it.

If I hadn't taken that rest I don't think I would have found his cabin yet. I know I passed within fifty or a hundred yards of it at least twice before and I hadn't noticed a thing. Yet there it lay, not seventy yards away.

"I'll be damned," I said, lowly but distinctly.

The sonofabitch had built as perfectly camouflaged a cabin as I believe it was possible to make. Its chief feature was that he'd used four big growing oak trees for his corner posts. Looking at it, I guessed the cabin to be about sixteen feet by twenty with a roof flat enough to fit snugly under the overhang of the trees, yet with enough slope to shed rain. It was board-sided and the old planks were so grayed and weather-beaten they were almost undistinguishable from the growing wood they were nailed to. Had it not been winter with her barren tree limbs, I don't believe I'd have seen it amidst a heavy growth of leaves. Apparently, he'd stripped the trunks of his corner posts to a distance of about fifteen feet high. This put his roof line right at the base of the large branches up in the top of the oaks where they came to their fullest blossom. I'm sure in the spring and summer the limbs hung down and hid all but the sides of the cabin. And that would have been taken care of by the thick underbrush that grew around the sides.

I'm certain I still wouldn't have seen it had my eye not been caught by the metallic gleam of the tin flashing he'd used to roof around the tree trunks. That was the only distinguishing feature, and I don't think a man walking by would have even noticed that. Certainly I hadn't, and wouldn't, if I hadn't chosen to rest right at that particular spot.

Then I noticed his chimney. It was ordinary looking enough at first glance, but I saw that he had four pipes running out of the top in different directions. The effect was to vent off the smoke into smaller, less noticeable quantities so that instead of having one big contrail of smoke coming out he had it broken up and distributed so that it was highly unlikely that it'd be noticeable at all once it cleared the tops of the trees.

"I'm a sonofabitch," I said. I got to my feet, brushing off the seat of my pants. For a moment I stood looking around, carefully noting landmarks so that I could find it again without any trouble. It was growing late. I walked south for a quarter of a mile, to make certain our paths didn't cross, then turned east for the creek and my own camp.

There were many things running through my mind as I made my way back. Chiefly, there was the thought that this man, whoever he was, was concealing himself just as I was. I didn't know his reasons, but he'd gone to a great deal of trouble to make himself hard to find. He wasn't just some squatter lurking on someone else's property; the effective job of camouflage he'd done on his cabin proved that. The smoke venting system was a touch of genius, one that I wished I'd thought of. Then there was the way he lived in one place and raised his food supply in another. That too had been thought out. He might get cut off from his cabin, but he'd still have his garden. Or he might get cut off from his garden, but I was willing to bet he had food supplies laid up to see him through a long rough siege. This was no hermit, this man. He was hiding—from some one or some thing. And he'd been doing it for a long time, that was evident.

I kept pondering all these new things once I got back to my camp. I made it just at dark, and I had to scurry around and get in some wood to build up my fire. I was cold and I huddled by the fire while the flames slowly caught up some of the bigger wood and began to put out a decent warmth. A bottle of whiskey was setting just inside my tent flap, and I reached in and got that and had a long pull for comfort purposes.

I didn't know—all these new things. What I'd learned made me feel uneasy about the man. It made him seem dangerous for some reason. I'd certainly been correct in my estimation of him as being purposeful. He was that all right. If he'd gone to so much trouble to hide, there was no telling what he might do when he caught sight of a stranger in his midst. I'm sure he'd consider me a danger and do whatever he could to eliminate that danger. Right then it seemed very important to get into that cabin and see what I could learn.

I ate quickly that night and banked the fire down until it was putting out very little glow. I'd been careless in the past, but that time was done. Other considerations had entered the picture. And I knew, then, that whatever had to be done was going to have to be done quickly. Otherwise I'd lose my element of surprise. It was just a matter of time before he found out he had company.

The cabin door was secured by a rope loosely tied to the jamb. I looked at it a long time before I shifted my rifle to my left hand and cautiously began to loosen the knot. I'd been moving slowly all morning. After watching at the creek and seeing my man on the way to his farming, I'd made my way to the cabin and taken up a vigil from a safe distance. For two hours I'd watched the cabin, alert for any movement or noise. For all I knew, the man might have a wife or partner who stayed in the cabin.

When I'd eventually made my way forward I'd done it gingerly, alert for any trip threads or raked areas or other telltales he might have rigged to let him know if he'd had a visitor.

Now, at the door, I was especially careful. The door would be the most likely place to put a telltale. You do that with a little piece of paper or a string or twig—anything you can jam in the side of the door when you're leaving. If the door should be opened in your absence the telltale will fall to the ground and you'll know, when you get back, that someone's been in your place.

That is, you'll know if the person opening your door doesn't replace the telltale.

I eased the door back and got a glimpse of something falling out of the jamb. But I didn't pay attention to it, not then. I wanted to see what was waiting for me inside the cabin first.

I swung the door all the way back and stood there, my rifle at the ready.

The cabin was empty. It was so sparsely furnished I could see that at a glance. There was a cot in the left-rear corner, spread with an army blanket. Directly to the back was the fireplace. It had a small hearth with several blackened pots and pans sitting around it. In the middle of the room was a rough table. And, stacked against the far wall, were the man's supplies—sacks and boxes and a little heap of old clothes and blankets and such. Hanging from the ceiling were fishnet sacks of onions and potatoes and even some late corn.

I looked down at the ground, looking for the telltale that had fallen. I saw something, and without moving my feet, bent down and picked it up. It was a 22 bullet, and I immediately knew why he used it.

For the moment, though, I turned my attention back to the interior of the cabin. I studied the floor, trying to decide if I'd leave tracks by walking in. The floor was hard packed dirt and looked to have either been brushed or swept clean. Whether this was neatness or cunning I didn't know. But I decided to take my boots off first. I did so and then took a step inside. Without moving I lifted one foot and looked at the floor. I couldn't see where I'd left any impression.

I looked at the bed first. It was just an old mattress, faded and stained, spread with two army blankets with a quilt for a bottom sheet. I bent and found an old, brass-bound trunk underneath. I would have liked to have looked inside, but there was no way to open it without pulling it out from under the bed and I knew that would have left distinct marks on the dirt floor. I turned next to the fireplace. There was a good bed of coals, ashed over, still working. They'd last until evening and then be useful for starting the supper fire. One blackened skillet had a thin film of bacon grease in the bottom. The rest were clean and empty.

The cabin had a window on each side except at the front. I hadn't noticed any the day before because they were ingeniously cut so that they were hidden by hanging limbs. But you could see out all right. In the shadow and the dim light of the forest, a man could peer out of one of these windows with little fear of being spotted.

There were two big tow sacks stacked in the corner. I opened one, it was just loose tied with a miller's knot. Inside was rough ground whole grain flour. I lifted up a handful and sifted it between my fingers. It looked stone ground, but I couldn't think where he might have gotten such flour. My main interest in the cabin was to ascertain if my man had much contact with the outside world.

The flour looked good. I'd been out of bread for about a week and I thought what good bread I could make with such flour. But I decided against taking any; it would probably be missed. Instead, I replaced the handful and then tied up the sack and moved over to the crates and boxes.

The first box held big tin canisters of sugar and salt and pepper. I opened a particularly heavy one and quickly replaced the lid. It was mother—a name for working yeast—and I didn't want to give it too much air. That'll stop the bacterial action. The yeast made me think the man seldom went to town—or else he just liked sour dough bread. But the canisters of condiments made me believe he did make frequent trips in. They were too small, especially the sugar, to last for more than a couple of months at the most. Of course, he might not use much sugar. Or he might be getting it from someplace besides a store.

I kept going through the boxes, looking for recent purchases of perishables, like pancake mix or cigarettes or chewing tobacco or bottled whiskey. There were none that I could find.

In one crate I found several boxes of shotgun shells. Ammunition must be labeled with a maximum effectiveness date, and I turned one of them until I saw NOV 1963. That made the shells very old and could have been an important clue as to when he'd come into hiding. Certainly he hadn't gone out later and bought them. The law required all ammunition six months past its expiration date to be removed from the shelves. This is so because powder can crystalize and become unstable, like nitroglycerin. It seldom happens, but it can.

There were some sacks, cloth, in the same crate with the boxes of shells. One was about a ten-pound sack of smokeless powder and there was Double-O buckshot in the other. My man reloaded his shotgun casings, which was no big surprise. Of course, I doubted if he fired that shotgun very often. Certainly, I hadn't heard it in the time I'd been on the mountain. And you could hear a shotgun for a long ways in the stillness of the forest—miles.

One box was full of personal effects, pictures and a few old books and some faded letters written in a spidery hand that I couldn't make out. I took up one of the framed pictures. It was a studio photo of a young soldier. I couldn't tell if it was my man or not. I guessed the age of the young man in the picture at about the middle twenties. The uniform certainly wasn't recent, but it could have been of World War II or Korean vintage.

There wasn't much to tell from the face. It was just a young man staring into the camera, the expression impassive, the eyes noncommittal. Probably it had been taken at the base photo studio from the looks of the color retouching. Even though the colors had faded they still held the garish, overdone touch of the amateur. The young man's skin tone was too high, his lips a little too red, the eyes too brown. I turned the photo over and it said, simply, Fort Hood.

The next picture I looked at was a family group. They were around and on what I recognized as a 1954 Chevrolet. Behind the car was an asbestos-sided cabin. I couldn't tell how far back in the country the cabin might stand, but I could tell it wasn't in any town.

There was a boy of about fifteen perched on the hood of the car on his knees. On top were a little boy and a little girl, sitting upright with their legs stretched straight out. Standing by the side was an older man and woman that I took to be the parents. The man had on a double-breasted suit and he looked uncomfortable. The woman's dress length corresponded to the year of the Chevrolet. Beside them was a young man of nineteen or twenty. I studied the soldier's picture and the face of the young man to see if they were the same, but the family photo was too indistinct to tell.

I put the pictures away and leafed through several of the books. One was a high school algebra book, another was a novel I'd never heard of, and a Bible. The Bible had writing in it; on the front page, in pencil, was written the name, Wilfred Hines. I, of course, couldn't tell if that was my man or his father or brother or someone he'd gotten the Bible off of.

I'd now been in the cabin for a half hour and I was getting uneasy. I decided to quit; I was certain I'd learned all the cabin could tell me. With a last look around, I backed carefully to the door, stooping every now and then to see if I had made any disturbance. But the floor was so hard packed that I hadn't left a sign. And, of course, I'd been careful to replace everything just as I'd found it.

At the doorway, I pulled the door halfway closed and studied the edge. The door fit fairly loosely in the jamb, which was why a 22 bullet would work as a telltale. But the reason he used the bullet was so that it would leave a little lead mark on the while wood of the door. You might replace the telltale, but if you didn't put it back in the same position he'd know. I stepped carefully back out through the sill, pulling the door to me as I did so. I could see a little mark on the jamb where the bullet had been and I pulled the door to by the rope, holding the bullet against the jamb until the door caught it and squeezed it in place. Then I pulled the door tight, tied the rope, and put on my boots.

Once outside I started getting nervous. I was pleased that I'd gone about my business calmly and thoroughly, but I was suddenly feeling the strain of time and the fear of being caught. I wanted to melt away into the forest as rapidly as I could, but I made myself stay and examine the ground carefully to be sure I'd left no revealing marks. Assured, I finally picked up my rifle and started home.

I decided not to think while I walked. It would be better to be on full alert and I could better think back in camp. I'd just let everything I'd learned lie ripening in my subconscious.

I had come to respect my unknowing adversary. I admired his talent for the game; if anything he was a good deal more advanced at the skills of staying alive and staying free than I was. Sitting in my tent that night I thought of all the reasons why he could have taken to the sort of life he had. He could be an escaped criminal, an army deserter, a man who'd run out on his family, a homeless person who was illegally squatting on someone else's land—he could even be doing as I was, fleeing a civilization he no longer trusted. But I doubted the last, just as I doubted several other explanations. The best rationale I could arrive at was that he was either an escaped criminal or an army deserter. Either situation would make him an extremely dangerous man to fool around with. Thinking it over, I knew with solid certainty in my heart that he and I would not be able to peacefully coexist on the same mountain. Both of us obviously had too much to lose to risk trusting the knowledge of their whereabouts to someone else.

The one thing I wanted to satisfy myself on (and knew I couldn't) was the extent of his contact with the outside world. If he were an army deserter or a criminal, he might be hiding out with the connivance of his family and friends. And if that was so there was certainly some intercourse between them. Either he went out and met them somewhere (getting supplies and news and moral support) or they came in to see him.

The one reassurance I felt was the length of time it appeared he'd been in the mountains. From all signs it seemed years. Maybe all his family and friends were dead; maybe he was an aging relic, long forgotten, who stayed hidden out because that had been his life for so long that he knew nothing else.

Except where did he get the sugar and salt and other condiments? It was a damn long walk to the nearest town—and where would he get the money to buy such things?

I rather liked the theory of the army deserter, for no other reason, I guess, than the nothing look on the face of the soldier in the photo. Not that I knew that was my man, I just had an instinct about it. Sergeant York notwithstanding. I knew that these mountain folk did not take to organized environments like the army and that many of them had run away and run back home. I would have bet there were families in the very region who'd been sheltering deserters all the way back to the Civil War.

But none of this kind of reasoning had me any closer to a solution than I'd ever been. All that was emerging was that I was going to have to do something about Wilfred—I was calling him that in my mind—before he did something about me.

I certainly admired his cabin and his garden. It looked to me to be a perfect set up. What a lot of trouble and work it would save me, I thought, if old Wilfred would just set sail over the mountain and keep on going. I could move right in.

I went to bed that night in the cold dark. Again, I'd banked my fire down so it wasn't visible. I didn't like making such a cautious camp, but I knew that it was necessary. Strangely enough, I didn't feel so lonesome knowing old Wilfred was out there somewhere. In reading about World War I, I'd noted where the troops on each side developed a certain affection for the unseen enemy in the trenches across no man's land. Remarque had expressed that very well in *All Quiet on the Western Front*. I hadn't really been able to understand it then, but now I felt that I did, just a little.

Chris was always on my mind when I laid down at night. I lay there, missing her, yet hardening my heart all that I could. I wondered what she was doing at that moment, whom she was with, what she was thinking about. I wondered if she missed me. It was a very painful thought process, and I shut it off as soon as I could and went to sleep.

Something unexpected was happening to me. I'd been on the mountain a little over three weeks now, and I found myself avoiding the idea of leaving. My food supplies were getting low, and by human nature, I should have been looking forward to a trip into town to replenish them. Astonishingly, that was not the case. I was out of fresh meat, out of fruit and vegetables, out of bread, almost out of whiskey, and while I had a good supply still on hand, my canned goods lacked variety both from a nutritional and appealing standpoint.

But the point was I was shying from the idea of leaving the woods. I liked my mountain, liked the solitude, liked the bigness, the rawness, even some of the frightening things. But that was just part of it. I also didn't feel like I wanted to be around people; people, buildings, civilization. You'd have thought I'd have been eager to talk to someone after such a duration by myself. Even hear traffic. Talk business. Watch television. But that wasn't the way I was feeling at all.

Not that it meant I wasn't still planning on going home. I was. Around the camp I wasn't making any permanent moves or plans. Short of building the planter boxes, I hadn't done a single thing that could be considered homesteading. And always, in the back of my mind, was the idea of going home, back to Chris. I wasn't sure what was holding me up, what was keeping me from loading up and leaving.

I supposed that when the loneliness became too much or when

the time began to drag on my hands or when I became too
worried about Chris, the inertia would leave me and I'd go.
Until then it wasn't such an unpleasant life. I got up in the
morning, had breakfast, and then piddled around the camp. I
was gradually widening my camping circle by clearing away the
underbrush and smoothing off the dirt and removing the larger
stones. These I used to reinforce the base of my tent. I'd laid
down enough so that I had the beginning of a pretty good surrounding wall supporting the canvas. If I stayed long enough
I'd have it as high as the roof. The effect was it didn't snap and
thump so much in the evening wind.

Firewood was still no problem though I was having to go
farther and farther afield each day. I burned so much that I'd
gradually cleared out all the downed wood within fifty yards
of my camp. Mornings I usually got in enough to last the rest of
the day, plus a little extra to make a stockpile. That was the
extent of my camp chores except for cooking and cleaning up.
There was a little spring about fifty feet from the camp where I
got my fresh water. It was the same one that ducked back under
ground and emerged through the side of the gully; the place
where Chris and I had had a drink. But I got my water where it
surfaced, just at the crown of a little knoll. It didn't pool, just
ran about an inch deep for a few yards and then went back un-
derground. Each morning I'd force myself out in the cold and
go over to it and wash my face and brush my teeth. Later, I'd
fill my water jug and take it back to camp so I'd have fresh
water for the day. What was left from the previous day I'd heat
and shave in. I'd made one or two efforts to wash some clothes,
but it was such a lot of trouble, not having any pots really big
enough to handle the chore, that I'd decided the hell with it
and confined my washing to socks only. I expected when my
clothes got so dirty as to be uncomfortable I'd figure out some
method.

What I really missed was something to read. I hadn't packed
any books or magazines and, except for a newspaper that had
been left in the pickup, hadn't had any formal reading material
at all. I'd read that newspaper until I knew every item by heart.
At meal times, I'd get down a few cans of this or that and read
the labels. I was an expert after a few days on what went into

most tins. The one thing I was amazed at was the quantity of artificial flavorings and preservatives they all contained. It was no wonder, I thought, that they all tasted so similar.

I had the big Hallicrafter radio that I'd paid five hundred dollars for, but I couldn't get it to work. I suspected there was something wrong with the batteries. I got what little news I received over the pickup radio, but the reception was very poor. Only when there was a low cloud cover (I suspected the signals bounced off that and down to me) was I able to hear at all. The news didn't change much, staying the same, it seemed to me, as it had the last five years. But one evening, I was amazed to hear that the country had gone on national gas rationing. For a time I was agitated and excited, but gradually I decided it wasn't anything likely to bring about the "economic breakdown" I'd predicted. But the country was in bad shape, there was no doubt of that. It would make me frown to hear the news and I'd begin to feel guilty about Chris and to worry if she were all right. That didn't say a lot for me as a man—that all I did was worry—but then it was a complicated situation.

Other than Chris I spent a lot of time thinking about people like Nick and Morton. I didn't want to admit such a thing, but I halfway hated to go back for fear of facing Nick. I didn't want to hear the things he'd say. He'd appear to be very understanding, but the cuts and the sarcasm would be no less painful for their subtlety. I kept remembering what he'd said about greenhouse plants, how they'd grown and flourished in the wild once, but that now they couldn't go back. They were too civilized, too dependent on the artificial environment, that if you tried to move them back into the wilds they'd die. Well, I was back in the wilds, and I wasn't dead. Not yet. But even as I said it to myself I could see Nick with that knowing smile on his face, saying, "Ah, yes, but then you brought so much of your environment with you. And, too, you haven't really been tested yet by time or extremes, have you?"

I suppose I missed Morton Dowd the most. That big dummy could make you laugh if nothing else, and now and again I could have used some amusement. Something to take my mind off what a really goddamn situation I'd gotten myself into.

But then I had Wilfred. And he was my main occupation, my

hobby, my study, and my preoccupation. I didn't, thus far, know what to make of him, but I didn't feel he was too much of a danger, though I wasn't taking any chances. I was still very interested in keeping my place and myself a secret. I hadn't entirely given up on the idea of the fort. I had been thinking about that a great deal, and I'd come to the conclusion that a great deal of good might come out of the way things had happened. My timing had been wrong, I concluded. I nonetheless believed there would come a time when we'd need such a place. The fact that I'd been here and had experience at it would prove very valuable in the future. I was going home, but I might be back and I didn't want anyone knowing about me.

So it wasn't just a game I was playing with Wilfred. I considered it very important that I learn all there was to know about him. For all I knew, he might be crazy and might kill me on sight. So for that reason and the others, I was extremely careful.

Stalking him was a good deal easier than I'd thought it would be. The unwary, purposeful way he went about his business made him an easy trail mark, but it also made me faintly worried. He certainly didn't act like a man with something to hide. Of course, he could have been hid out for so long that he'd decided he was secure forever. That sort of thinking, I knew, was the faultiest kind. You are never secure, and there is always a danger that can attack you from the most unexpected source. I'm sure, in his most meticulous planning, Wilfred had not counted on something like me. It was a lesson to me, looking at it, to know that you've got to take the wildest, most unheard of possibilities into your schemes.

I tell you, I couldn't come to any conclusions about Wilfred. For seven days I'd been following him. On one occasion, I tracked him to his garden and spent the better part of the day lying behind a tree, just watching him. He was a good worker. We'd had a little thaw in the cold, and he'd worked hard enough to bring on a pretty good sweat. I could see the dark V it made down the back of his workshirt. He'd hoe for fifteen or twenty minutes, moving steadily down a row; then he'd stop to rest, wiping his forehead with an arm, leaning on his tool, sending occasional glances around the encircling forest. But they were just curious, haphazard looks, not the kind a wary, alert man shoots over his shoulder.

All right, if he wasn't an escaped criminal or a deserter, if he was just some sort of withdrawn hermit, that made the danger no less to me. If he wasn't hiding, then he was going into town occasionally, and once he was aware of my presence, he'd be talking about me. A stranger is an odd commodity in such a sparse area, and having nothing better to do, gossip and loose talk is an easy leisure. Once the word got out, curiosity would be aroused and someone would be coming to look into my business.

One evening, I trailed him home and watched his cabin until well into the night. There wasn't much to see. When night came he hung some sort of blackout curtains over his windows, making the cabin well nigh invisible in the darkness. Earlier in the evening I'd noticed he had a fresh dressed-out hog carcass hanging from a tree in front of his cabin. The weather was still cold enough that the meat would keep. That's where the expression "hog killing weather" came from. Before refrigeration, you didn't kill a hog until you were sure of a long cold spell, usually in late November or early December. But this was January, and I wondered if it were my man's first pork of the season. I hadn't seen any cured meat around his cabin when I'd made my first visit.

What I couldn't figure out, though, looking at the carcass, was how he'd killed it. I was certain I hadn't heard any gunshots, and I was equally certain that I would if one had been fired within a five-mile radius. Perhaps he had some hogs all through the area. The early settlers had let their hogs run loose and many of them had never been caught or killed. The razorbacks, as they were called, that had sprung from that early stock were as wild as any bobcat that roamed the woods. I'd seen signs of some of those old tuskers, but I'd never caught sight of any. The thought had been on my mind to go hunting in earnest for one, but of course, I didn't want to fire a gun. Several times, I'd wished for something like a bow and arrow, something I could do some silent hunting with. I was completely out of fresh meat and hungry for some. One thing, you didn't take on one of those babies bare handed. A wild hog is as lean and quick as any fighting bull and will charge just as readily. Some of them have tusks eight and ten inches long and they can cut the legs right off a man.

I wasn't watching Wilfred's cabin that night in an attempt to learn anything as much as I was forcing myself into the dark woods to build up my courage. There was a future ahead of me that might hold anything, and I felt I needed hardening and training. It may seem silly that a grown man could be afraid of the black forest, but you must remember that I'd become very soft in my years with Chris. All the nights I'd been in my camp, I'd never once ventured outside my circle of light. Going to Wilfred's cabin had been a goal and a purpose, one that would have a beginning and an end.

I forced myself to last it out until ten that night. It's strange how the darkness seems to come in and envelop you, making you a part of whatever it is. All of its hidden dangers are right beside you, all its unknown terrors, its stealthy noises seem to lie next to your skin. I didn't watch Wilfred's house as much as I kept my head on a swivel, looking over my shoulder, to the left, to the right, and then, quickly, back to the front door for what might have materialized while my attention was elsewhere.

The walk home wasn't so bad. At least, then, I was moving. I did stumble quite a bit, and once I fell over a tree root and banged my knee up.

When I got to the camp, I went in and turned the lantern up to full brightness and sat on my cot and trembled a little. I let myself have a quarter of a bottle of whiskey. I was down to three fifths now and I was rationing it closely. It was ludicrous in a way, because I was sitting on a billfold that contained a little over eight thousand dollars. I could have bought out the entire liquor supply of any of the surrounding towns with that kind of money.

On my tenth day of following Wilfred, I lay in my lookout roost at about four o'clock in the afternoon, waiting for him to come home from his farming. I knew his schedule now like a book. I'd watched him cross that morning, gone back to my camp, and now I was here to await his return. I was a good deal like the suburban wife who puts her husband on the commuter train in the morning and then whips down to pick him up in the evening.

He came out of the woods in almost the exact spot he always

did and started down the grassy slope toward the creek bed. I
had my rifle lying in front of me, resting on some small rocks.
When the man was by me enough so that he wouldn't see the
motion, I eased the rifle up to my shoulder and looked at him
through the scope. He was at about a three-quarter back angle
to me. The cross hairs marked him right at the base of the neck.
Without thinking about it, I let my finger curl around the trigger. The safety was already off and all it would take would be a
slight pressure. I swung the rifle with him as he walked. It
wouldn't even be a hard shot. I could hit him at the neck or
down a little lower or even in the head. I let the rifle ease up,
centering just behind his ear. I could kill him so easily.

He had reached the creek bed. The cross hairs on the scope
tracked him faithfully as he clambered down the bank and strode
across. I was holding just the slightest pressure on the trigger.
Just a little more and *bam!* My mind toyed with the idea of how
the shot would sound, how he'd flinch in surprise and shock, how
he'd pause in mid-step, one foot still raised, and tumble backward. Perhaps he'd rear once, but then he'd fall back and lie
still in the fine sand of the creek bed. I could feel my finger
tightening on the trigger.

Then he was at the opposite bank and scrambling up. I felt
a frost of perspiration coating the palm of my hand. I could feel
it where it rested against the stock. Then Wilfred had disappeared, obscured by the brush he'd suddenly passed through.

Slowly, I eased my finger off the trigger and sat up. I put the
rifle down on the ground beside me and started to tremble all
over. Shock and dismay were running all through me. Dear God!
I'd been going to shoot the man! If he'd had another yard to go
my finger would have kept tightening and I'd have shot him.
I'd have shot him! A stranger, a man I had nothing against! I'd
have murdered him.

I got up slowly, leaving my rifle lying on the ground. Aloud
I said, "You better go home, Horn. You better go home as fast
as you can! These mountains are getting you. You've gone crazy!"

I sat back down and lit a cigarette. I was deeply troubled in
my mind. I still couldn't believe what I'd almost done, and I
ran it through my mind a half dozen times. No matter how I
tried to rationalize it, the fact still was that I had very nearly

pulled the trigger and killed the man. My whole body was shaking, like it will after a very near accident.

I sat there for an hour. Finally, I picked up my rifle and started for camp, my mind still working, looking for a way out of what had almost happened.

That night I tried to take serious stock of the situation, my situation. I began with the very beginning, when the idea had first come up. From there I moved through every event, every change, trying to add them together to see if they'd give me a sum of where I was going. But it was too much. My mind couldn't hold it all. Or at least, it couldn't give me any answers. I let myself drink more than my ration of whiskey. I was back to a time of wanting not to think and whiskey was the best stuff for that.

About two o'clock the next afternoon, I set out, resolved to get the situation straightened out. I was going to quit acting like a Boy Scout playing headhunter and go straight to Wilfred and have a talk with him. I should have done it in the first place, but I was still playing panic in the street and breakdown of the economic structure. Of course, I blamed part of that on the mystique of the wilderness. It did things to you, primordial things. I could feel some of the changes it had wrought in me. Here, it had seemed almost natural to sight in on an unknown prey and shoot him. Here, it had seemed almost natural that I should hunt him because he'd be hunting me.

Almost.

But not quite. Now I was going to stop all this foolishness and go to the man and get the matter straightened out. I'd find him ignorant, but willing to get along. He'd just have to know about my place. That was all there was to it. The alternative was what I'd almost done, and I wasn't about to take a chance on a repetition of such an incident. Not while I still had my sanity.

I walked briskly along. Wilfred would be at his garden, most likely, and I'd just go there. I'd holler him up from the edge of the clearing, so as not to startle him, then I'd walk on out and we'd talk.

I didn't know how to get to his place directly from my camp

so I was quartering down toward the creek. Once I broke out in the relatively clear valley land, I'd turn up northward and from there on I knew the route.

I had my rifle along, but I was carrying it only because you didn't go walking through such country unarmed. I didn't expect to need it with Wilfred. The birds and squirrels were making their usual amount of racket, but I didn't pay them any mind, just went on along. I was carrying my rifle at port, my head swinging back and forth, checking the bush around me as a natural course.

Then I broke out of the tree line into the little grassy lowland. I turned right and started toward the brush that flanked the northern end. As I approached it, I was startled by a crow suddenly emerging from a tree just at the edge. I looked up, watching him. He was cawing frantically. Crazy bastard, I thought. Then, from some part of my eye, I caught a glimpse of the brush swaying. I whirled, leveling my rifle as I did. At that instant Wilfred stepped out.

There was an instant flurry of confusion. He saw me at about the same time as I did him, and his shotgun came up level too. My mind was a blank. Part of it recognized him and part of it didn't. I tried to yell. I think I got out, "Hey!" I thought he made some sound, a yell or something, but it was drowned out by the roar of his shotgun. Half pausing, half whirling away, he fired off both barrels. They went *boom! boom!* in the quiet of the forest. It startled me. It frightened me so I went stumbling backward, losing my balance. I tried to yell something but he was already running back into the bush. And then I fell over backward. As I hit, the jar set off my rifle. I was still holding a finger on the trigger and my elbow hit, and it went *kapow!* with that high-pitched explosion big hunting rifles make. The recoil slammed the butt into the ground and the rifle jerked and got away from me. By the time I'd retrieved it and come to my knees Wilfred had disappeared. I could see the bushes still shaking where he'd passed through.

I didn't know what to do. It was not the time to chase him. My one thought was to get out of the open, and I immediately scrambled around and fled back to the tree line. There, I crouched behind a tree trunk and peered out into the clearing.

There was no sign of Wilfred. After watching a moment, I turned and made my way cautiously but swiftly back to camp.

After building up the fire, I got out the whiskey bottle and lit a cigarette and sat down on the camp stool.

Finally, I said, "Goddamn" lowly and disgustedly. Now things were in a pretty mess. It might be a little difficult to approach Mister Wilfred at this juncture for a nice civilized talk about coexistence in the woods.

But at the same time, I was beginning to wonder if such a thing would have been possible in the first place. The minute he'd seen me, he'd upped with that scatter gun and blasted away. I might have been very lucky. I might have stepped out in his garden clearing and got my head shot off before I could comment on the weather. He'd shot at me and the only reason he hadn't hit me was because the range was just about ten yards too far for a shotgun. I still had the vague recollection of something hitting my pants legs like spent pellets.

And then had come my shot. He was already running, so he couldn't have known that mine had been an accident, that the barrel was pointed straight up in the sky. All he'd have heard would have been the bang, and he'd have run on, ducking and dodging, expecting another.

Say, I thought, this game has turned serious. That guy might kill me on sight. I tried to summon up the flashing image I'd had of him in the confusion. All that would come was the picture of a purposeful man whirling, leveling his gun, crouching to make a smaller target. Then letting off two quick shots and breaking for cover. That sonofabitch had tried to kill me! And would have if I'd left twenty seconds earlier that afternoon or had walked faster or even if I hadn't stopped to see what the crow was making so much noise about.

Well, one thing for sure, I was going to have to consider him dangerous until I found out different. For a time, I idly considered leaving. It would be an ideal time. I obviously had a good reason now. Even one that I could accept and act on. But I resented that. I wasn't going to leave just because some crazy squatter was running around loose with a shotgun. Goddamnit, I had a right to be where I was. No, my God, I wasn't going anywhere. Not until I got this matter straightened out. The hell with him. We'd see who could win the shoot-first, ask-questions-later sweepstakes.

But I was going to have to be more wary. I even considered pulling down my camp and making a much smaller, better-concealed hideout. But that would be too much trouble.

I went to sleep that night thinking it'd be the last time I'd be able to sleep in my tent for some time. My man wouldn't be doing too much reconnoitering just yet, but once he stopped running, he'd be coming to look for me, and I had no intentions of providing him with a sleeping target. Instead, I'd have to take my sleeping bag and a ground cloth and sleep off a few hundred yards in the darkness. Wilfred was causing a lot of changes in my life, and I didn't like it.

And then nothing happened. It started raining that night and simply kept on. It was a heavy, soaking downpour and neither Wilfred nor I was going to go stalking about through the woods in it. Mostly I sat in the door of my tent with the flap back watching the rain come down unremittingly. It made a very bleak scene, the rain and the trees and the brown, dead undergrowth. It wasn't as cold as it had been, wasn't even below freezing.

Of course, my fire was out so I heated my tent and cooked on a butane stove. Not that that could go on very long, since I didn't have a great supply of butane. In fact, I was getting low on quite a number of commodities. It was amazing to me how much stuff just one man could use up. I was okay on canned goods for some time, but I was getting deathly sick of canned spaghetti and hash and beans and that sort of thing.

On about the third day of the rain, I went over to my supply tent to rummage around and see if I couldn't find some little treat I'd overlooked. My goods and supplies were still in jumbled confusion for I had never really gotten around to straightening them out. Most of the boxes and crates were where I'd dropped them when I'd stumbled around unloading them in the hell of that day. In a back corner, I found several crates I hadn't looked into. As I stacked them straight, I noticed a very familiar-looking wooden box lying at the bottom. For a moment I wasn't certain I was seeing what I thought I was. It was dim in the tent and I took the box to the door to examine it more carefully. It was a case of 1959 Château Latour. A Bordeaux wine from Paulliac.

I carried it carefully back to my living tent and sat it on the ground in front of my camp stool. Then I sat down and looked at it. I hadn't the foggiest idea how it had gotten there. Supposedly, I had sold all my wines. One of my endeavors had been the importation of wines. With most of them, I'd simply acted as a middleman, but on certain years and châteaux, I'd laid down a number of cases for personal investment. Most people don't know that the great wines appreciate in value at a greater rate than, say, the stock market or some gilt-edged seven percent investment. The case I was looking at was worth seven or eight hundred dollars.

But I still couldn't figure out where it had come from. To raise money, I'd sold off my own personal stock—a little over thirty cases. How this one particular case was overlooked, and more puzzling, how I had managed to load it in my pickup, was a question I couldn't answer.

But there it was.

I pried off the top and looked at the bottles, lying so beautifully in their individual cradles.

Nineteen hundred and fifty-nine had been a great year for the Paulliacs. I tell you, I'd hated to sell off that wine worse than anything else. I'd had some of it for ten years. It was so precious to me that we very seldom would drink a bottle, and then it had to be a fabulous occasion. Oh, we drank good wine, fourth and fifth growths—a Brane Cantenac or Talbot or such—but that was our consumable wine, as I liked to refer to it to Chris. But the real reason was that I just loved that wine, as you can love a fine painting. It was a joy to me to go to my improvised cellar—one of the back rooms where I'd installed an independent temperature regulating system—and look at the wine, read the labels, and hold the bottles up to the light.

Well, there wasn't any point in not drinking a little of it now. For all I knew, I could be dead before I even got halfway through the twelve bottles. But I wasn't going to drink it like some drunken soldier. Fine wine demands food, and I'd fix the best meal that I could devise to go along with it.

First, though, I wanted to open the bottle so it could breath. It had been in that bottle a long time, and it deserved a chance to release its spirit and flow and run free.

Of course, I didn't have a corkscrew. I tried to devise one out of a nail, but it was a complete failure. Finally I just shoved the cork down in the bottle. I hated to do that—it's an insult—but I had no other choice.

I was going to decant it, naturally, since you've got to do that with an old wine. I didn't have a decanter, but I finally hustled around and found a clean one-quart mason jar. I grinned a little as I poured the wine in the jar. I imagined I was the only man in the history of the world who'd ever decanted a Château Latour into a mason jar.

When I had the wine decanted, I held it up to the light. It had a slightly brown cast, but even as I watched, the color began to mature off and to deepen to a luxuriant ruby claret.

"Ah, yes," I said. "Ah, yes." Finding that case of wine had elevated my feelings a hundred percent. I was smiling and grinning and I hadn't done that for some time.

Next I turned my attention to the food. There wasn't much to choose from. In the end, I made a sort of mess out of canned chicken and mushrooms.

I let my stew simmer for about an hour and then dished it up. For a wine glass, I had a thick water tumbler. Not the most perfect vehicle for wine, but it was all I had.

I pulled one of my ice chests over and used that for a table. Sitting there, in the flap of my tent, looking out at the dark woods, I ate passably and drank great.

It was ridiculous. It was so ludicrous I started laughing. Wine is the most civilized thing we put in our mouth; wine has been the flower, the nectar of civilization. Wine is the drink of gentle people, of cultured, intelligent people who only want to enjoy life and to be allowed to live quiet, pleasant, fulfilling lives.

I sat there drinking wine in a tent in the remote mountains of the Arkansas Ozarks. I sat there, a man planning to hunt and track and maybe kill an Arkansas hillbilly, a man maybe about to be killed by an Arkansas hillbilly, a man as isolated and desperate as anyone can get. It was absolutely silly.

I started laughing and couldn't stop. All the rain, the tent, old Wilfred over across the creek, no wife, no future, no nothing.

I kept laughing. Old Nick had been right when he'd said how ridiculous the embellishments of civilization looked on most of us. "About like dressing a gorilla in a wedding gown."

Good old Nick. Still laughing, I raised my heavy glass and made him a toast. "Here's to you, Nick. No hard feelings."

The rain abated on the fifth day, and I faced the prospect that I was going to have to do something about Wilfred. It came down to some simple choices. I was either going to have to find him and talk to him and convince him I meant him no harm and that we could coexist peacefully, or else I was going to have to render him harmless in some way. Killing him would be the easiest and safest prospect, but I fled from the idea. At the same time, I couldn't see how I was going to get the chance to negotiate. Even if I had him cornered, he'd fight or run without giving me a chance to say one word. I had proof of that.

I left camp that day armed with my rifle and the .357 magnum pistol. I also took along a little knapsack with a couple of days' food supply in case I got cut off from my camp for some reason. The pickup worried me, but the best I could do was remove the distributor cap and hope Wilfred didn't damage it just to immobilize me.

I was going to his cabin. That was the logical place to start. He'd have had to taken shelter from the rain and cold. And if he weren't there and didn't show up in a reasonable amount of time, it'd be a pretty good indication that he had another retreat somewhere else.

As I walked along, I wondered what I'd do if I suddenly ran up on him. It was important to have my mind made up, for there might not be time for decisions in a sudden confrontation. I hated to just shoot him. But I didn't want him to shoot me either.

I went very cautiously through the woods. If the rains' end had brought me out, it would have brought out Wilfred for the same purpose. The woods were wet, and even the rocky soil was mushy and muddy. There were little runlets of runoff water all over the mountain, some heading east and some west, but all getting off the mountain.

I was just coming up out of a little ravine when I got a fright that almost unnerved me. There was a little clearing right in front of me, maybe ten yards wide. All of a sudden, from the bushes on the other side, came an explosion of noise; grunting rushing thrashing noises. The bushes were quivering and shaking. It lasted an instant, but it was an instant in which I imagined myself being charged by God knows what. I let out a scream—an actual scream—and somehow, weakly, I tried to get my rifle up. From the bushes there burst a large sow followed by four or five piglets. They went racing across the little clearing, five or six feet from me, and disappeared in the next line of underbrush.

I sat down on the ground, my heart beating wildly. For a second I laughed, then I got disgusted with myself. It was no joke, not really. If that had been Wilfred or anyone else intent on doing me harm, they'd have found me frightened and weak and defenseless. That wouldn't do, that wouldn't do at all. A man's got to keep his nerve and react when he has to or else he's lost.

After I'd smoked a cigarette I went on my way, not as pleased with myself as I had been.

When I got to the creek, I was astonished to see it had water in it. There wasn't much; it was running maybe a foot deep, but it was running swiftly and I could see from all the runoff feeding into it that it was going to get deeper.

After having a careful look around I waded across. In my waterproof boots, I wouldn't get my feet wet, a thing I was careful of because it was turning colder again.

I moved even more cautiously on Wilfred's side of the woods. When I got to the locale of his cabin, I reconnoitered it carefully before moving up. There was nothing stirring. I didn't think Wilfred was there. The latch rope was tied, for one thing, and it would be a pretty good trick if he could do that from the inside. Also, his hog carcass was missing. He might have taken it inside to smoke or something, but I didn't think so. For a time, I considered approaching the cabin and having a look inside, but I fundamentally shrank from that. Old Wilfred could be lying out somewhere just waiting for me to make such a dumb move.

That night I spent a miserable, uncomfortable time laying out about a hundred yards away from my camp. I had my air mattress and my sleeping bag, and I'd made myself a cozy little niche under an overhang down in a ravine, but it rained again about midnight and I had to get up and move to higher ground. I spent most of the night huddled under a tree, trying to cover myself and my sleeping bag with the ground cloth. But I still got wet. When dawn finally came, I was immensely glad to see it.

The evening before, I'd taken some black thread and made a little picket line around my camp. In the dark it would be invisible and an intruder wouldn't even feel it when he broke through, since I had it set up only about a foot off the ground. The first thing I did was to check that. I was disappointed to find it still intact. Listen, I was getting tired and nervous from the uncertainty. I would like to have known what Wilfred was doing and if he were even still in my woods. As stiff and sore and irritable from the lack of sleep as I was, I believe I'd have shot him on sight.

I hung around the camp most of the morning, checking various things. My little seedlings had sprouted and I took a great pleasure seeing their green heads breaking through the rough potting soil of my planter boxes. I regretted not having any clear plastic. If I'd had some I could have covered the tops of the boxes and then left them outdoors all the time. That covering helps retain the moisture and the oxygen and makes them grow faster.

About noon I decided to go down to the creek and have a look around. With the muddy ground, I was able to detect a good many animal tracks, most of them hogs, and now and again the print of a deer. I resolved to shoot some game the next time I jumped anything. Wasn't much point in not firing a gun now. Of course, though, I'd do it as far from my camp as was possible. Maybe go on a hunt over to the next mountain. With it below freezing, the meat would keep nicely wherever I dropped it and I could just skin it out and cut off what I could conveniently carry back to camp.

The creek was really up. With a stick I checked its depth and estimated it to be three feet by the bank and deeper in the middle. It was running very swiftly, and I had no interest in trying to cross it. For a time I walked up and down the bank, looking for prints my man might have made in the soft, bare soil. I couldn't find any, though I was leaving plenty of my own.

I was perplexed. Where in hell had he gone to? He might have cleared out, either to town or to friends or to some other part of the mountains, but I doubted that he'd go and leave everything he'd built up. Besides, if he'd gone to other people, they would have come looking for me. In his mind I was sure he'd thought I was trying to shoot him. That's a natural thing to think when you see a man you don't know aiming a rifle your way. Thinking that, he wouldn't just go off and leave me in peace.

I decided that there might be some answers in his cabin. If he'd cleared out, he'd have taken some of his possessions with him. Well, there was nothing I could do about that, not with the creek in the state it was. I'd just have to wait a few days, being patient and alert. A few days of dry weather would also serve to tell me if he were coming back with friends or not.

I started to go back to my camp, but the sun was still so high that I thought an expedition to his garden might not be a bad idea. I felt positive he wouldn't be there, but it was something to do.

His garden and the area around it were as quiet as a church. There was no sign of him, nor any that he'd been there recently. The ground obviously hadn't been worked since the rains. I lay behind a tree, just at the edge of the clearing, watching and listening. I could see the tops of some mature-looking turnips and some carrots and even some young onions sprouting. There's not much I like better than little green onions. I hadn't noticed those before. I lay there staring at the truck. What I ought to do, I thought, was skin out there and get me an armload of stuff and carry it back to my camp. I could take my big coat off and make a pretty good sack out of it. Serve old Wilfred right, having his provender stolen. That'd make him come out from behind the log.

I went out cautiously, constantly looking the woods over through a full 360-degree turn, my rifle at the ready. Nothing moved; there was not a sound. In the garden I waited and watched even more, alert to fling myself to the ground at the slightest sound.

Finally, I fell to work. Laying down my rifle, I stripped off my jacket and began to pull up turnips and onions. I decided against more than one cabbage. They took up too much bulk, and I wasn't that fond of cabbage. The turnips, and especially the onions, were beautiful. The onions were about an inch in diameter at their smooth, white heads. A perfect size for eating. I had a bunch in my hand and was shaking the dirt off the roots when I happened to glance over my shoulder. There was my man. He had just come out of the tree line and was creeping along in a crouch, his shotgun at a firing angle. The reason he hadn't fired on me from the cover of the trees was that the range was too great for his shotgun. But I didn't stop to think about that. The instant I saw him I instinctively threw myself to the ground. I hit on my shoulder, rolled, grabbed at my coat, and came to my feet running. Even as I was up, I heard the roar of his shotgun. He fired twice, *boom! boom!* I felt something tug at my calf muscle, but I was running as hard as I could. In an instant I was into the trees. I ran blindly for a few moments, jumping downed wood, dodging trees, tearing through the underbrush as fast as I could go. But I couldn't keep up the pace. In a moment I had to stop and rest. I leaned against a tree, my breast heaving, my heart jumping wildly. I had my jacket clutched up in my arms, wadded against my face to still the sound of my heavy breathing. In that instant I realized I'd left my rifle.

Well, that was a hell of a note. Before I'd had the advantage of range, my rifle against his shotgun. Now he'd have my rifle. He wouldn't have many cartridges, but one would be enough.

Goddamnit, I felt like beating my head against the trunk of the tree that was propping me up. I had another rifle, but it didn't have a scope on it. Of course, in the heavy underbrush, a scope wasn't that much use. But a man ought not to go around giving his weapons away to the enemy.

I went on after another moment, cutting down south, angling in the direction of my camp. I needed to get back there and get rearmed. I had the .357 magnum in my hand, but I wanted a rifle.

It was a frightening walk. At every sound, I thought I was going to be shot. But that's rough terrain to try and take a man unawares, and this time, it was on my side.

Just before I got to my camp, I knelt down to rest and noticed blood on the leg of my pants. Pulling the pant leg up I saw that one of the shotgun pellets had gone through my calf muscle. I could see at a glance that it wasn't anything, but it put me in a vicious rage. The sonofabitch had drawn my blood! Goddamn him! He'd shot me!

I went into my camp, resolved now on only one thing. I was going to kill him. I was going to hunt him down and kill him dead.

Wilfred seemed to have disappeared again. I'd ventured out several times, but there'd been no sight or sign of him. His cabin door was still tied and the place looked deserted. I had to assume, from that, that he wasn't in residence in his cabin. The windows were too small for him to get in through, and unless he'd chopped a hole in his roof, there was no other possible means of entry.

I checked his garden several times, but I was careful not to go in the clearing. I sure as hell didn't want him playing that little joke on me again. It was for that same reason that I never entered the clearing his house was set in.

But where was he? Where had he gone to? After a few days of intensive searching, I became apprehensive and pulled back to my camp, venturing out only on short excursions. I was afraid he might use one of my tents for an ambush place. But I was also afraid he might come in and destroy everything, set fire to my tents, wreck the pickup, carry off my supplies.

Sitting around one day, I suddenly thought of that last thing Nick had said to me—that I was not civilized enough to take up such a life. I really hadn't thought much of it when he'd said it, but it'd stuck in my mind. Thinking on it, I decided that he'd say what was happening right now—the business with Wilfred— was exactly what he'd meant. Here I was, contemplating shooting a man, and to Nick that would mean I was reverting. Well, in my mind I challenged that premise. What was happening was reality; it wasn't some of Nick's fanciful philosophizing. And I would have liked to have had him tell me where I'd had a choice in any of the events that had led us to where we were. Of course, he would have said I should have pulled out, gone home where I belonged in the first place. That would have been Nick, all right, that would have been his solution. But it wasn't mine.

And, anyway, was he really right? Was I reverting? Was I going savage, ape? I hadn't shot Wilfred, hadn't even shot at him. And was I really and truly going to shoot him? Never mind all the surface resolutions, was I, down deep, going to kill him? Shoot a man, kill a fellow human being? Take a life? If Nick could say that I was, then he knew something about me that I didn't. But where was Wilfred? Where the hell was he?

I didn't believe he was gone. I decided on that once before and nearly got myself killed for such foolish thinking. No, he was hiding out in some secret lair he'd prepared long before. I had a secret lair too; the place I slept out at night. And I was getting damned tired of it. The place was whatever piece of flat ground I could find to spread my sleeping bag on. I changed it every night on the odd chance that he might be lurking about and be on to what I was up to. It was certainly a lot of trouble. I had to go out after it was good an' dark, so he couldn't see me, carrying my ground sheet and sleeping bag and air mattress. I didn't like that stumbling around in the black, tripping over roots and rocks and skinning up my shins and my face from low hanging branches. And I didn't like laying out in that black. It scared me. I couldn't sleep soundly at all. Every little noise would have me jumping out of my skin. Once some small animal blundered into me, and I nearly died of fright.

Hell, I was in a war. I was in an actual killing war. Never mind the numbers, never mind that it was just two men. Never mind that I was the general and the infantry and artillery all rolled into one. It was still a war. If I got killed, I'd still be just as dead as if I'd been involved in an atomic holocaust along with eight million other people. There may be comfort in numbers in some things, but death is not one of them.

I decided I ought to name my war. Hell, they always named wars. You couldn't have a really first class war unless you named it. There'd been all the world wars—they'd been easy to name, though I thought the names didn't really show a lot of imagination. I liked names like the Sino–Soviet War, or the Crimean War, or the Boxer Rebellion, or the French and Indian War. These were names with color. I thought of naming my war the Wilfred–Franklin War, but that sounded a bit trite. Finally I settled on The War of Dry Creek. That had a hell of a ring to it and would look good in the history books.

But it was seldom I felt the least bit of humor about my situation. Besides Wilfred and the danger and discomfort he was causing, my supplies were now dangerously low. I'd finally run out of whiskey. I still had a few bottles of the wine left, but I was being careful with that. More importantly, I'd misjudged my food supply. It had looked like a lot when I'd inventoried what I'd brought. But it's amazing how much a man can eat in a relatively short time. Also, there was a disparity in the supply of the foods I used the most of. For instance, I had only one case of canned meat left, but I had four cases of chunk-style pineapple.

I was also low on fuel for my stoves and heaters and lanterns. Since Wilfred, I didn't keep my fire going. Obviously, it would be a beacon. And in camp, I stayed in the tents as much as possible. Otherwise, I'd have been an easy target moving around in my own clearing. But I had to have heat and light in the tents and the use of a stove to cook my food.

One day I killed a wild boar. I was walking near my camp, just casually looking around. Ahead of me, maybe forty yards, I saw what I took to be a big boulder. The light was poor and the brush obscured my vision. But as I neared, the rock turned its head and looked at me, and I saw it was a big hog. God, he looked immense. I was carrying the 30.30 lever action Winchester and I eased that up to my shoulder, making as few movements as I could, so as not to frighten the pig. But I'd no more than got the rifle to my shoulder than the boar suddenly wheeled, with a roaring grunt, and came charging right at me. It panicked me and I started firing. I couldn't hit him. He was running like a broken field runner, cutting left and right, feinting, faking. I could see the bullets kicking up rocks and dust right at his feet, but I couldn't hit him. He came on, and over the rifle sights, I suddenly realized how close he was. Without an instant to spare, I jumped behind a tree as he went rushing past. I tell you, I had a clear vision of those huge, yellowed tusks as he made a thrust at me.

He didn't get past very far. Almost instantly he jerked to a stop and wheeled. For a second he paused. I don't think he could distinguish me from the tree. He wasn't ten feet away. All of a sudden, I jerked out the .357 magnum revolver and shot him. I hit him in the shoulder, for he squealed and twisted his snout around, trying, like a dog, to bite the place. For an instant, he staggered sideways; then his legs buckled and he fell over. That .357 magnum is a hell of a shell, much bigger than a 30.30. But he didn't stay down long. Instead, he jumped up like he wasn't hurt at all. I shot him again, this time hitting him dead on the brisket. I was getting my nerves under control and aiming a little more coolly. The shot hit him hard and sent him backward. Still grunting and squealing, he slowed around in a little circle before he fell over. Just once he tried to raise his head then, as the blood pumped out of him, he got still and I saw that he was dead.

I'm hell with that .357, I tell you.

I walked over and looked at him. He must have weighed four hundred pounds. He had long, curving tusks, yellowed and old-looking, sticking out the side of his jaws. They must have been five or six inches long. If he'd got me in the leg with one of those, with all that speed and weight behind it, he'd have laid me down and been able to come back and kill me at his leisure.

Well, I'd killed a wild pig, and I wondered what I was going to do with him. I realized, looking at him, that I didn't know anything about dressing out a hog. I knew you scalded them or something like that, but I didn't know how to go about it, even if I'd had a big vat full of boiling water. I sat down beside him, trying to think out the problem.

God, he looked awful. His skin was scaly and bristly and scarred. I could see ticks all over him. He didn't look like anything I wanted to eat. But I knew I couldn't just leave him like that. I knew he could be eaten. I'd killed him, and I was going to eat him. Otherwise, it had just been senseless.

Well, I knew you had to bleed a hog. You had to do that with any carcass. But in order to do it effectively, I was going to have to get him head down and cut his throat. He was lying right under the tree I'd jumped behind. Looking up, I saw that I could get a rope over a limb and then string him up by his hind feet. I could effectively gut him and dress him out in that position too. But how was I going to pull up a four-hundred-pound hog without a block and tackle?

I wasn't but about two hundred yards from my camp. I walked back, looking the terrain over. It was rough, though not as bad as some, and I thought I could get the pickup over. I got a coil of stout rope, started the pickup, and drove over to my hog. Once there I tied his back feet securely to the rope, threw the rope over a handy limb, and then tied the other end to the bumper of the pickup. I put the pickup in gear, eased a strain on to the rope, and then started forward. My pig came up just as nice as you please. When I had him suspended about four feet off the ground, I put the pickup in park and got out and set to work.

I'd brought along every knife I thought I could use, and they were good knives. I was glad I did because dressing out a huge boar is neither a pleasant nor an easy task.

First I cut his throat and let him bleed a while. While that was going on, I sat and smoked a cigarette. He had an amazing amount of blood in him.

Next I gutted him and cleaned out the abdominal cavity. It almost made me sick, but I was determined. I was finding I wasn't quite the hardened individual I'd thought I was.

When all that was done, I just stood and looked at him. A little thin stream of blood was running down his snout and dripping to the ground. The ground directly under the carcass was all over blood. I'd almost slipped in it a number of times.

I didn't know what else to do. I didn't know if you skinned a pig or not. Anyway, I wouldn't know how to go about it. I made a few tentative cuts with the skinning knife, but I didn't have much luck.

Finally, I decided to just cut off a ham. I'd tied his rear feet in such a manner that I could undo one and still leave him suspended by the other. I did that, and with one huge rear leg hanging down, I went to work on separating the ham from the carcass.

It was a hell of a job, taking better than an hour. When I was finished I took the damn thing over and threw it in the back of the pickup. It must have weighed seventy or eighty pounds and the meat didn't look like any ham I'd ever seen. It was bloody and red and very unappetizing. But, then, all the ham I'd ever seen had come from the supermarket.

I decided to leave the rest of the carcass right where it was. Untying the rope from the end of the pickup, I muscled it over and was able to tie it off to a nearby tree.

One of my natural springs was nearby, and before driving back to camp, I walked over and washed up as best I could. I was able to get most of the blood off my hands and arms, but I was still heavily splashed down my shirt front and pants.

I drove back to camp with the ham in back. The first thing I did was change clothes. Having blood all over you is an uncomfortable feeling. It dries and cakes quickly.

That night I had a ham steak along with a bottle of the Latour. I had to laugh at the contrast. I fried the steak on my stove, frying it hot and long to be sure I killed all the parasites. It was awful. It didn't taste anything like ham. It had a wild, gamy flavor and it was stringy and tough. I took the occasion to use up a can of the chunk-style pineapple. That's supposed to go very well with pork.

Pork should be smoked, smoked until it's cured, I knew that from reading my government bulletins. Next day, I was going to have to figure out how to go about smoking my ham. The rest of the carcass would keep very well in the cold, and there was little likelihood of any varmints getting to it, strung up like it was.

I'd read that fresh pork is not good for you, that it will upset your stomach. I discovered that this was so and spent a very uncomfortable night laying out in the woods.

Wilfred was making me very nervous. A lot of time had passed since he'd trapped me in his garden patch and shot me, time in which, except for the business with the hog, I'd spent cautiously patrolling the surrounding woods up to a distance of three miles. There was no sign of Wilfred. I found myself going around, saying aloud, "Com'on, Wilfred, a joke is a joke. Now quit hiding and come on out and play."

I don't know, the bastard acted like a trained psychologist intent on a war of nerves. If that was the case, he was winning. I got jumpier and jumpier every day. Already I'd whirled and fired on a bush that was doing no more than flutter in a vagrant breeze. I just couldn't figure out where he'd gone to or what he was doing. Why didn't he have a run at me? Jesus Christ, he'd shot at me twice and hit me once, which didn't leave much doubt about his intentions. I couldn't keep up my guard forever, it was too much of a strain. Was he waiting to see if I were just some casual visitor who'd leave? How could he know I wasn't some solid citizen who'd go into town and return with the sheriff?

Thinking on that, I decided that was why he was hiding out. He was waiting to see what I was going to do. He had him some very secret place somewhere and he was laying up there waiting to see if I'd go for the police. When he was sure I wouldn't, that I was just like him—a hideout in the woods who wanted no part of the police—then he was going to emerge and kill me.

Meanwhile he was playing hell with my life. I couldn't move freely around my camp, and it was going gradually to pot from lack of attention. My seedlings were retarding in their growth because I wasn't setting them out regularly every morning. I wasn't paying as much attention to my person. Before I'd resolved to shave everyday and keep myself neat, but that sort of thing is hard to maintain when you're being hunted and are on a manhunt yourself. I still hadn't washed any clothes, but now I'd stopped washing socks and underwear. And I really hated sleeping out in the woods at night. It seemed now that it rained every night at about two in the morning, and I'd wake up in a soaked sleeping bag.

I thought about going into town during the interim, but I was scared to make the move. In the first place, I didn't want to go, nor did I want to feel as if Wilfred were running me off. But more importantly, I didn't want to go off and leave my camp for fear Wilfred would come in and destroy it. I couldn't repack all my things in the truck, even if I'd wanted to. They'd been unboxed and uncrated and the truck wouldn't hold them. Besides, it would have been a hell of a lot of work.

For something better to do, I began smoking my hog. I say, for something better to do, for I'm not certain I had any intentions of ever eating him. I smoked him right where he hung by digging a four foot pit beneath him, building a small fire, and then lowering him just into it. First, though, I cut off his head— a gruesome job—and his legs and made an attempt at skinning him. I got most of the hide off, but it was a miserable job and one that left me almost unable to stand myself. I ended up burning the clothes I'd been wearing.

I'd worked up a bed of coals at the bottom to which I added some big logs arranged in such a way that they wouldn't blaze up too readily. I soon had a dense cloud of hot smoke enveloping my hog. Of course, it would have been better to have had him in an enclosed place, such as a smokehouse, but I didn't have one and didn't have the materials to make one. It was just something to do, anyway.

I'd sit, all day long, hidden by the brush, my rifle across my knees, watching my hog cook and hoping the climbing tower of smoke would bring Wilfred to come and see what it was all about.

Actually, it was working out very well. By judicious addition of logs, I kept the fire smoking, but not blazing up. That it was working I could tell from the sizzling drops of hot pork fat that fell down into the coals at a steady rate. Maybe I'd take a week and just smoke this baby down to hard, lean pork, something you could slice razor thin, like a Virginia ham.

God knows I wanted something good to eat. My meat diet was down to Spam, and there were just so many ways to fix that. Of canned vegetables, I had a half case of asparagus, a few tins of beets, some mushrooms, several cases of tomatoes, and several cases of beans. I had the pineapple, a few tins of apricots, some applesauce, and a couple of bottles of pickles. I had plenty of salt and pepper left, was low on sugar, was almost out of coffee, and still had the tins of English breakfast tea that I'd bought for Chris. I'd long been out of such things as fresh oranges and lemons and apples.

One day, while my hog was still smoking, I went over to Wilfred's garden on a raid. I was very nervous, but I was also about half angry and completely depraved for a fresh onion or turnip. I circled its perimeter three times, working in decreasing circles until I was certain no one was about. Then I dashed in, swooped up what I could carry in my hands, and raced away into the woods.

I was half expecting him to have come up and raided my hog while I was gone, but such was not the case. The meat was still cooking nicely.

That night I had a positive orgy on the fresh vegetables. I sat there, eating those succulent onions and turnips and thinking. Even in my haste, I'd been able to see that someone had been at the garden plot. It hadn't been worked, but someone—and it had to be Wilfred—had been there harvesting some of the vegetables.

I tell you, that hog gave me something to center myself around. I planned to smoke it for about a week. You understand that the fire wasn't hot enough to actually burn the outside meat. The way I was doing it, the effect was a warm, penetrating heat that worked itself all the way through the carcass. Of course, I knew it wouldn't cook evenly, hanging in one position like that. But it was still far too heavy for me to spit, even if I'd been able to devise a way to do it.

I slept near it at night, getting up at all hours to tend the fire. That might have seemed risky, but it wasn't. I had my bed roll back far enough that I wouldn't be easy to discover, and the fire didn't put out enough glow to silhouette me when I was working over it. Wilfred could have been ten feet away in the darkness and he'd still have had a hell of a hard shot hitting me in that ink.

During that time, I never wandered far afield. Of course, I was at my camp constantly, checking it. And once I went down to the creek. Surprisingly, the water was still up. It wasn't very deep, though, and the current was now logy and turgid. I imagined that most of the water was now a result of a backup out of the Buffalo, caused by heavy rains up river. Soon the Buffalo would regain its normal banks and our little creek would be dry again.

I saw several square-toed tracks that Wilfred had left, but I couldn't tell how recent they were. Sometimes I wondered what he must think of me. As far as I could tell, he hadn't visited my camp. He'd seen me twice, but other than my rifle he didn't know anything about me. He must have been curious.

Finally, I couldn't smoke my hog any longer. Even I recognized it was done. I brought up my pickup, lowered it into the bed, and drove back to my camp. There, I strung it up over a tree limb in the same manner I'd derricked it up in the tree to bleed. The tree was just outside the entrance to my sleeping tent and the smoked carcass looked very good hanging there. I intended to butcher it and store it away in my ice boxes.

I had some that night. It was all right. It was better than the fresh ham I'd had, but it was still very tough and strong tasting. Probably it would have been better if I'd rubbed salt into it while it was smoking, but I hadn't thought of that until too late.

I now fell into a sort of lethargy composed of sorrow and boredom and loneliness. I even started sleeping back in my tent at night. Several weeks had passed since the action between Wilfred and myself at his garden plot. He was, I decided, a timid soul who was going to hide back in the forest, gnawing at roots, until I left. He didn't have any friends or relatives. If he had they'd have come in and routed me out long before this. And he hadn't been into any town talking about the stranger. That would have brought the sheriff.

A lull had come in The War of Dry Creek. Who the truce seemed to favor I wasn't sure. Nor did I seem to care.

18

I decided to go into town. I had to make a move of some kind; I was so lonely and nervous and depressed that I couldn't stand it any longer. All I did all day was sit around and brood and jump at the slightest sound. A man can't live that way, he just can't. It all came over me one day. All of a sudden I was very tired of the woods and the mountains and the silence. I wanted people and noise and the sounds of honking horns and telephones and televisions and the sight of buildings and concrete and store windows. Hell, I'd have settled for a good car wreck as the peak of excitement. A riot would have been pie.

I was going to risk the camp. I considered hauling most of the stuff off in the surrounding brush and hiding it, but after only a few loads, I gave that up as too much work. All I finally did was strike my tent poles, letting the canvas settle to the ground. There were still some bulges and ridges from some crates left underneath, but the whole blended in well with the landscape. I didn't even bother to knock down the little wall of rocks I'd used to surround my living tent.

Actually, I wasn't too worried about leaving. Wilfred had had plenty of opportunities to do it in before, and he hadn't availed himself. He probably wasn't even in the neighborhood. The odds, I thought, were heavily in my favor. I'd calculated that it would take me no more than eight hours to run into town and back and a lot of eight hours had passed with his running loose and no harm had come. There was no reason to expect anything now.

I left about ten o'clock in the morning, very excited. It seemed strange to be driving the pickup again after such a long lay off. I bumped my way out of the forest and over the rocky mountain path and then got on the well-traveled road into town. I was going to Searcy, which was about seventy miles away. Yellville would have been much closer, but I thought I might as well follow my original plan of secrecy in the general neighborhood.

I drove along, my spirits soaring, in eager anticipation. Everything looked strange and new. I couldn't believe that I was so glad to see civilization again. I even wanted people. I wanted to see people badly. I wanted someone to talk to.

God, I was excited. I'd shaved and dressed that morning as if I was going out on the biggest date of my life. Chiefly, besides the pleasure of going, I was craving; I was craving chocolate and whiskey and fresh meat.

My whiskey had been gone for sometime, though I still had a few bottles of the wine left. Of course, the wine wasn't like the whiskey; I wanted that hard bite, that sudden calm. And I wanted some beef, some edible beef. I'd fixed that Spam everyway I could think of, and I was tired of it in all ways. I could barely stomach my pork anymore. I'd set out to eat some, but it'd seem to grow in my mouth. Swallowing would become so difficult that I'd end up spitting most of it out. I didn't even like the sight of it hanging from the tree.

God, I was hungry for so many things. I'd been out of sugar for a few days, but what I really wanted was chocolate. I'd sucked the juice off of a few cans of that damnable chunk-style pineapple, but that hadn't helped. What I wanted was some chocolate-covered cherries. I wanted to eat a whole box of those, then drink a bottle of whiskey, then sit around and talk to a bunch of people. I didn't care what they said; the simpler the better. I didn't want any smart, sophisticated talk. I just wanted to hear about the baby's colic and what they were paying for day labor and what the hay crop looked like and when they were going to fix the streets.

God, I hadn't known how much I wanted it until I got going. I drove madly, going faster and faster the closer I came to my destination. I wanted to get out of that truck as I passed through each little town, but I wouldn't let myself.

What jumped out at me as I passed through that first little town was a phone booth by the side of the road.

Call Chris.

Telephone Chris. Call her up and say, baby, this is your wandering man. How you been? I love you. Let's forget all this. Let me get out of these wild mountains and shake the leaves out of my hair and quit fighting a crazy hermit and come home.

Call Chris.

I drove past the first phone booth and then a number of them as I passed through more little crossroad towns. It seemed that Arkansas had a lot of roadside phone booths. It seemed that there was one around every curve.

Call Chris.

Telephone her and say, baby, I don't know what came over me. This whole scheme was insane from the very first. I'm sorry I treated you this way.

There wasn't much traffic on the roads, just an occasional pickup with a calf or pig or sacks of feed in the back. I passed a couple of hitchhikers who glared at me as I swept past. But my mind was on something else.

Call Chris.

Call and say, baby, I was wrong. Please forgive me and let me come home. You were right all the time. You did the right thing *not* to come with me. You were right to leave me in that café by the side of the road. I should have gone back with you. I should never have put you in such a position where you had to make a choice.

I gripped the wheel with both hands, squeezing it until my knuckles went white. All the while, I was boring down harder and harder on the gas pedal. The pickup flew along the road, accelerating with the pressure. I came to a long curve that switched back as it wound around a mountain. Halfway through it, I felt the truck going out of control. I could feel it slipping sideways, toward the side of the mountain. Trees and rocks were whizzing past, almost a blur. Almost reluctantly, I came out of my deep cloud and got off the accelerator and began bringing the truck back. I got it slowed and under control, though not until we'd gone fishtailing down the middle of the road.

After that, I sat back and breathed heavily for a moment. Then I let my breath all the way out and relaxed. I always had to do things, think things, look at things, as an absolutist. Ah, my many faults. My many, many faults.

The town looked all strange and new. As I stopped at my first red light, I couldn't get over how differently, how strange I felt. You'd have thought I'd been back in the mountains for ten years. "Com'on, Horn," I told myself, "stop rhapsodizing. Detroit hasn't even had time to come out with a new model in the time you've been gone, and that's no time at all." As I said it, I had the uneasy feeling that I was talking as Chris sometimes talked to me.

First thing I did was to hunt up a wholesale butcher and arrange to buy a side of beef. I went there first so he'd have the afternoon to cut and wrap it while I ran some other errands. I'd given up on the idea of hanging a side from the tree out in front of my tent. That'd be more picturesque, but having it individually wrapped and stored in my ice chests would be a hell of a lot handier.

The butcher took me back in his cold storage locker to pick out a carcass. He had scant few and what he did have was stringy, too lean-looking beef. The meat was obviously off small, young, range cattle that hadn't been on a feeding program.

"What's this?" I said. "These look like packer-canner grade."

"It's good beef," he answered uninterestedly.

"Where's the USDA stamp?" I asked him. "Hasn't this meat been inspected and graded?"

He turned on me defensively. "Listen, this is good meat. If you don't want it there's plenty others that do. Where you been buying meat?"

Then he quoted me a price that was outrageous.

I shrugged. "All right," I said. I really had no choice.

As I placed the order, he gave me little appraising looks. I'd shaved and washed and done what I could for my appearance, but I knew I still must appear a sight. For one thing my hair was very long and shaggy. I'd thought of hacking it off myself, but decided that would only have made it worse. And my clothes were pretty much a mess. I'd already decided I'd get some new things. It'd be easier than trying to wash. But I did place a big wash tub on my list of necessities. Something heavy enough to boil water over an open fire in. That's the way I'd remembered my grandmother washing clothes in the backyard.

Next I went to the liquor store and bought seven cases of bourbon and one of rum. I don't know why I bought so much whiskey; it just made me feel good to have a lot of it on hand. The owner added up the order and whistled. Then he glanced up at me, taking in my hair and general appearance. "Must be gonna have some party."

"Hunting party," I explained. "I'm taking a hunting party in."

"Oh, yeah?" He looked at me, even more suspiciously I thought. "Where you from? I thought I knew all the guides around here?"

"Mountain Shoals," I said, naming a town about sixty miles away. I had planned on telling this story. I didn't want anyone knowing too much about me. First, because there was the matter of the fort, and second, because I didn't know how the business with Wilfred might end. I had correctly predicted that I would arouse some curiosity in the town. It was just as I'd told Chris it would be when she couldn't quite understand my interest in secrecy and the reason we wouldn't be able to run into town every jump out of the box.

I handed the man seven 100-dollar bills. I expect it was the biggest order he'd ever handled. He looked startled at the money. Finally he took it in his hand and glanced suspiciously at me again. Then he said, "Just a minute" and went into a back room.

I started feeling nervous. I had no reason to, I hadn't done anything; yet it was coming over me stronger and stronger every minute that the man was gone. I had visions of the police coming in and arresting me on suspicion. Suspicion of what? Suspicion of planning to shoot Wilfred if he shot at me again? What the hell was I so nervous about, so jumpy, I asked myself? I didn't know.

The man finally came back, made change, and then helped me carry my order out to the pickup. As I drove away, I had the feeling he was standing there staring after me, memorizing the license plate number. I looked back and he was standing there staring after me.

Then I went to the barber shop, parking my truck right in front so I could watch it. The whiskey was just in the back. At first, I thought the shop was full and I turned to leave, but one of the barbers waved me over to his chair. "You're next," he said, popping out a cloth. The men waiting were just there to read and talk and gossip.

When I sat down the barber took a handful of long hair and flipped it up in the air. "Whew!" he said, "you're pretty shaggy. Ain't even sure I can cut that."

"Just cut it," I said tensely. I felt as if everyone in the shop was watching me.

The barber was a greasy-looking thirty-year-old who probably went to the Baptist Church and belonged to the KKK. He took another handful of my hair and flipped it. "You one of them hippies?" Then he laughed to show he was just kidding.

I didn't like it. I half turned in my chair and gave him a hard look. "Just cut the hair, fella. I been in the bush—" I broke off. I didn't owe him any explanation. "Just cut it," I finished. "Work. Don't talk."

He finally set to work, mumbling all the while that he couldn't be expected to do a very good job on such a mess. It was all making me even more nervous and tense. Once, through the plate-glass window, I saw what appeared to be a police car go cruising down the street. It seemed they slowed and looked the pickup over very carefully.

And there was one man, a loiterer, sitting in a chair opposite me against the wall who stared at me the whole time. He was chewing tobacco and he never took his eyes off my face, his jaws going in steady, regular rhythm.

When the barber was finished, I paid and left. From there I went to the meat house. My order was ready and I was glad. I'd had enough of the town. I was ready to leave. I'd do the rest of my shopping in the towns on the way back.

I stopped in Bald Knob and bought some flashlight batteries and a number of cans of butane fuel and finally satisfied my craving for chocolate-covered cherries. I bought six boxes—all they had—and then stopped on the road outside of town, killed the engine, and sat there eating the chocolates and drinking bourbon straight from the bottle. I ate almost half a box. When I was finished I felt a little sick, but I also felt better. I supposed that was the effect of the whiskey, however.

I sat there for quite a time, long enough that the sun started to fade and night wasn't far off. I was a little surprised. The day had gone very fast. Well, I'd had the whiskey and the chocolates, but I still hadn't had the human companionship, not a good kind. Perhaps I could stop at some little café or bar on the way back. Maybe even hang around a service station and talk to the night man.

There was something else on my mind that I'd been shoving back as far as I could in my subconscious.

I needed a woman. I hadn't had sex in almost two months and that is a period of time I haven't gone for since I became a man. All those days in the mountains, I'd tried my best not to think about it. Most times I was successful, for I knew that by that path lay vulnerable weakness. But sometimes the remembered vision of Chris's luscious body would steal over me and it would be damn near more than I could stand. I would remember things we'd done, the sensations we'd shared, the hotness, the juicy loveliness of it all. I'd remember her slowly taking off her clothes, her body against the sheets. I'd remember the sight and the feel and the taste of her. I'd remember that passion that rose faster than I could capture it.

I needed a woman to release some of that remembered vision that had built up until it was almost a pain.

Of course, I wasn't going to find a natural woman, someone I could meet and take to bed as a result of mutual attraction. There wasn't time, nor were these the circumstances for that.

In Batesville, I suddenly pulled into a service station. Batesville was a town of about five thousand, and I thought what I sought just might be on sale there.

A young man, of about twenty, came out to greet me as I went over the little hoses that go ding ding. They had a sign out front limiting the gas to each customer to five gallons.

"Yes sir," he said, "gas?"

"Yeah," I said, my throat dry.

When he'd filled the gas, I paid him with a ten dollar bill. As he was counting my change out I asked him, as casually as I could: "Where do they keep all the women around here?"

He looked blank. He was a very country looking young man. "Well," he finally said, "I guess they's mostly at home. Tendin' to home."

"No," I said, "I mean whores." I almost shouted the word. "Doesn't a town of this size have any whores? At least one."

He shook his head, looking puzzled, as if he'd never heard of such a thing. "I don't think so, sir," he said. "I don't believe we have any of them. I don't think the law stands for it."

"Thanks," I said. I put the truck in gear and pulled out, my face fiery.

I didn't want to stay around Batesville and buy anything, not after such an experience. Instead, I turned off onto state road 14 and headed on for camp by way of Mountain View. There I bought a few more incidental things, bread mostly. The weather would freeze it for me, and it would keep for some time.

It was coming on dark as I pulled out. Already the sky was darkening and little fingers of deep purple were reaching across the sky. When they joined, it would be night.

I stopped in Mountain Home, which is something of a resort town, and bought more supplies. I didn't buy too many fresh vegetables because I knew they wouldn't last. But I did make a heavy dent in the canned goods department of one store. It was a big chain supermarket, so I was able to buy quite a bit of the out of the ordinary. I bought all sorts of things—truffles, marinated artichokes, cheap caviar, canned clams, canned oysters, canned shrimp, ripe olives, anchovy paste, pâté—anything I could think of that I might develop a taste for. Of course, I bought any number of cans of the standard stuff. But I'd been doing that all along. My bill came to over three hundred dollars and it took four stock clerks to carry it out to my pickup.

As I pulled out of the supermarket parking lot I noticed a phone booth by the side of the road. I steered the pickup over and stopped right in front of it. I didn't kill the engine, just put the truck in neutral and sat there staring at that phone booth. I ought to call her, I thought. I really ought to call her. I wanted to, but at the same time I didn't. Was I afraid to call her? Was I putting it off out of shame, shame that I'd done the wrong thing by her, shame that I'd failed? Or fear? Fear that things could never be right between us again?

I really wasn't worried about her. She was a lot stronger, a lot tougher, I'd found out, than I'd thought. She was all right.

All I knew was that I didn't want to call her, not yet, not when I wasn't sure about so many things. The motor throbbed mutedly in the cold night air. I sat hunched over the steering wheel, looking at that goddamned phone booth.

Finally, with a sense that I was leaving something, I put the truck in gear and pulled out on the road.

Oh, God, I was suddenly so unhappy I didn't think I'd be able to stand it. I didn't think I could face that camp again. I didn't think I could go back there and take up the kind of life I'd been living. Ahead of me were a few more small towns, then Yellville —which I wouldn't want to stop in by any means—then the dirt road out and then the path and then overland to the camp.

I passed through Lone Rock and Calico Rock and Fifty-Six. I just kept driving, feeling terribly depressed. Then I came to Cotter, a small mountain town strung out along the state highway. As I came into the town I noticed a light in one of the few buildings. It was good and dark now and cold. I'd turned the heater on in the truck. I saw the light was coming from some sort of café. As I passed I noticed it said, Cotter Café and Dominoe Hall. I immediately put on the brakes and steered over to the curb. I'd gone on past and I had to back up to come abreast of the front.

I had to see someone, talk to someone, feel human again. I looked through the glass window of the café. I couldn't see much since it was fogged up. It appeared to be just an ordinary café with a bunch of men, maybe six or eight, sitting around playing dominoes.

I considered the risk and decided the hell with it. There was no point in locking the pickup. I had about two thousand dollars' worth of stuff in the back, exposed, and, if anyone were going to steal anything, they could just walk off with it.

Feeling shy and nervous, I opened the door and went in.

No one looked up at my entrance. The room was overheated, as most places where old men hang out are. Ahead of me was a little short bar with three or four stools. It was a typical beer bar with little racks of potato chips and pretzels on top. There were also big jars of beer sausage, soaking in vinegar, and pigs feet and pickles. There was one man sitting at the bar. Around the rest of the room were scattered a number of tables. Some of them were café tables, some were the slate-topped kind you see in dominoe halls. They're slate-topped because the players keep score wih chalk on the tabletop. Hell, in my rambles in the oil fields and the trucking business I'd been in a hundred such places in Texas and Louisiana and Arkansas. I could speak the language.

I sat down at the bar. The old boy down the row from me never paid the slightest bit of attention, just went on drinking his Falstaff. The bartender or the owner or whatever he was got up from one of the tables where he was playing dominoes and got behind the bar. "What'll you take?" he asked me.

"Gimmee a bottle of Bud," I said.

He got the beer out, uncapped it, and set it in front of me. I paid him and while he was counting out my change, jerked my head back toward the tables and asked, "What are they playing?"

"Dominoes," he answered briefly.

"I know that," I said, "what kind?"

"Moon."

"I play a little moon. I'm just passing through, and I'd like a little time off the road. Would they let a stranger play if a seat came open?"

"Ask them," he said, and was gone back to his own game.

I drank about half my beer, just sort of watching the games over my shoulder, and then finally wandered over and sat down by a table. There were two old men and one young guy playing. The old man I was sitting by had on a work shirt buttoned up to the collar, a gray button-type sweater over that, and then a wind breaker on top of the whole thing. I'm sure he had a set of heavy underwear on underneath. He was old and weathered, and there was a bristle of gray hairs over his jaws. He had a cold cigar clamped between his teeth.

They took no notice of me when I sat down. Finally, I asked, "Are sweaters allowed if they keep their mouths shut?"

The old man gave me a gruff look. "Not if you do what you say."

"I can handle that," I told him.

They played with terrible intensity, slamming the dominoes down with force, making a hard, sharp sound. I'd already figured out that they were playing twenty-five cents a game, twenty-five cents a hickey.

After I'd watched a couple of games I said, conversationally, "I'm just passing through. On my way up across the Missouri border."

They didn't take the slightest notice of me. I might as well have been talking to the next table. I wasn't surprised or discouraged, I expected it. But I also knew how to handle the situation. "Cold as a witch's titty," I said. "Fucking heater has gone out on the truck, and I had to get off the road and get a little warm."

The old man grunted. Without moving his lips he asked, "What're you hauling?"

"Aw," I told him, "I'm just in a pickup. Just taking a bunch of stuff up for my boss and his rich friends. He's got a fishing and hunting camp up across the border. I'm just one of the fetch and carry hands."

"Huh," the old man said. "He's rich and you're on the road with a bum heater. When I voted for him in 1938 I thought FDR was going to put a stop to all that kind of foolishness. But we still got them rich ones who look out mighty well for themselves."

"Aw," I said, "I don't mind. It's a good job for somebody like me that ain't got no education or much sense."

The younger man spoke up and asked me, "What do you do when you ain't fetchin' and carrying?"

"Just general work around the place," I said. "He don't stay there year round so I have it pretty easy most times. A little thing like a heater goin' out ain't gonna drive me up no tree."

The other old man, who was thin and weather-beaten, said, "Now I like to see a man loyal to his work and glad to earn his money. Ever'body wasn't to go around knockin' somethin' these days."

Amos was the old man with all the sweaters and coats on. He said, in a querulous voice, "I never said no different. Goddamnit, Harley, you are one to put words in a man's mouth!"

But I'd established myself with them. A few minutes later,

they let me buy a round of beer and then I was part of the table.
I even started commenting on the game. The old man, Amos,
made a bad lead and went set on a bid. I said, "If you'd come
little, led your deuce ace, you could have knocked down the calf
and that puts the other man in a switch about his cow. If he
goes small you've got him. If he holds you, trump back in and
lead your trump double and knock out his cow. Then all you
lose is one trump trick and your off and you've got your five."

He gave me a hard look, but all he said was, "You're mighty
late with that advice."

"I thought I'd better wait until the hand was over," I said.

They laughed.

God, I was enjoying myself. Sitting in an overheated café in
Cotter, Arkansas, sweating a two-bit moon game, and I was enjoying myself. Life is a very strange proposition.

After a little, the younger man left and they invited me into
the game. We played for two hours. I won a little, but I made
certain to give it back by buying the beer. I didn't do it in an
overbearing manner, just in the casual sort of way a stranger
might who's glad for the warmth and the comfort on a hard
night. When the game was over and I got up to leave, the old
man, Amos, said, "You get through here you stop in and we'll
show you how to play moon. You's just lucky tonight. Me and
Harley are most nearly always here."

We shook hands all around and even the sour-faced bartender
called so long as I left. I got in the pickup, my breath coming
steamy in the cold night air, and started up the road. It was almost ten o'clock and I still had another hour to my camp.

Eventually I turned off the old rutted road and went creeping
overland toward my home. At best, through that terrain, you
can make ten miles an hour. It was dip and climb with the
headlights now boring into the ground and now bouncing crazily
among the dead tree limbs.

But I felt good. I was a little drunk, but very mellow and at
peace. Perhaps I'd have been feeling even better if I'd found
something to fuck, but I doubted it. I've never been that way as
a man. From the moment I'd met Chris, she was my woman. If
I had found a whore, I think her naked body would have only

meant anguish in the comparison. I think it would have brought back sharper memories than I wanted.

I jounced along over that ground, my mind hazy and good feeling, thinking about it all.

At a point I stopped, getting out of the pickup to urinate. My water ran steaming through the cold night air. I'd stopped in a clearing and I could see the black night sky above, decorated with bright stars. "Ah," I said aloud, "there you are."

I didn't know what that meant. I just said it, feeling good.

And then, all of a sudden, standing there staring up at the stars in the black velvet sky, taking a piss, weaving a little from all the whiskey, just standing right there I knew something. I knew I was going home. Just like that. It would take me a day or two to get all the loose ends gathered up, but then I was going to turn the nose of that pickup for home and fly like a bat out of hell.

I laughed out loud. Then I laughed again, louder. "Love is all there is, Franklin," I said a little drunkenly. "You got to realize that. You ought to have realized it all the way. You got to go back to your love. The only way. Hey! Hey, Wilfred!" I was yelling out at the night. "You hear me? You can have it! You can take these goddamn mountains and stick 'em up your vegetable garden. I'm leaving! Hear? I've had it—had it—had it—had it—had it. . . ." I made an echo and laughed at my own humor. How had I gotten so stupid. If there was going to be trouble, then the only way was for Chris and me to handle it together. Christ, I'd been dumb!

"All yours, Wilfred!" I yelled once more and got back in the truck, still laughing like a maniac. I put the truck in gear and pulled out.

The terrain quickly became familiar. As I went along, I recognized trees and certain grades of land and I knew I was getting very close to camp. Finally, I climbed the little hump whose top housed my tents and came into my clearing. My windshield was fogged up, and for a second, I didn't quite know what I was seeing. I remember thinking: Oh, hell, I didn't bank that fire down far enough, and it's got out of hand and spread. When I got out of the pickup I saw little patches of fire burning in several places. I still didn't know what to think, I still thought my fire had caught the camp on fire. Then I began to walk quickly around the area and I knew, immediately, what had been done. The good drunken feeling drained straight out of me. All that was left in its place was rage.

I'd been wiped out. My camp had been destroyed. My tents had been burned. There were scattered remnants around the ground, slowly being consumed by the fire. The supplies I'd left looked as if they'd been made into one huge bonfire and burned. I found the melted remains of my plastic ice boxes. All my hoes and axes and rakes and such had been added to the bonfire. The wooden handles, of course, had burned, but the iron heads lay in twisted and tortured evidence among the ashes.

All my food supplies were gone. Whether they'd been burned or simply carried off I didn't know. Apparently, they'd been carried off for there were no cans or tins among the ashes.

My radios were gone; my heaters and lanterns and stoves and flashlights were gone. All my cooking utensils were gone. Everything I'd left, everything that I'd brought to the mountain was gone.

I suddenly remembered my sleeping bag and air mattress. Like a fool I hadn't carried them off to a hiding place. They'd either been burned or stolen. Either way they were gone.

Fortunately, I hadn't left any guns or cartridges in the camp. All of those I'd hidden except for the 30.30 and the 357 magnum and an appropriate amount of cartridges that I'd taken along with me, hidden under the truck seat.

The rage was mounting in me, though it was no longer fury. There wasn't any doubt in my mind about who'd done it. Old Wilfred. That meant he'd been watching my camp the whole time. Apparently, I'd been right in thinking he viewed me only as a visitor who'd someday leave. When I'd driven off, leaving my camp, he'd taken that opportunity to speed my going.

Well, the sonofabitch had done it now. He'd done it good, and it was going to be his death.

I understood why he hadn't picked me off from ambush. He'd been thinking about me in the same way I'd been thinking about him. He'd assumed I had friends and family, who knew where I was and who would come looking for me if I didn't eventually turn up. And he didn't want that, any more than I did in his case. But it was all right to burn me out, to scare me. Maybe that way I'd leave.

Well, the motherfucker had made a hell of a mistake. I understood Wilfred much better now. Now the lines were clearly drawn. There'd be no outside forces to reckon with. It was just him and me. Just us. Just a little contest to see who the best man was. Winner gets to live.

I liked it. I stood there among the dying ashes of my camp, and I liked it very well. I could kill him now with no compunctions or worry or even very much regret. All my life, I've had to fight enemies that I didn't quite understand and where the rules and procedures were dim and poorly drawn. All my life, I've been restricted by laws and unwritten laws and boundaries that I could not see, but knew must not be crossed.

All that was gone now. Here was a clear-out fight. Here was something that I could handle by my rules. I could make up my own laws to suit this situation. There'd be no outside opinions to cloud the issue.

There was no point in going off to sleep in the woods. I didn't have anything to sleep on, in the first place, and I wasn't going to leave my pickup unguarded. I had no doubts but that Wilfred was out there, just out of sight in the black, watching me. I couldn't move the pickup, not across that terrain without headlights, and he'd see the lights and know where I was. So that was pointless.

Finally, I just crawled in under my truck and settled down for the night. I had the 30.30 and the 357 and the cartridges. I might doze a little, but I wasn't going to sleep. If Wilfred tried anything further this night, he was going to get mighty sick from the ulcers I intended to put all the way through him.

The cold helped me keep awake. I dozed off and on, but the slightest sound, even the creak of one of the truck springs settling, would bring me to full alertness. I slept with that 357 at full cock. I wasn't spooked about anything anymore.

I came full awake with a start. Looking out from under the truck I could see that it was daylight. I glanced quickly at my watch. It was nine o'clock. The time surprised me a little, but not much. I'd dozed off and on until daylight. When I'd seen light coming down through the trees, I remembered thinking, well, now he won't dare show himself. I guess that had reassured me enough so that I'd gone off.

It was good, for I'd needed the sleep. Now, though, it was time to get to work. I scuttled backward out from under the truck and quickly flattened myself against the side of the cab. The 357 was in my hand. The surrounding woods looked peaceful, but I gave them a careful, lingering scrutiny. I looked at each tree, each bush, making my mind recognize what a man would look like hiding there. Little trails of smoke were rising from the scattered fires of what had been my camp.

I went crablike again and scuttled backward into the tree line. From there I went on a charging search around the immediate perimeter of my camp. I ran with the 357 pointed in front of me, ready to shoot anything that moved. There was nothing but trees and brush. I took a second turn, deeper and slower this time, checking for sign, for movement, for anything. At long last, I'd satisfied myself that I was alone, and I went back into my camp and looked around.

It was the same mess; worse, if anything, by daylight. "Okay, Wilfred," I said. So, in his mind, I was some dude who could be spooked and run off by destroying my camp. I supposed I was to imagine Big Jack and forty mad renegades running wild through the woods. If I did what he wanted and expected, I'd immediately get the hell out of the country and leave it to him and his solitude.

Well, I thought the best thing would be to give him that impression. From then on we'd play a stalking game. Oh, yes, Wilfred, I was packing up and getting out. You just keep on thinking that, buddy, until you feel that lead bite home. Then you wouldn't have to think anymore. I intended to relieve him of all his responsibilities.

He'd shot me and he'd burned me out. If you want to think I was crazy to plan his death, you go right ahead. But don't forget, all the signs indicated that he'd kill me given the chance. Hell, he'd even broken and burned my three remaining bottles of wine. I found one of the broken necks with the cork still intact. The goddamn barbarian hadn't even understood what he was destroying. He'd burned my seedling planters. I found the little humps of prepared soil where he'd dumped them out and then thrown the planter boxes onto the fire.

It is not an easy thing to decide, finally and fully, that you're going to kill another man—though governments seem to be able to do it with impunity. But, I ask you, what choice did I have? I hadn't really declared war on him. I'd been walking warily around his borders for weeks, trying to find some way for peaceful coexistence. He'd taken that prerogative away from me. Every act of aggression had been on his part. He hadn't left me any choices.

There was a lot of work to do, but I had to eat first, make myself strong. I built myself a little fire out of oak twigs, right amid the shattered remains of my camp, and broiled a steak out of the meat that I'd brought from town. I had to eat it with just my fingers and my pocket knife for I didn't have any other utensils, not even plates. I ate it like an animal, without salt or seasoning.

After that I began to haul in the supplies I'd carefully hidden for my trip to town. I didn't touch the cache I'd made when I'd first come to the mountains. I went and checked to make sure it was secure, but I didn't disturb it. That was my last refuge.

I went about the business of bringing in the supplies with a secure feeling. Wilfred, if he were watching, would be able to see that I was loading up the pickup for departure. He obviously didn't want to kill me except as a last resort. He wanted me to leave.

When I'd loaded everything in the truck, I walked over and stood in the middle of my camp like a man taking a last look around. Some of the fires were smoldering a little, and I stamped them out as best I could.

There was no residue in my mind of what I'd decided the night before. That had gone with the whiskey and the night and the fire my camp had made. I only had one thing on my mind now. I felt one little stab as I turned for the truck, but that was all. I got in the truck and made a circle and then headed out the way I'd come. I drove as fast as the terrain would allow. If Wilfred was trying to follow me, I was going to make it hard on him. I drove all the way to the little road, then up it for about a mile or two. There I was able to do twenty miles an hour, and I knew I'd lose Wilfred. When I thought I'd gone far enough I turned off, south, back into the woods. I was on the big tract of land that had me land locked on three sides. I drove along carefully. I was looking for a narrow, deep ravine, something I could hide the pickup in. It took some doing, but I finally found a gully I thought would suit my purposes. I wanted to back the truck in so that I could come out easier and faster if I had to. It was going to be a ticklish business. I backed the truck to the mouth of the ravine and then got out and worked about a half an hour moving what rocks I could out of the way.

I got it down in the bottom by taking it very slowly, a foot at a time. Once I drug high center on a rock and thought I was in trouble, but I gunned in a little more power and she came loose with a grating screech. The sound hurt me. I felt like I was tearing the guts out of my truck. When I had it settled in, I got out, walked off a few yards, and looked back. The top was below ground level. You'd have to walk right up on it to see anything.

But I was going to do better than that. Fortunately, there had been a couple of axes and a machete in the pickup, and I went to work with those, cutting brush. It was long hard work and took most of the afternoon. It takes a surprising amount of brush to cover a pickup. And, too, I hadn't wanted to cut brush right in the immediate vicinity; that would have been a bad sign to leave.

When I was finished, I stepped back and looked at it critically. It looked like a brush-filled gully. Unless you looked closely, you wouldn't notice the cut ends of a lot of the brush, and unless you were seeking it, you wouldn't know there was a truck down there.

It was late when I finished, and I was tired. I crawled down under the brush and sat down by my pickup and had a few drinks of whiskey. Finally, I roused myself enough to open a can of meatballs and spaghetti. I ate it cold, not liking the taste, but knowing I needed food. It was almost dark by the time I finished, and I spent the rest of the light hurriedly making up a pack. I put in a number of canned goods, some onions, three bottles of whiskey, three boxes of cartridges each for the 30.30 and the 357, a flashlight with extra bulbs and batteries, the machete, and a small hand axe. I'd be leaving before daylight, and I wouldn't be able to pack then without striking a light of some kind—and I certainly wasn't going to do that.

Finally I crawled into the cab with the bottle of whiskey and the 357. The steering wheel had a horn rig on it, and I rigged a cord to that and both door handles so that the horn would blow if someone tried to open either door. Then I had a few more drinks of whiskey and lay down to sleep. I set my mind to wake up at 4:00 A.M. That's a trick I used to be able to do. I wasn't certain it'd still work, because I'd been out of practice for so long. But I needed to be up early. I had a lot of traveling to do the next day, and I'd need all the time I could get.

It was very cold. I really missed my sleeping bag and blankets. Hell, I didn't even have any more clothes. The bastard had either burned or carried off what I'd left at camp. Fortunately, I'd taken my big coat. It was warm, but without a sleeping bag, I was going to get mighty uncomfortable if I had to sleep on the ground too many nights.

I missed four o'clock by ten minutes. The moment I opened my eyes I was awake, and I saw by my watch that it was 3:50. It was black dark, but I could still see how fogged up the windows were from my breathing and body heat. God, it was cold. I sat up stiff and chilled. The thought of a cup of coffee came to my mind, but I put it aside. I couldn't even have a cigarette, for I didn't intend to strike a light for any reason. The best thing to do was get moving; that'd warm me up.

After I'd untied the cord attached to the handle, I eased the door open and slid out. It was much colder outside the cab. It came up and hit me like a physical force. For a second, I didn't think I'd be able to stand it and I longed to crawl back into the relative warmth of the cab. But I forced myself to strap on my knapsack, pick up my 30.30, stick the 357 in my belt, and start off.

It was rough going in the black, but every yard I made before daylight would be worth it. I was traveling by the luminous dial of a little pocket compass. I'd need that until I got back on familiar ground. I was heading for Wilfred's cabin and I figured it to be about ten or twelve miles away. I thought I could average at least two miles an hour and be there between nine and ten o'clock.

I did very well on the time. I was traveling as fast as I could, and consequently, I took several falls and scarred my legs up against rough boulders and downed logs.

By daylight, I was on known ground. Stopping to rest, I looked around, noticing various landmarks, and decided I was about a mile south of my former camp. I was dead on route and ahead of schedule. It made me feel proud, this forced march. God knows, I couldn't have done it two months before. I was willing to admit that Wilfred was probably my superior in wood skills and strength and endurance. But just by admitting this, I brought us closer to parity, for it would force me to use other methods and make him fight my kind of fight. I didn't believe Wilfred was as smart or as cunning as I was. I had no intentions of chasing him all over the woods walking into some trap he'd carefully laid. Or getting picked off from ambush. And I had no doubts in my mind that Wilfred, the next time he saw me, would have murder on his mind. He'd know, then, that I hadn't left and didn't intend to leave, and there'd be only one course open to him. I had my hopes about half pinned on the thought that I might have bought a day or two by my ruse of leaving. I wasn't going to count on it for that would have been foolish and unwary. But if it had—well, then I'd have an advantage that could prove very valuable.

I was going to go to Wilfred's cabin and I was going to wait for him there. If he showed up I was going to kill him, just as quickly and safely as I could. He had to return to his base sometime, and I intended to be there waiting for him. I'd prepared myself for a long, lonely vigil.

The creek was almost dry again. I crossed it easily, not bothering to check for footprints in its damp sand. The ones Wilfred made would be a mile north of me. I was deliberately taking this roundabout route to preclude any chance of running up on him. If he was doing what I thought he'd be doing, what I'd be doing in his shoes, he'd be over watching my camp to see if I were going to return. According to his past habits, I judged he'd be away from his cabin during the midday hours.

I got to his cabin a little after nine. Once I saw how far ahead of schedule I was running, I started to take it easy.

I should say, I got to the area of his cabin. I stopped a quarter mile short and began working my way around it in a wide perimeter. When I didn't see anything to make me suspicious, I tightened the circle about a hundred yards and went around again. I kept gradually homing in on his clearing until I'd satisfied myself there was no chance of anyone lurking about in the area I'd searched. There was no danger to it. The brush and trees were so thick that I couldn't possibly have been seen from the cabin.

I ended up opposite his front door, hidden in the edge of the tree line. His rope latch was securely tied, and there was no smoke coming from his chimney. There was no sign of activity at all. If the bastard was in there, he was doing a good job of faking it.

Nevertheless, I watched for one hour by my watch. Nothing happened. There wasn't much point in delaying further. I got up, and using the trees for cover, worked my way around to the back. Without hesitating I broke from the cover and sprinted up to the back wall of the cabin. I leaned there for a second, breathing heavily.

Not a sound besides my own breath.

I tried to see through one of his little windows, but it was too dark inside.

I'd brought along a piece of cord, anticipating the need, and I used that to make a sling for my rifle. Then I slung the gun over my shoulder and started climbing one of the bog oaks that formed a corner post for the cabin. It was easy climbing. The oak was old and gnarled and many-branched. When I was high enough, I crawled out, as quietly as I could, onto the roof. There I paused for just a second, not so much to listen as to let my heart slow down. Hell, it was too late to worry if anyone were inside: I was committed. I was a sitting duck and the faster I got inside the better off I'd be.

He'd roofed his cabin with old-fashioned cedar shakes. They were thick and long. I got the small axe out of my knapsack and worked the blade in under one and pried it up. It ripped loose with a grating sound as the rusty old nails screamed in protest. A foot of the interior of the cabin came into view. I looked inside, but still couldn't see anything.

Working rapidly I ripped off several more. They came loose easily. The shakes were so big that I didn't have to take off over ten to make a big enough opening for me to get down through. But that was easier said than done. First, I dropped my knapsack and rifle through. Then, gradually, I worked my legs and lower body down the hole. If Wilfred were in there he'd have no problem just hacking me up with the nearest thing at hand. My testicles were tingling and shriveling in fear. Finally, when I was down to my armpits, I slipped one arm through and then just let myself go. It was a longer fall than I'd anticipated, and I landed hard. For a second, I thought I'd sprained or broken an ankle and that scared hell out of me.

The cabin was empty—or empty of Wilfred. There was plenty of other stuff there. Over in one corner were stacked a lot of the cases of food supplies I'd left. Lying against the wall were my rakes and hoes and shovels. He hadn't burned everything, not by a long sight. My rifle was even there. He had it mounted over the fireplace, which I thought was a nice touch. I wondered why he wasn't armed with it, but I suppose he preferred his shotgun. He couldn't carry both and he wouldn't have any extra cartridges for the rifle—just the five it contained.

I looked the stuff over hurriedly but carefully. My lanterns and heaters and stoves were stacked neatly in a corner. I was glad to see them, though a little surprised. They couldn't be of much use to him, there not being any fuel. But I guess he just couldn't bring himself to destroy them.

What I was trying to determine was if everything was accounted for—either by being burned or stolen. It was a long trek from my camp to his cabin and some of the stuff was heavy. He'd been plenty busy during my absence, but my guess was that he hadn't tried to bring everything in; instead, he'd taken most of it a little ways out in the woods and hidden it, to be recovered at his leisure. Of course, he was going to have to see what I'd do first. But I felt, almost certainly, that he was busy at that very moment hauling back plunder that he'd cached out. I'd, frankly, been surprised at his burning me out. That hadn't made any sense. But that hadn't been what he'd done. He'd burned just enough stuff for show, stuff he couldn't use—like extra farming implements and plastic iceboxes. What the hell did he want with a plastic icebox? He wasn't going to be getting any ice delivered.

I went over and sat on his bunk and rubbed my ankle. I hadn't really hurt myself, just jarred it a little. I'd have been in a hell of a mess with a broken ankle.

After a moment I noticed that the bunk felt extra soft. I jerked back the old army blanket and saw he had it rigged with my air mattress and sleeping bag. I smiled a little at that. But I was glad to see that sleeping gear.

If I had it figured right, Wilfred could be coming back at any time. He'd want to spend some time watching my camp, but he'd also want to make at least a couple of trips back and forth with the stuff he'd stolen from me. It was a little after eleven by my watch. If I'd been him, I'd have wanted to get back with one load by early afternoon. That way I could go back, watch some more, and come home just before dark.

If that was the case he could be showing up at any time. I needed a place to hide, for I wanted him all the way in the cabin and completely unaware when I sprung myself on him. There didn't seem to be any place except under the cot. I got down and looked beneath it. By sliding out the trunk, there'd be just room for me to wedge in behind. I'd be well-concealed and protected if he started shooting. It would make tracks in the dirt floor when I moved out the trunk, but I didn't think he'd notice that immediately.

Next, I considered if he could be forewarned of my presence. He wouldn't be able to see the hole in the roof, not unless he got up there; it was too flat for that. I'd been careful not to leave any sign outside. His door rope was still tied. I concluded that, unless he'd laid some sort of telltale that was too subtle for me to recognize, he couldn't know I was inside. He might look in the windows first, but he wasn't going to see anything that way. If I got under the cot and stayed quiet and still, there'd be no way for him to be aware. It would be a cramped, uncomfortable wait, but I could do it. Hell, I had to do it.

I prepared myself by eating first. I had a can of cold corned beef. Wilfred had taken away all my eating utensils, and I retrieved a spoon from one of the boxes, glad not to have to eat off the point of my pocketknife. It gives all food the metallic taste of carbon steel. Eating utensils are apparently treated to hide that taste. I had never known that before.

Concord High School Library
2331 East Mishawaka Road

When I finished eating, I had a couple of drinks of whiskey and then crawled under the cot, pushing my knapsack and rifle in ahead of me. I had my 357 in my hand. That was what I intended to use on him.

It was cramped under the cot. I'd only moved out the trunk about six inches and I was wedged between it and the wall of the cabin. I could have moved it further, but that would have made it dangerously conspicuous.

Lying there, I was just able to get the whiskey bottle up to my mouth and take little nips. I wasn't nervous, you understand. I didn't need the whiskey for that. In fact, I felt quite calm and resolute in my mind about what I was going to do. I was a little tense, but that was only a natural part of the situation. The tenseness came from the need to have everything go off all right, not from any qualms about what needed to be done.

The time drug on. It went very slowly. I'd look at my watch, convinced that hours had passed only to be shocked to see how early it still was.

Why didn't he come on?

Lying there I had a lot of time to think. I didn't feel particularly lonely or sad. I guess you can become inured to anything. I wasn't missing Chris, for instance, any more than I'd been missing her in the past. You'd have thought I would be, being at some kind of moment of crisis and knowing how dependent I'd been on her. I mostly just lay there and thought about random things—things out of my past that didn't seem to have any applicable relation to the present situation.

For instance, I thought about trains. We always seemed to be traveling when I was a little kid. That was during World War II, and we were either on the bus or the train. They were all crowded. Of course, we were poor so we traveled day coach. I could remember we always seemed to be sitting by some soldier who'd curled up in the corner of his seat, sleeping in wrinkled khakis. His tie would be pulled loose and he'd have his barracks cap down over his eyes. The cars were always smoky and hot. And so crowded that I never had a chair of my own, just had to share the edge of my mother's. But I'd see the rich guys coming through from the Pullman section, going up to the dining car to eat. They always looked cool and comfortable. Even at an early age, I remember vowing I'd make a lot of money and then I'd be one of the ones coming up from the Pullman cars. Of course, I never did it. By the time I got money, people didn't ride trains anymore. That was a thing of the past. Besides, I didn't care that much about money by then.

Oh, I'd come from poor, and I'd done just like all poor boys. I'd gone out and tried to make money. That's standard. But I think I realized, sooner than most, that money isn't all it appears to be. It's pleasant to have, but it can't fix your life up for you.

I started scrambling when I was young. When I was fifteen, I was roughnecking in the oil fields. That's hard and dangerous work, but I was glad to get it.

Another thing I remembered happened to me in about the fourth grade. I'd been invited to a birthday party for a little girl that I had a terrible crush on. I think my present to her was a little white purse. During the party, I kept following her around, asking which present she liked best. When she finally said she liked mine third-best, I was enormously pleased. I guess she got about ten presents. I don't know what a trained psychologist would have done with such a memory, but all it meant to me, thinking about it, was that I was still in the running with that little girl.

I was wishing very hard that Wilfred would come on. I wanted to get our business over with.

In the town I grew up in, there used to be a couple of brothers —bachelors, recluses. They farmed a place just out from town, and they were very frugal and hermitlike. They never spoke to anyone that I know of, and no one seemed to know much about them. They walked where they went. You'd see them coming into town—walking in single file—wearing faded old work clothes and old felt hats. They just came in to buy their groceries and other supplies, and then they'd vanish for another week. Their place was nice enough, though they had newspapers pasted over the windows so you couldn't see inside. Everyone said they had a fortune hidden under the kitchen floor—or some such floor. It was a standard story and probably was the same in every town in the country. They were old, and they died while I was in high school. Sure enough they had a fortune. Inside the house, there were about five thousand books; they left all these plus over a hundred thousand dollars to the local library. But the money wasn't under the kitchen floor, it was in the bank. A lot of people were indignant about the money being left to the library. For a while, that was all you heard around town, what those brothers should have done with their money. A lot of people thought there were any number of more worthy causes. But the will stood. There was a mild movement to change the name of the library to their name—I forget their last name—but it never came about.

Then I thought about Clinton Pyle, who hadn't crossed my mind—to my knowledge—in twenty-five years. Pyle was a big, tall, raw-boned boy who'd been a couple of years ahead of me in school. I think what made me think of him was that he stepped along a lot like Wilfred did. He always wore high-topped work shoes and old clothes. His family, if anything, was poorer than mine, and he was on the extreme edge of the lowest strata of society. He was considered a menace, and if he was talked about, it was only to predict his bad end and warn young people to stay clear of him. He did, indeed, come to a bad end. He raped a Negro girl and was sent to prison for the offense. I remember he got in a fight with Lester Radcliffe, and the principal made him and Lester walk around for one week, each holding the end of a twelve-inch ruler. I guess the thought was to force them to communicate, and therefore, work out their differences. It was wasted effort. Lester Radcliffe drowned that very year in the municipal swimming pool. I remember wondering how that was possible, to drown in a municipal swimming pool. It was the only time I'd ever heard of it happening, anywhere.

It had gotten to be one o'clock. It was really too early to be apprehensive about Wilfred, but I was wishing he'd come on. I'd gotten into the cabin with supplies enough to last a week. And I was prepared to do so. But finding the situation and working out his movements and logic as I had, I'd decided he ought to be along very quickly. But that was just rationale and needn't be true. Nevertheless, I wanted it to be true and I wanted him to come on. I sipped at the whiskey and waited and thought.

Was I going to shoot him when he walked through the door or stand him up at attention and talk to him a while? If I did the latter, it'd mean I'd have to kill him in a fairly cold-blooded way. But I hated just to shoot him. I was curious as hell about

the sonofabitch. I'd been speculating about him for months, trying to piece him together, and I wanted to know a few things.
But the last was a dangerous course. If I got to talking to him, I
might not then be able to just walk him out and put a bullet
through his head.

The cold and the waiting seemed to give an individuality to
each object. They seemed to stand away from the cabin walls as
if they were there, in some sort of disembodied spirit, alone by
themselves. I could see each hoe, each rake, each box as a separate entity, standing there, stark and alone. I think that cold,
still air was causing it to seem so. In the hours I waited, I
learned to know that cabin very well, what I could see of it. Obviously, it was very well-built. The boards were tight, but they'd
been caulked with long strips of oakum to make them even
tighter and more weatherproof. The dirt floor was hard-packed
and smooth. It must have taken quite a little time and effort to
get it so. Out in the middle was a table. It was just a topped off
stump set over with planks to make a tabletop. It was rustic and
crude, but it worked very well. What else would you want in a
table? It appeared to me that Wilfred had been able to cast himself among nature without really interfering with the natural
way of things. Man generally comes in, slaughters everything in
sight, sets himself up on a concrete pillar, and then wonders why
the grass isn't green anymore.

That was a question that had been in my mind for some time.
Should man feel a guilt about what he does to nature or is it
just there for his benefit, to be used however he feels like? I
mean, does nature, the natural things, have a soul, a spirit that
cries when we do harmful things to it? Are we ruining something godlike and spiritual when we pollute and misuse and
strip and destroy? Or was it just put there like an expendable
toy—something to keep a destructive child pacified while he
destroys it? Understand, I'm not talking about destroying nature
to the harm of others that want to use it—I'm talking in the
philosophic. Obviously, it's wrong and greedy and self-interesteed
to destroy anything before others can take pleasure from it. But
we do that in so many ways and efforts that it would seem
pointless to make nature just the one keep-off that we have. The
question was in my mind because of the way I'd heard people

talk about a river or an unspoiled wilderness or a deer or some such thing. They talked about it as if a cathedral or church or something holy had been defaced. That was the only reason I was wondering. I have to get most of my opinions from other people, and I couldn't decide what they meant. I don't want to see a river fucked up, because I love the sight of a stream of clear, pure water. I love the feeling its virginity and youthfulness and freshness and sparkle can give me. It's alive; it's gay. And then to see another stream, polluted and rotten, old tires in it, awash with beer cans, skimmed over with scum, stagnant and reeking—it's like an old man with the smell of death on him. I know I love the one and hate the other, but I don't know why that is. It just makes me wonder if that stream has a soul that is offended, or is it my own soul that hurts?

One of the wisest, most interesting men I'd ever known was an old man named Owen Durstenburger. He was a retired geologist that had occasionally forayed out in to the backwoods of the world to make his fortune. I knew him when I was on hard times and living in a small town up in the highlands of Arizona. We'd become friendly, and I think he recognized a kindred spirit, though there was a great disparity in our ages. I was in that town alone and trying to figure out what to do next, and it was coming on Christmas. He sent one of his sons in to me with a hand-lettered invitation to come out and take a cup of Christmas cheer with him. Notice I said that he sent his son in with a hand-lettered invitation. He didn't phone and he didn't write by postage. He sent me an invitation in his own beautiful, ornate script on heavy, cream-colored bond paper. I remember what a thrill it was to get such a thing, to be treated with such classic courtesy. I read that invitation a dozen times, turning it over and over in my hands just to enjoy the feel of the paper and admire the beauty of the old man's scroll.

I went out the afternoon of Christmas day. The old man's wife had died years before. He lived with two of his three sons in a great big, old-fashioned two-story house out in the country. We sat in his main living room in front of a huge fireplace—the thing must have been eight or ten feet across—and sipped bourbon so old and so prime that the bottle didn't even have a label on it. The day was immensely cold and the house was cold. If you left the area of that huge fireplace you'd be immediately uncomfortable with the cold. We sat on a leather couch, a heavy leather couch. Everything in his house was heavy and very real. Mister Durstenburger did not believe in phoniness for appearance's sake. One of his sons, the one who was not home, was in medical college in another city. The other two were still undergraduates. One was studying to be a lawyer, the other was taking agriculture and business. He'd told me, "I've got the perfect number of sons, Mister Horn. One for the land, one for the law, and one for the care of the body. They'll be able to take care of each other when I'm gone."

Nothing of any real importance got said, but I can still remember the quality of that day in that dark room, the fireplace leaping with huge logs burning, the cold, the great bourbon, the way the old man could make the most commonplace remark a string of separate jewels. He knew how to live, that Mister Durstenburger. His courtesy, his graciousness, his gentleness, and his treatment of me as if the occasion of having me out were something special touched me and swelled me and made me into more of a person than I had been before I'd come. He was a noble man, that Mister Durstenburger. I lay there, cramped up under that cot, and wondered where he was at that moment. I supposed he was dead.

It got into mid-afternoon. I don't know whether it was the whiskey or the lack of sleep from the night before, or just relaxing from all the tenseness, but I began to doze. I'd go off for a minute, catch myself, and come awake with a start. It sort of made me want to laugh, that I could get so relaxed, considering my circumstances and my purpose.

About three o'clock, I was dozing a little when I heard a sound. It wasn't anything I could identify, but I came immediately alert, straining every fiber to hear. There was something at the door. Then came a noise like someone dropping a heavy load to the ground. As quietly as I could, I shrank back, pulling myself further under the cot. I had my gun hand laying just in front of my face. Softly, I cocked the 357. I was on my chest, my head up, watching the door intently.

There were other noises—I think he was untying the rope—and then the door swung back.

It was Wilfred framed in the opening. He'd leaned his shotgun up against the sill, and he had a couple of boxes of my provisions setting in the doorway. With a grunt he picked up the two crates and brought them into the cabin and set them against the wall. Then he went back, got his shotgun, and pushed the door to.

I just lay there, watching him covertly.

He came into the middle of the room and stopped. He had his shotgun by the barrel, the stock resting on the dirt floor. He stood there, looking around. I supposed he was letting his eyes adjust to the dark after the winter sunshine outdoors. He reached up to scratch at the stubble on his cheeks. At that second I let my head and arm come out from under the end of the couch. I pointed the 357 straight at his chest.

"Freeze," I said.

He shifted his head around and down, seeing me. Shock and dismay were all over his face. His arm made a subconscious move to lift the shotgun.

"Freeze, or I'll kill you!"

He seemed to relax a little.

I told him, "Drop that shotgun."

He didn't move.

"Drop that shotgun!" I said louder. "Or I'll shoot you! Drop it!"

He sort of half crouched and let the gun gently down to the floor. I could understand that; that gun had been a friend too long for him to mistreat it.

"Straighten up!" I ordered.

He did.

I stared at him over the sights of the 357. They were fixed unwaveringly on his heart area.

"All right," I said.

I let a moment pass. We were frozen, he and I; he standing there in the position I'd put him in, me huddled up behind an old trunk, under a cot.

"Who in hell," I finally asked, "are you? And what's your business?"

He didn't say anything.

"Goddamn you," I told him. "I want some answers or I'll kill

you right now. You burned my camp. You shot me. Now, goddamnit, you tell me what I want to know. Who are you? Tell
me, goddamnit!" I shouted.

His mouth opened and he went, "Oh na wa so ma sha las na
fra."

It was just gibberish. I looked up at his face, startled. Then I
understood what I was hearing. I'd been staring at his chest so
intently, ready to shoot him, that I hadn't noticed his mouth.
The whole right side of his face, beginning at the corner of his
mouth, was pulled back in a hideous grin by a huge scar that
ran almost to his ear. You could see, the way the side of his face
was opened, the gnarled gums where teeth had been.

"What the hell," I said. "Can't you talk?"

He went, "Wa sham lo spe fa na shamana."

"You can't talk," I said. "What the hell happened to you?"

He started some more of the gibberish, waving his arms
around as if I could be made to understand by that.

"Hold on," I said. "Let me get out of here and I'll try to figure this out." I began to wriggle forward, trying to get out from
under the cot. I was trying to pull myself along by my elbows
and, to do that, I dropped my gun hand down to get some pull
with that arm.

At that instant he bolted. He caught me so off guard that I
believe he'd have gotten away free if the door hadn't been shut.
He was across the cabin before I could even react. God, the bastard could move! But the second it took him to fling back the
door was what gave me my chance. I was trying to traverse on
him, get a shot, but he was moving too fast. Then he had to
pause to open the door and I fired. The pistol made a hell of a
boom in the little cabin. I hit him in the thigh. The way I
was positioned under the cot made it impossible for me to raise
my arm high enough to shoot him in the upper body. But the
bullet went home, and the 357 has such power that it knocked
him through the door and down. I had a glimpse of his falling
as I tried to jerk myself out from under the cot.

I couldn't get free. It was all so hectic and fast that, for a second, I didn't understand that my pants were hung on a sharp
corner of the trunk. I just went on struggling, blindly, until I
heard cloth tear and felt a sharp pain in my thigh.

Insane with haste I backed up an inch, kicked the trunk out further, and began pulling myself out by my elbows. Time was passing. I could no longer see his boots, as I had when he'd fallen, just outside the door.

It took me a full minute to get out from under that damnable cot. By the time I got to the door he was gone. I looked wildly around, but he was nowhere in sight.

But there was a clear blood trail on the ground in front of me.

Calm down, I told myself. Take your time. Take yourself a deep breath. We've got him. Just take it slow and carefully. He can't get away. Don't make a foolish mistake now.

I forced myself to stand there a full minute, getting my nerves back under control.

The blood trail was very solid and distinct. He was losing a lot of blood. Time was on my side. The more he bled the easier he'd be to take. He was unarmed and hurt. All I had to do was follow the blood very slowly and carefully and he'd be mine.

But I didn't want him doubling back on me and getting a weapon. I went back inside and got his shotgun and my 30.30 and the automatic he'd put over the fireplace. I gathered them up in my arms and took them a few yards out into the woods and hid them under some underbrush. Then I went back to the front of the cabin and studied out the job in front of me.

Where he'd fallen there was a good pool of blood. I tell you, that 357 will tear a hole in you.

I could see where he'd struggled to his feet. A line of blood, splotchy and scattered—it was running down his leg and dripping off his boot—led out of the clearing and into the forest on a northwesterly course. There was plenty of daylight left. I could get him before dark easily.

I set off to follow the sign, the 357 in my hand and at full cock. I went very slowly, checking all around me at each step. Don't misunderstand, I knew the man was wounded and unarmed, but I still had a strong respect for him. He was dangerous, and I didn't want him suddenly jumping me from behind a tree and breaking my head with a sharp rock.

God, he was losing a lot of blood. The trail got more distinct the further I went. Every yard I expected to find him lying dead.

This can't be, I thought to myself. No man is that tough. He's got to fall.

I went on for almost a quarter of a mile. I was working through dense forest, but it was no problem to trail him.

Then, unaccountably, the sign began to thin out. After a little there were only smears and scattered drops of blood to go by. I was concerned. It made me more apprehensive and I stepped very warily through the winter forest. All of a sudden, I broke out of the trees and faced a cliff face rising in front of me. No, you couldn't really call it a cliff. Its rise was too gentle for that. But it was the beginning of a stony mountain. There was no underbrush or trees growing on it, just rocks and hard, crusty dirt. It rose away, at about a thirty-degree angle, a growing mountain that peaked far off in the distance.

That's where the blood trail stopped.

I cast ahead a few yards, then rounded back and tried in several directions. There was no sign. Frantic, I retraced my steps and made certain of my direction. The trail, though scant, was visible to there, then it stopped. I looked up the slope, seeing nothing but boulders and tortured ground.

All of a sudden the hair began to rise at the back of my neck. I was standing just outside the tree line and I suddenly thought that the bastard had climbed a tree and was waiting for me to get directly under him so that he could fall on me.

Slowly I turned around and raised my pistol and looked up in the trees. I couldn't see anything. Ready to shoot at the slightest movement, I rounded back to the end of the blood trail and looked up in all the trees around me. There wasn't a thing. If he'd been up in one, he'd have been easy to spot on account of the bareness of the limbs. He simply wasn't there.

Goddamnit, I thought, he didn't climb a tree and then swing off through the forest. He wasn't Tarzan, not with that 357 slug through his thigh.

I was weary, and I sat down and tried to think. It hit me that he might have gotten a tourniquet on his leg and stopped the bleeding. But his pants and shoe were bloody. Wouldn't they have left some sign?

Well, maybe he'd understood that and rolled his pants leg up and taken off his shoe.

But how could he have kept on going?

Goddamnit, he'd lost a gallon of blood. I sat there, trying to think of how much blood a man has in him. A hog's got a lot, but a man's not a hog. How far can he go spilling out that kind of quantities?

I realized it was coming on to dusk. The mountain was taking on that blue-brown cast it gets when the sun announces it's about to go down. If I let night steal up on me without figuring out the problem, he might get away and I couldn't have that.

God. That bastard was tough. I shivered in the cold, not wanting to have him recovered and waiting for me.

Well, I knew I was going to have to camp right at the end of the blood trail. The blood he'd lost would soak into the ground and turn brown, and I'd never be able to follow it the next day. When morning's daylight came I'd have to be at the final point I'd lost him. From there, I could cast about until I ferreted him out. The night was on his side, not mine.

And dusk was coming fast.

With a growing feeling of peril, I hurried back to the cabin, grabbed up my knapsack, ripped my sleeping bag off Wilfred's bed, and retraced my steps to the end of the trail.

There, just inside the tree line, I found a level piece of ground and settled down to wait out the night. I didn't intend to sleep, I was too wary for that. All I was going to do was wait, in what comfort I could, for daylight.

He couldn't be far, I felt sure of that.

I ate a cold can of beans, took a few sips of whiskey, and then slipped down inside my sleeping bag. I lay facing the direction Wilfred had fled in. I had the 357 in my right hand, that arm cradling my head. I knew I could lie there the whole night without any fear of dozing. I let my body relax, let it rest itself. My mind would do the work tonight. Tomorrow I'd need my body.

I don't know at exactly what point I became aware, really aware, of the glow on the cliff face. I know I'd been seeing it, or half noticing it for some time, but I think I dismissed it as moon reflection or gas emission or something else. The glow was very faint. It was about a hundred yards up the slope, two hun-

dred yards from me, and looked more like a reflection than anything else. I think the thing that finally claimed my attention was
the way it seemed to flicker. Sometimes you could see it, and then
it would pale to the point where you were convinced you were
imagining the whole thing. Then it would come back.

I finally sat up in my sleeping bag and stared hard at the spot.
It was something, all right, but whether it had anything to do
with Wilfred I couldn't guess.

"Goddamnit," I said lowly. I knew I was going to have to go
see, and I didn't want to do it. It was bitter cold and I'd been
warm and comfortable in my blankets. I felt the way you do,
you know, when you're about half asleep but know you've got
to get up and take a piss. You'd much rather the need went
away and let you get fully comfortable again, but you know it
won't. So finally you throw the covers back and get up and go
stalking into the bathroom.

I unzipped my sleeping bag and threw the top half back. For
a second, I sat there scratching my head, staring at the very faint
glow. It probably wasn't anything—pyrite catching the moon's
image, a discarded tin can. Even as I watched, the glow lessened
and dimmed. I almost laid back down again, willing to forget it
in the comfort of my sleeping bag. But then it flickered up again.

Hell, I thought, no reflection flickers. Not with the moon
shining steady.

I was fully dressed and had the 357 in my hand, so there
wasn't any preparations to make except to get out of the sack
and crawl up the cliff.

The first fifty or sixty yards were easy. I was just walking. Since
that part of the mountain was not forested the moon gave a
good glow and I was able to pick my way very ably.

Then the cliff started rising more and more steeply. It was
never a climbing job, but then neither was I able to walk upright. I got down on my hands and knees, sticking the 357 in my
waist band, and moved steadily toward the glow. It became more
distinct with each yard I closed.

I could feel the tension start to rise. This was no reflection.
This was no mirage. They don't increase in intensity the nearer
you get.

At twenty yards away, I began to pick my way very carefully, being certain not to disturb any loose rocks or make any noise. My main problem was with my breathing. The adrenaline was flowing and I was unable to control the panting that arose from my chest.

I was almost there, and I could see and understand what I'd been seeing. It was a declivity of some sort in the face of the cliff, a cave or cavern or just a big hole, to my right. If I'd been sleeping a hundred yards to the left, I'd have seen the full glow as soon as it got dark. As it was, all I'd seen was really a reflection, the effervescence of the light source.

My man was in that hole. I knew it in certainty.

I crawled up very slowly. When the mouth of the cave was just a yard or two above me, I stopped and tried to slow down my breathing. I needed to think about what to do. I could possibly crawl up behind the boulder and look in, but I might make noise that way. The only other alternative was to get right at the lip of the hole and then suddenly spring in shooting.

I chose the latter.

My 357 was not at cock, and I shoved it up under my coat to deaden the sound, and as gently as I could, I pulled the hammer back. It made a very tiny clitch-clack. It would be inaudible a few yards away.

Pulling myself along, I worked my way up until I was right at the lower lip of the hole or cave or cavern or whatever it was. All I was going to do was spring to my knees, aim into the light, and shoot anything I could see.

I waited a moment, steeling myself.

I told myself, "He'll kill you if he gets another chance. You better make sure of him this time or you're done."

Shoot him. Don't hesitate. Shoot him.

Oh, God, I was a divided soul in those few seconds. Part of me knew that I had to do what was necessary and part of me cried out against it.

But why did I hesitate. That was the part I couldn't understand. Why not kill him? I'd already shot him, all I needed was a better shot to finish him off.

I had to quit thinking. I just went ahead and came to my knees and dove forward. I had my right arm, topped by the 357, out in front of me like a spear.

"Hold it!" I yelled like a maniac.

For a second I stared and then I got slowly to my knees and half walked, half crawled into the little cave.

Wilfred was there all right. Just him, lying over in a corner of this little cave. It was only about seven or eight feet long, maybe four feet wide, and about five feet high. There wasn't room in which to stand fully erect. Still on my knees, I stared at him, the 357 pointed straight at his chest, my finger on the trigger.

He was lying back over in the corner, his head pillowed on a pile of old raggedy clothing. Beside his head was a flickering stub of a candle fixed to a handy rock. By its shine I could see his face. He was deathly pale, his skin so white and drawn that it looked like the sheen you'd see on a block of wax. For a second, he didn't seem to be even aware of my presence; just lay there, his eyes half-closed, not looking at anything. He'd unbuckled his pants, I guess to look at the wound, and then pulled them back up without bothering again with his belt. Around his thigh was a rough cloth tourniquet twisted tight with a stick. Below his leg I could see a big pool of congealed blood.

I watched him carefully, ready for any defense. Finally, I could hear his breathing; it was short and shallow and very weak.

When he still didn't look at me, I got slowly to my feet. The ceiling was so low I had to stand in a crouch. Still fingering the 357 nervously, I took a few cautious steps until I was standing over him. I stared down in his face. His lips, or what remained of them from whatever horrible wound he'd taken, were parted to better help his breathing. After a long moment, his eyes flickered open and he stared up at me.

For just a moment. It wasn't a long look, but I thought they were very young looking eyes in that old, seamed face that was so pale. I think it made his eyes look bigger, browner, more sad, more something or other.

I stood there, fiddling with that pistol, feeling like a fool to be holding it on the man. Finally I shoved it in my belt and sat down beside him. There wasn't a sign of a weapon near him.

We were there in silence for I don't know how long. Maybe ten minutes. He kept his eyes closed. I looked around the cave. There wasn't much to see, a few stumps of other candles, some old clothes, a few jars of preserved food. Near the entrance was a pile of brush. I imagined he normally used that to conceal the opening when he hid himself out. I imagined he must have been too weak to put it in place when he crawled in wounded.

The candle was flickering low. I got another one, lit it off the going one, and set it down on the same rock. It made the cave brighten up.

I stared at those two candles, mesmerized by their flame, thinking. It was the candles that were making me feel bad. Hell, if he hadn't lit that candle I'd have never found him. But I understood, though not wanting to, why he'd done it. He hadn't wanted to die in the dark. He hadn't wanted to crawl up in this hole in the rock and die like some animal. He knew that candle would lead me to him. I couldn't take lying there in the dark with another dark, the big one, about to come.

Goddamn, I suddenly felt bad.

When I couldn't take it any longer, I cleared my throat and said, "You ought to loosen that thing. You'll get gangrene if you don't."

It was a long time coming, but finally his eyes flickered open. I nodded my head at the tourniquet. "I don't know how often you're supposed to do it, but I think it's about every fifteen minutes."

His only sign was to lift one hand weakly and let it fall back.

"You want me to do it for you?"

I thought I saw a slight movement of his head, so I reached over and cautiously untwisted the stick, watching carefully for any fresh blood. When none came and I'd eased the pressure he seemed to relax back a little.

"I'll watch it close," I promised him. "If it starts bleeding, I'll twist it tight right away."

His eyes came open and he looked at me. There was nothing in his look, nothing I could read.

I still couldn't tell how old he was. Perhaps I could have if he hadn't appeared so weak and fragile. I suppose, were it not for the disfiguration of his mouth, that he would at one time have been a handsome man. He had a prominent forehead and high cheekbones and a long, tapering jaw.

"I guess you feel pretty bad," I said awkwardly.

He lifted his hand again and let it fall.

"Well, goddamnit!" I suddenly burst out. "What was I supposed to do? You took a shot at me. You tried to kill me. Didn't you? And didn't you burn my camp out? And steal my property? Goddamn, what did you expect?"

After that I didn't speak for a few moments. The one candle flared up and then burned out. I got another one and lit it and then another one. I didn't want the dark to come either.

"Let me have a look at your leg," I said. "Do you mind?"

He made a movement of his head. He did it very weakly, but it was the strongest sign he'd made. I got my pocketknife out and carefully slit the cloth of his trousers around the hole the bullet had made. When I had his thigh exposed, I could see how bad it was. Damn, that 357 slug had made a mess. I'd got him quartering from the rear, and it had come out near the inside of his thigh. It was a gaping wound, the edges torn and tortured. Looking closer, I could see pieces of bone embedded in the shattered flesh. "Shit," I exclaimed, "your leg is broken!"

His eyes flickered open.

"I'm a sonofabitch," I said. How the hell had the bastard made it away from the cabin and then up the cliff face with a broken leg? Oh, God, the man's courage or will or whatever you want to call it made me almost want to cry. I said, instead, "I think it's the femoral artery. I think it is. That's the big one in the leg. That's why you've bled so much. I read up on a lot of medicine." I was talking nervously and fast because I didn't know what to say and I didn't want to just not say anything.

Gradually, I began to realize how cold he must be. He wasn't shivering, but I was conscious of being chilled even in my big coat and he was lying there, on the cold rock, in just a shirt and torn pants.

"Look here," I said, "I've got a sleeping bag and whiskey just a hundred yards or so from here. You're freezing to death. I'm going to go get them. Will you not try to run?"

He opened his eyes again, but they were still expressionless. For just a second, I thought I saw a flicker of humor, but that may have just been my imagination.

"You drink whiskey, don't you? A little whiskey would make you feel better. Just promise me you won't try and run off." I hesitated. "I'm not going to hurt you anymore. You don't have to be afraid of me."

I stood up, stooped. "Now don't move," I said. I was afraid to go. "Please don't move," I said again. When he still made no sign, I turned and hurried out the cave mouth. Once back on the cliff I had to crawl. But I went as fast as I could, stumbling and falling on loose rocks. At level ground I broke into a trot. The moon was still good, and I was able to see fairly well. At my little camp site, I grabbed my sleeping bag and the sack of food and the whiskey and then turned and rushed back toward Wilfred's cave. My haste was frantic, but I didn't exactly know why. Certainly, I didn't expect him to try and run away. He'd never be able to get out of the mouth of the cave. I just knew I wanted to get back there as fast as I could.

I scrambled up the cliff, heedless of the noise and my hands and shins. At the mouth of the cave, I went right in without pause. The thought had crossed my mind that he might have a concealed weapon and be waiting to shoot me as I entered. I'd gone on without caution anyway.

He was lying just as I'd left him. I went over and knelt by him. There was a little blood starting to seep from the wound.

"Oh, hell," I said. "I thought this thing had clotted. I'm going to have to screw down this tourniquet again."

I fussed over him like a nurse. "Damnit," I said, "you put it on in the wrong place anyway. It's too low. It should have been up higher, up near where your leg connects with your hip. That's the pressure point. Down here you've got all that muscle to go through and you've got to squeeze it down too tight." While I was talking, I moved the tourniquet up and twisted it until the runlet of blood stopped. "I know that doesn't feel good," I said, "but it's necessary."

Next I covered him with my sleeping bag, tucking it as far up under him as I could. "I hate to see you lying on that cold rock," I said, "but you'd have to get up for me to get this under you. That might not be good."

There was no indication from him. He didn't even open his eyes. If anything, he looked weaker.

"How about some whiskey?" I asked. "You ought to take some." I unscrewed the cap and held the mouth of the bottle near his shattered lips. "It'll be hard to drink, lying back like that, but I'm going to pour a little in. You try and swallow." I did, easing a thin stream in at the corner of his mouth. Some of it ran down his chin, but then his jaws worked and he appeared to be swallowing. "Let's get some more down," I said. "It'll warm you up." I poured him another mouthful. Again there was the weak effort of taking the liquor down. But he didn't cough or sputter.

"I'll have one now," I said. I turned the bottle up and had a long pull. It felt good going down and even better in my stomach.

For five or ten minutes, I alternated watching him and giving him a mouthful of the whiskey. Gradually, there seemed to be an effect. He appeared to be getting stronger. Finally, he was able to get his lips around the bottle and take a real pull. When I took the bottle away he made a sound that sounded almost like a satisfied, "AAAaah."

"Good stuff, ain't it?" I said.

He opened his eyes. They looked brighter, more alive.

"Take another one," I commanded. I put the bottle back up to his mouth and gave him a long drink.

"That'll make you stronger," I said.

I'd thought of pouring some of the whiskey in his wound, as an antiseptic, but had decided against it. What little we had was going to do him more good in his mouth. He wasn't going to die from an infection, wasn't going to have time.

The whiskey was having a quick effect. It couldn't be said that any color was coming back in his face, but he looked more alive. His features were becoming more distinct, as if there was a man living behind the face.

I had another pull myself. We still had half a bottle.

There didn't seem to be much to say. Here lay a man that I'd shot, that I'd intended to finish off, who was lying in my sleeping bag, being fed my whiskey and nursed by me. It was too contradictory.

We were there, together, in the lengthening night in that cave. It seemed to get colder. I had to keep giving him little nips of the whiskey. If I didn't, his face would soon start looking like a slab of wax.

"Wilfred," I said. Then I stopped. "Is your name Wilfred?

I've been calling you that in my mind, but I don't really know. Is it?"

I noticed, even as weak as he was, that he seemed careful to keep the damaged side of his face away from me. It would be impossible to say how, but I somehow felt that he was ashamed of it. I took a pull of the whiskey and gestured with the bottle. "How'd you get that? That torn up jaw?"

He lay there, and for a second, I didn't think he was going to respond. But then there was a slight movement beneath the cover of the sleeping bag and his hands came slowly working their way out.

"Here," I said, "don't push those covers off." I started to tuck them back, but he'd got his arms out and was making some sort of gesture with his arms. He was very weak at it, but he seemed to be trying to pantomime a man holding something out in front of him with both hands.

"A stick?" I asked him. "I don't understand. Somebody hit you with a club?"

For answer, he rolled slightly on his side, exposing a hip pocket.

"Something in your pocket?" I could see the outline of a billfold or wallet or some such thing. "You want me to look in your pocket?"

I could see he didn't have strength to answer me, so I just reached out and worked an old, worn billfold out of the rear of his trousers. "This?" I asked him. "You want me to look in this?"

But he was too weak to make any further signs. He just collapsed back and stared dully up at the ceiling of the cave. I looked through the old billfold. There were some faded snapshots and a few one-dollar bills. Finally, in the main compartment, I found a folded piece of unusual looking paper. I opened it and saw that it was some sort of government document. Holding it close to the candle, I was able to see that it was a citation for the silver star to Wilfred Hines, for meritorious and valiant conduct during the Battle of the Bulge in the Second World War. Acting without the compulsion of orders, he'd attacked an enemy position that had his squad pinned down, demolishing it. In the last of the engagement, he'd suffered a grievous face wound as the result of enemy bayonet action.

I read it through several times then refolded it and put it carefully back in the old wallet. I put that on top of the sleeping bag, on his chest. After a second a hand came creeping out from under the cover, clutched the billfold, and took it back inside with him.

"That's fine, Wilfred," I said. "That's just wonderful."

I gave him another drink of the whiskey.

"What are you doing up here in the mountains?" I asked him. "You've been here a long time. Ten years, twenty years? Longer. I know you've been here a long, long time. How come?"

He made no sign.

"I understand," I said. I wanted to ask him: Wilfred, are you hiding out up here because of the way you look? Are you ashamed for people to see your face because it looks so horrible? Is this your reward for charging an enemy machine gun position in the defense of the people you don't want to see you? Is this how you think it's supposed to work?

But I didn't say or ask any of that. I said, "Something's fucked up somewhere, Wilfred, for you to go through all of what you went through and then get shot by somebody like me way up here in a place you thought was safe."

Later I said, "Maybe if we could have talked this wouldn't have happened. But you couldn't talk, somebody cut your tongue in half. Somebody who didn't even know you. So we couldn't have talked. But maybe if we'd had the time, we could have figured out some way to communicate. I don't know. I'm not very smart, Wilfred."

The whiskey was getting low.

"I ought not to have shot you," I told him, "but I was afraid. I was afraid you'd shoot me. Maybe you would have. I don't know. But you didn't take that rifle of mine and pick me off at long-range. And you could have done that."

The thought was anguish to me.

There was only a quarter inch of whiskey left in the bottle, and I gave him all that in one pull.

"Could you eat something?" I asked him. "I've got a few cans of stuff here. I could heat them up."

He looked at me with his large eyes. They were getting luminous again, like cold, agate marbles.

"It'd make you stronger," I argued.

He didn't even bother to shake his head. After a moment he closed his eyes.

A long moment or two later I burst out, "Look here, Wilfred, I don't know what to do. Goddamnit! What do you expect?"

He didn't move.

"Look," I said earnestly, "I can't haul you into town. It's not possible."

It was getting colder.

I was talking desperately, painfully. "Listen, what am I supposed to do? My truck's fifteen miles from here. It'd take me ten hours to get to it in this dark. And then what would I do? I couldn't drive it anywhere near to this cave. You want me to try and carry you out of here? You want me to sling you over my shoulder and try to carry you to a doctor? That wound would open up in the first ten steps. Don't be silly, it wouldn't work."

His eyes were still closed.

"Why don't you try and eat something? I told you we were out of whiskey."

Another of the candles guttered out and I lit the remaining one I could find. I had three burning, but two of them were just bare stumps.

"All right," I said harshly, "I'm sorry I shot you. Goddamnit, does that make you feel any better? It doesn't me."

The cold was going all through me.

"I wish Nick was here," I said. "He's a doctor. Or he was. He's a preacher now." I looked at him, his poor, lined face seeming to sink into itself. "Goddamnit, Wilfred, I'm sorry as hell." I felt like crying out of frustration. "But what can I do? Tell me that. Tell me what the hell I can do!"

His breathing was sounding more irregular. I leaned my head close to his chest and listened. I couldn't hear anything from there, but he had his lips open, and there was a sort of rattle in the sound of his breath.

"I'm sorry I shot you," I said. Then I said it again.

I watched his chest rising and falling, listened to his shallow breath. I was abruptly angry. "But what am I telling you for?" I was furious. "What do you know about the reasons for killing?

You killed a bunch of Germans in a machine gun nest. What for? To make the world safe for democracy? Because some fucking idiot put you in that position and instilled the idea of killing? What better reason did you have for killing those Germans than I did for shooting you?"

I pulled my coat tighter around my body. It was so cold. I could see thin sheet ice on the walls around us where the limestone had sweated. Another of the candles had gone out.

"Oh, hell," I said, lowly, after a moment. I laid a hand near him. "Just look at you. Look at what's happened to you. Hell, Wilfred, look what's happened to me."

A little later I asked him, "Wilfred, have you got any people near here I could try and get to? I'll make a hell of an attempt if you have. I'll run all the way."

A candle flamed up, as they will do, and then went out.

In the waning light, I could see Wilfred move his head slightly. I didn't know what he was trying to answer.

"I could get your Bible. I saw it there one time when I came to see you."

He didn't move.

"Oh, God," I said, "why has this happened to me? Why have I caused it to happen?"

Wilfred made a little sighing sound and then seemed to relax.

Boy, I thought, that old bastard has lost a lot of blood. It grew later as I sat there on that cold rock floor.

"Wilfred?" I said. "Wilfred, do something."

He was very still.

"Wilfred?"

I looked at him closely; I got my head down even with his chest to see if I could see a rise and fall. He was very still.

"Oh, God," I said, "don't die. Don't be dead." I put out my hand and touched his face. It wasn't particularly cold. It was just a face. As I did so I realized I'd never touched him before. I'd touched him with a bullet out of my pistol; I'd touched him through the sleeping bag as I'd tucked it up underneath him; I'd touched him with the blade of the knife I was holding as I'd cut away his pants; I'd touched him through the cloth of that sad old tourniquet he'd somehow managed to rig; but I'd never really touched him.

This man I'd killed.

I pulled his eyelid back. His eye was there, but it wasn't seeing anything anymore.

I said, "Oh, God, forgive me."

I got up, wanting to hurry. The last candle was very low. I looked the cave over and finally found a piece of a candle about three inches long. I got that lit and set it on the rock and then went out of the cave. I didn't take anything with me. Without really noticing I made my way back through the forest, growing black now that the moon was dying, to Wilfred's cabin. I thought I could sleep in his bed that night, but I couldn't. I lay down for a few moments, but then the very blankets began to shroud me and I jumped up and raced out the door. I crept over to a tree at the edge of the clearing to wait for dawn. After a little I became aware of the weight of the 357 in my belt. I got it out and looked at it. Its shape was indistinct in the dark, but I knew it by feel. I only held it a second. After that I drew my arm back and cast it as deep into the forest as I could. Then I settled down to wait for the dawn.

Next day, when I was able, I climbed back up the cliff face to the mouth of the cave and began sealing it off with rocks. I didn't go inside, didn't even intentionally look inside. It was hard, desperate work in the insecure footing of that cliff face but I did it as thoroughly as I could. Nothing went through my mind. I tried to keep it blank. I made myself concentrate on the work, furrowing my brow over the selection of each rock and just how well it would fit into the wall I was building. I'd get occasional glimpses of Wilfred, stiff, I guessed, under my sleeping bag. The candles had long since gone out, and it was dim and dark in the cave.

When I had the opening sealed off I went back down to the level ground and gathered up some dead brush and arranged it across the face of the rocks. It looked out of place, on that bare cliff face, but I didn't care. You understand, I wasn't hiding what I'd done, I wasn't hiding Wilfred, I was burying him. The old dead bushes, if anything, were flowers.

When I was done I said a little prayer to God and then went back down the cliff and over to Wilfred's cabin. It was difficult to make myself go in, but I did after a time. I sat on the hearth. It was very cold and dim in the cabin, but I made myself sit there, smoking a cigarette and not thinking about anything in particular. Wilfred had a pile of firewood over in a corner, and I suppose I could have built a fire, but I didn't much want to do it.

All his old, sad stuff was still in its place against the wall. And the trunk, the trunk that had bought him a few more hours of life, was still in its askew position where I'd shoved it so desperately.

I still had a bottle of whiskey I'd left, and I got that out and drank some of it. After that I ate a can of cold hash. It was pretty bad, rough and greasy tasting.

Some days passed, I'm not sure how many. Probably about a week. I didn't do anything, just sat around and tried not to think. My whiskey ran out on about the fourth day. After that I didn't eat, though Wilfred had some provisions there. Mostly, I just sat out in the clearing and stared, either trying not to think or trying to figure out things I wasn't really equipped to handle.

I couldn't sleep on Wilfred's bunk. Eventually, the cold forced me inside at night, but I slept curled up on the floor, freezing to death. I couldn't even use his blankets. Those were nights of horror which would have been even worse had I not been dazed into a sort of insensibility.

One morning, I came awake with a certain amount of resolve. I wasn't really back to myself, but I was closer than I had been. Without thinking much about it, I started the long walk to my truck. I was very weak from not eating, but I pushed myself without mercy, going on, one foot in front of the other, until I'd simply fall over and have to rest. I crossed the creek and walked through my old campsite in a sort of funk.

My truck was as I'd left it. I slid down the side of the ravine, tore away some of the branches, opened the door and collapsed full length on the seat, so tired I wasn't sure I'd ever rise again.

It was nearly dusk. Before I'd made the walk in about six hours, but in my weakened condition, I'd spent a full day on the task. After a little, I went to sleep. When I awoke it was full day. At first, I wasn't hungry and I just picked at a can of Vienna sausages, but once I got that down, I suddenly was ravenous and I ate four cans of food just as fast as I could open them. After that I drank a little whiskey and felt stronger.

About noon, I cleared the brush off my truck and eased it up out of the ravine. It was a lot easier coming out than it had been going in. I found the road and drove back to my camp, bumping slowly over the old, familiar terrain. I felt as if I'd known it for a thousand years.

At my old campsite, I got out and looked slowly around. The weather and the wind had eroded most of the signs of what Wilfred had done, but there were still charred pieces of burned plastic lying around. I picked up a piece of a wine bottle and looked at it. It had been a shame to waste good wine like that. I cast it aside.

For a week, I slept and sat around. Without a tent or other shelter I just slept in the truck. The only effort I made was to clean the camp of all signs of the burnout. I did get my fire going again. I'd build it up big at night and sit there, my front warm and comfortable, while the cold wind swept over my back. I wasn't drinking an especially great amount of whiskey, but I was drinking enough so that my thoughts didn't have such sharp, cutting edges.

I would not use Wilfred's cabin; nor would I take from his vegetable patch. I was finding that we do not steal from each other quite so readily. Nor do we kill without paying an un-looked-for price. I was not crystal clear in my thinking, but I was beginning to believe there were things more important than survival.

Maybe that's what makes us different from the other animals. On a bright, cold morning I walked over to Wilfred's cabin. I didn't go inside. I just pulled his door to and tied the rope latch very tightly. Then I turned around and walked back to my camp.

I was going into town. I needed to buy some supplies to replace those that Wilfred had taken. They were in his cabin, but I wasn't going to touch them.

Also I wanted to buy a tent. I needed some sort of shelter. A tent seemed to have the same temporary quality that my life did.

I drove into Yellville and bought a tent and a sleeping bag and various lanterns and heaters in a sporting goods store. I stopped several times on the way back at other little towns to purchase what I thought I'd need.

Coming into a little town I got to thinking about the weather. It was still cold, hard cold, but there was a quality about the air that suggested a rebirth to me. I parked in front of a little feed store and went in and asked the guy what the date was.

"Fourteenth," he said.

I stared at him, blankly.

"Fourteenth," he said again.

I asked, "Of February?"

He laughed. "Boy, where you been? Fourteenth of March."

"Oh," I said. "I just forgot for a moment."

There was a roadside phone booth just at the edge of town. I had remembered it from the last trip. I pulled in there.

There was no hesitation about calling Chris. I was going to call her, had been planning on it ever since some feeling of life had begun to seep back into me. But as I approached the phone booth, I felt a certain sense of reluctance. It wasn't fear, it was embarrassment. I felt awkward. Which was a hell of a note for a man to feel about calling a woman he'd loved and been married to for nine years and who'd come to be almost as much a part of himself as his own life. I fumbled a coin out of my pocket and got the operator and gave her the number and my credit card number. Then I stood, holding the phone, wondering what she'd say to me, what I'd say to her. I didn't feel like the same man. I wondered if she'd be the same woman.

She answered on almost the first ring. Her voice was strong and clear, exactly as it had been remembered in my head. It was a second before I could speak and she said, "Hello?" again.

I cleared my throat. "Chris. It's Franklin."

"Oh!" she exclaimed, startled confusion in her voice. "Franklin."

"Yeah," I said. I hesitated. "Listen, I'm all right. I hope you are."

"I'm all right," she said. Then, with a little rush of breath. "Where are you?"

"I'm in a little town near the mountain. I—"

She broke in. "Are you sure you're all right?"

"Yes," I said. "Listen, my love, I— Well, I don't quite know what to say."

The shock was leaving her. "What happened, Franklin? What the hell happened to us? How did we let it?"

I shook my head, even though she couldn't see it. "I don't know, dear. Just confusion. I'm sorry for it. I'm very sorry. I have missed you until I'm almost out of my mind."

Her voice came sharp. "Then come home."

"I am, dear," I told her, "very soon. I've almost got things figured out."

"Come home now."

I was silent a second. Hearing her, hearing her voice, hearing her say things like that was putting a lot of good back in me. Some of the nightmare was starting to fade. "Soon," I promised. "Not right now. Not right away. I've still, still got some thinking to do. In about a week."

Then she was silent.

I waited; then I asked, "Chris?"

"I'm here," she answered. "I was trying to think how to ask you something."

"Ask it anyway."

"Well—How do you feel about things? I mean, are you satisfied now?"

"It's hard to answer, Chris. So much has happened. So much I can't tell you about now, that we'll talk about when I get back. But I'll be satisfied when I get back. I'll be satisfied to be with you. Anywhere. I made some mistakes, Chris."

"So did I," she said.

"I was afraid you wouldn't tell me to come home."

"Are you crazy, Horn?"

I smiled then, for the first time in a long while. "I love you," I said.

"I love you. Please come home."

"Very soon."

"Be careful. Please."

"I will. I love you."

Then I drove away, back up the winding mountain roads to my camp.

I parked at my old site and sat down to rest a moment before I unloaded the supplies. I lit a cigarette and stared out at the mountains.

I knew where I'd made part of my mistake. I could see it. I'd been afraid of something I called a society or a civilization or a system or something. And I'd forgotten that all that is is a bunch of individuals. I'd mistrusted the whole and forgotten to trust the individual. Which was a bad mistake for me to make. I'd got my numbers confused.

But there had been other mistakes, a lot of them. I had been wrong with Wilfred. Poor Wilfred. I guessed I'd never get completely over that. Which was as it should be. Because he wasn't going to get over it either. I had blamed him all the way as the aggressor and that hadn't been true. I should have communicated with him. Somehow I should have reached him with reason so that we could have talked it out. He couldn't communicate, but I could. Yet, I'd gone along blaming him for not communicating with me. And that had been a mistake. I should have raised my voice and kept talking until some solution could be reached. For I could talk. No one had cut out my tongue. The fault was mine.

But the biggest mistake I'd made had been not to trust myself. I had talked very big about my birthright. Then I'd turned around and denied it. I'd run off to hide. It was indeed important for a man to survive, but it was more important that he survive on his own terms.

I looked around me, at the woods, at the mountain. Now, this close to the ground, I could see clearly the signs of spring. The woods would soon be green again. It was a pretty place. It'd make a good summer camp to come to when it got too hot in town. I felt sure that Chris would no longer be afraid of it, not when she understood it. And I would see it differently too.

"Hell," I suddenly said aloud. "I'm going home." I got up and looked around for another second and then went to the pickup. I got in, started it, made a circling turn, and headed back for the road, back to my home.